The Royal Griffin

JULIET DYMOKE

THREE CASTLES MEDIA

First published in Great Britain in 1978 by Nel Books.
This edition published in 2017 by Three Castles Media Ltd.

Paperback ISBN 978-1-52142-170-3

10 9 8 7 6 5 4 3 2 1

Cover design by Fourteen Twentythree

For Moira and Frank Alder

PART ONE

THE KING'S SISTER

CHAPTER ONE

'I do not think I want to go,' the Princess Eleanor said and twisted her head to see her reflection more clearly. 'Would you not have been a little afraid, my lady?'

'Of what?' her cousin asked. 'When I was your age I looked forward to my marriage. Three husbands my uncle Richard considered for me and not one did I have. I promise you I would have given half my jewels for the sight of two pillows set side by side on a bed.'

'Forgive me, madame, I had forgotten.' Eleanor lowered her gaze, setting the silver mirror down on the table. She had not meant to offend her namesake, this old Princess Eleanor known for so many years as the Maid of Brittany, but it was impossible not to be aware of her own youth, to deny the fact of her growing beauty.

The Maid had once been beautiful, they said, but now Eleanor could see little lines on her face, the hair beneath the stiff white wimple quite grey, and she wondered what it must be like to have been a prisoner for so many years. Curiosity as well as old memories had urged her to ask permission of her brother the King to visit this solitary lady before setting out to meet her bridegroom. Somehow the Maid was tied up with her childhood and in a few days that childhood would be over. She would lie all night with a man and while her stomach turned over with nervous excitement at the thought of it, at the realization of her new status as a wedded wife, nevertheless she was afraid, conscious that she was stepping from a spoiled and happy youth into responsible womanhood. For a moment, rather than talk of it, she asked the Maid which she would have preferred of her prospective husbands.

The Princess laughed. 'Dear child, any that would be joined to me. Perhaps the idea of Saphadin was the most romantic, though marriage has little to do with romance, God knows. He was the great Saladin's brother, you know, and my uncle Richard- "Coeur de Lion" they called him, and rightly- wanted to settle the fighting for the Holy Places by making us King and Queen of Jerusalem. But Saphadin would not turn Christian, so that was the end of it. One of Saladin's messengers told me he was very handsome.' She gave a little sigh. 'Then my grandmother, Queen Eleanor of Aquitaine, took me to Austria when my uncle was a prisoner there, hoping to wed me to Duke Leopold's son, but nothing came of that either. You are like her, my dear.'

'Like Queen Eleanor?'

'You have her dark hair, a look of her in the way you hold your head, but your eyes are true Plantagenet blue, as mine are. I wonder if I might have done more for you if I had married Louis of France? But then my uncle died and your father became King. He shut me up in Corfe Castle and that was where I first saw you.'

'I wish I could remember,' Eleanor said.

The room was littered with her bride-clothes, travelling trunks open to reveal fine silks and velvets, sendal and sarsinet, shoes and veils, golden fillets and crespines to hold her hair, belts and gloves, including a pair embroidered by the Princess herself, and there was a box with two locks to contain her jewels.

The Maid was fingering an ell of dark green cloth, her face shadowed. 'This is very good quality,' she remarked inconsequentially. 'You should have a riding gown made from it. Your brother sent me a similar piece last Candlemas.'

'Henry likes giving presents.' Eleanor, however, wanted to pursue the subject that interested her. 'Was he at Corfe when we were there?'

'No, he was with your mother at Exeter. Your father feared for your lives, as well he might, when he was fighting the barons and Louis of France as well. But your brother Richard and your sisters were there. I used to play with them and I taught them to dance, but I was a lonely time for me, barely twenty and never allowed outside the castle walls. Corfe is so high on its rock that I could see the sea through a gap in the hills, and I used to sit there looking at it and wondering if I would ever see my own Brittany again – which I never did.'

'You think my father was cruel? Everyone seems to have hated him.'

'Yes, he was cruel,' the Maid said, but the years had taken the edge from her bitterness. 'He slew my brother, Arthur.'

'Henry says no one ever knew for certain – '

The Maid laughed with sudden sharpness. 'My dear child, one thing you must learn is never to run from the truth, however hard it may be. King John murdered Arthur, or his minions did, in Rouen Castle. My Lord Hubert, de Burgh will tell you the truth of that.'

'Then you must hate Henry, and Richard and all of us.'

'Hate you? You were not responsible and you are not in the least like your father, except', a little smile crept into the Princess's eyes, 'perhaps you have something of his pride.' You were a mere babe when he died.'

Eleanor nodded. She had no memories of her despised father and few of her mother Queen Isabella who had fled to France after his death and married Hugh de Lusignan, Count of La Marche. Now she was busy raising another family and Eleanor had seen her only once, but at the English court she had been petted by great ladies and her brother the King made much of her. 'I'm glad Henry sent these figs,' she said at last, selecting one from a silver dish. 'He allows you to keep a great household.'

'Oh yes,' the Maid agreed. She too took a fig and peeled it with delicate fingers. 'He knows how fond I am of fruit, and I believe there is a case of almonds too. But you have seen, child, that though I ride out often, it is never without a suitable escort of knights who are also my gaolers. You will, please God and

His Holy Mother, have a happier life than I, my sweeting.'

Eleanor considered this for a moment. 'I suppose I shall be happy with my lord of Pembroke. I have seen so little of him since our wedding. I was only nine then and these last five years he has been in Ireland for most of the time. What did you mean when you said you might have done more for me? Isn't this a good marriage?'

'Well enough,' the Maid agreed, 'but you are a princess, daughter of one king and sister to another, and I would have looked higher for you than William Marshal.'

'But he is Earl of Pembroke and his father was a very great man, was he not?'

'Old William Marshal was perhaps the best knight who ever lived,' the Maid agreed. 'My uncles all cared greatly for him and I'm sure his eldest son is as good a man in many ways, but I would have chosen royal blood for you as for your sisters. However, the thing was done five years ago so there is no point in repining. Are you afraid of him because he is so much older than you?'

'I don't know.' Eleanor kept her head turned away. 'My lord William is so big and so important. The few times I have seen him he has treated me as a child and now – '

'Now he is to be your husband in more than name, eh? My dear, I can tell you little about marriage and I have never taken a lover, for that would have delivered me into my enemies' hands, but I remember William's mother. She married his father when she was no more than sixteen, barely two years older than you, and her bridegroom was in his forties then. Yet they were very happy. I am sorry she did not live to see you and William bedded.'

Eleanor nodded. The day of her brief wedding ceremony was rather hazy in her memory; she had been too young for it to be consummated and had left her bridegroom on the same day, to live under the care of the Dowager Countess. She had grown very fond of the Lady Isabel and had grieved for her when she died scarcely a year later. Since then Eleanor had lived mainly at court and she wondered to which of his vast holdings the Earl of Pembroke would take her after the feasting. Perhaps they would be happy as his parents had been, but the romances she read telling of l'Amour Courtois had nothing, so the Maid said, to do with marriage. She had been reading a new poem, for her brother had had her well taught, called Le Roman de la Rose and her head was full of it so that the reality of becoming a wife seemed almost a mundane thing, a burden to a woman. One's husband would not, after all, sing ballads as the troubadours did to one's eyebrows or liken one's breasts to slopes of lilies, yet he would make demands, frightening demands that were a dark unknown to her.

'I wish I could have waited a little longer,' she said impulsively, 'stayed the summer with you.'

The Maid gave a melancholy smile. 'Youth is too precious to let slip away in waiting, dear child. Have you not heard the couplet –

"But 'yet and yet' goes on and on
And 'wait a little' grows too long."'

Eleanor smiled. At fourteen, with all life stretching before her, she could not envisage it slipping away. She glanced at the Princess, seeing the saddened eyes, the smoothness of skin gone, the figure beneath the heavy silk gown sagging a little. And this room – it was the room of a lady of high birth yet solitary. No child's rattle had ever lain discarded here, no baby clothes had ever been lovingly stitched here, nor had a new life come in the great bed that no husband had shared, no lover either if the Maid was to be believed, and Eleanor did believe her. There was a loneliness, a waning of beauty, all opportunity denied, life worn away in captivity, albeit a gentle captivity.

And suddenly she had no more desire to stay, to dream away the summer by the slow flowing river under the willow trees. Life was for living and now she wanted the Earl and Countess of Gloucester to come, she wanted to see them riding in under the gatehouse with a train of knights and ladies and men-at-arms to escort her to Winchester where her brother would formally give her to Earl William. After the feasting she understood the Earl would take her away for their 'lovers' days', and she would begin to learn to rule one of his great houses.

She stood up, holding the Maid's mirror at arm's length to see as much of herself as she could. This gown of blue sarsinet matched her eyes and the trimming of marten fur edging the white surcoat was not too wide to make its appearance heavy. Gold thread embroidered a pattern of leaves about the hem and sleeves and the low-slung belt was of gold chain, a gift among many others from Henry. As became a young virgin her hair was unbound but a blue fillet held her white veil in place and there was sufficient colour in her face to keep her from becoming sallow. She had never been overfond of sweetmeats, and vanity made her refuse them for she had fine white teeth and no mind to lose them. The Maid ate marchpane or sugar plums constantly and her front teeth were almost black. Eleanor nibbled another fig and her impatience grew until at last she heard the sound of hooves, many hooves, clattering over the drawbridge. She ran to the window, sucking her fingers clean. 'They are here, Madame, they have come!

It seemed to her the bailey was alive with colour, the banners and pennons of the knights, the wedding attire of the company bright with scarlet, green, blue and gold. Men were dismounting, women being lifted down from the saddle, while servants ran back and forth with great leather jugs of ale to refresh them. The halt was to be brief for they were to rest the night at Bradford-upon-Avon, and only the Earl and his wife came up the stair to be ushered into the Maid's chamber.

Gilbert de Clare, Earl of Gloucester, was about thirty, a somewhat choleric young man, very conscious of himself and his position. He was anxious to be on the road again, to see his young charge safely in lodgings for the night, for it was still early enough in the year for darkness to come in the late afternoon, the April days bright enough in the morning to allow an early start. He bowed over the Maid's hand and gave a few formal words of greeting, but his wife was more forthcoming. She curtseyed but before she was more than half risen, she and the Princess were embracing each other. Isabella de Clare had been Isabella Marshal, daughter of the great William Marshal and had consequently spent much of her time at Pembroke, permitted to visit the prisoner with a frequency allowed to no one else.

She turned to look appraisingly at Eleanor while the Maid called for a page to bring wine. Gilbert muttered something about time, and fifteen miles to cover before dusk, but the Maid would take no refusal and the tall and imperious Isabella said calmly, 'We shall have time enough and more, husband,' whereat he subsided, but he cast a glance at the open chests.

'God's death, lady, did you have to unpack all your bridal gear?'

'Of course,' Eleanor said. 'I wished the Princess to see everything. My brother has been most generous to me.'

'Well, they'd best be carried down at once,' he grumbled, 'or we shall be here all night.'

The Maid nodded to a hovering serving woman to see that it was done and while a couple of attendants came to struggle with the heavy chests a lad carried the iron-bound box that contained Eleanor's jewels.

The wine, sent by the King, was excellent, and Gilbert drank in silence while the two women chattered about bridals and Eleanor sat on a stool between them, her hands clasped, as anxious now as the Earl, though for other reasons, to be gone. At last the cups were empty and the Maid rose reluctantly, embracing Isabella once more.'

'This dear child will be your sister. Have a care for her.'

'Of course,' the Countess said warmly. She had much of her father's natural kindness and she looked down at the eager, nervous girl with an indulgent smile. 'Eleanor will have five sisters now. Matilda is not with us, though she hopes to reach Winchester for the wedding, but Sybilla and Eva are below and Joanna will be waiting for us at Winchester. My brothers Anselm and Waiter are here too – you are part of a large family, my dear.'

Eleanor lifted her head. 'And my husband, madame, has the King for brother-in-law.' They should see that the Marshals, great though they were, were not conferring a greater favour on her than she on them, for she was a Plantagenet and everyone knew that before he had achieved so much fame and honour the senior William Marshal had been a landless younger son, a mere nobody.

Isabella laughed. Her own husband was, with the one exception of the Earl of Chester, the wealthiest and most powerful man in the kingdom and she could afford to indulge that little spurt of pride. 'Well, so he has. I wish my next brother Richard were here but he is always so busy about our inheritance in France. Do you recall him, child?'

Eleanor shook her head. She did not need reminding of the extent of the Marshal holdings, but Richard Marshal had been out of England so long that she had no interest in him. She glanced at the Maid and saw a great sadness there. Young as she was, it seemed to her that the Countess's talk of her sisters and brothers only served to heighten the isolation. She went to the Maid and kissed her.

'Dear madame, when my lord takes me to Pembroke we will come and see you. You have been so kind and I'll not forget.'

The Maid held her face for a moment between her hands. 'You will have many new duties, Eleanor, but if you can visit a lonely old woman I shall be glad. I do not think your brother would deny me that great pleasure.'

'Well,' Gilbert picked up his gloves. 'We'd best be gone. Your servant, my lady.' He gave a brief bow and opened the door. Eleanor clung for one last moment to the Princess and then was about to run out when her arm was caught and held.

'It is not becoming to run,' the Countess said. 'Pray walk and as elegantly as you can to show off your gown. There are a great many knights and ladies waiting below to attend you and you must not appear a mere hoyden.'

Eleanor curbed her steps impatiently but when she emerged from the door of the great hall, followed by her attendants Doll and Megonwy, and her old nurse, Ellen, who had also nursed her brother, it was as a royal princess going to her bridal. Her groom, Finch, was standing by her white palfrey and as he locked his hands for her small foot she sprang lightly into the saddle. Her two sisters-in-law, Sybilla de Ferrars, Countess of Derby, and Eva de Braose greeted her warmly. Lady Derby had her two little girls with her, riding one behind the other on a small pony, and they smiled shyly at the Princess Eleanor. Their father carried the bride's banner while William de Braose made as if to range himself on her other side until he realized that place was to be occupied by the Earl of Gloucester and reined back, somewhat red in the face.

Then they were moving out and Eleanor turned for one last glance at the chamber above the great hall. She saw the Maid at the window and waved her gloved hand, but remembering Isabella's injunction turned it into a royal gesture. Slowly the cavalcade took the road east and her excitement began to rise, Mabille trotting well to keep pace with the Earl's black destrier, the mules laden, with her baggage left some distance behind. The countryside was bright with the green of young haw- thorn, the buds of oak and beech ready to burst, violets and primroses in the banks. The sun had some warmth in it and by noon Earl Gilbert was sweating in his furred mantle. They halted to refresh the horses by a stream, servants bringing ale and meat and bread for the company. A peasant woman from a rough wattle cottage came out and asked if the young princess would like a drink of milk. Eleanor took the bowl gratefully. The Maid had told her that milk kept the skin white and clear and Eleanor was determined never to lose the beauty she had Aquitaine had still been beautiful even in old age.

Finch came to adjust her stirrup and she smiled at him, wanting him to share in her happiness this day. He was a short, sturdy young man, sent to her some years ago by the Maid with a recommendation; he had thick brown curling hair and he was immensely strong, yet very gentle with horses. He had been born a 'mantle-child'; his mother had died at his birth whereat his father had disappeared and the abandoned infant was fostered by one of the Maid's serving women.

Eleanor had asked him whether Finch was his father's name or his given name 'and he had scratched his head, saying he didn't think either, but a bird had been singing on a nearby bush when he had been found on the chapel steps at Bristol and his foster mother thereafter called him Finch. He was only a few years older than his young mistress but from the first he gave her the unstinting service of a single-minded young man who had his bread to earn. It was he who had taught her how to handle her mount, he who had found this spirited mare Mabille at Gloucester horse fair.

Eleanor handed the bowl back to the peasant woman and he helped her into the saddle once more. The gentle countryside rolled by, groups of peasants in the fields turning to watch the great cavalcade pass, and at last as the sun went down and the spring evening grew chilly they rode into Bradford-upon-Avon. Isabella complained of being stiff but her small son Richard, who was six years old, slid down from his pony crying out that he could have ridden on all night.

Eleanor slept in a great bed at the manor, sharing it with both Sybilla and Eva, the only other chamber being occupied by the senior Earl and Countess, and the rest of the company accommodated where they could find space to lay a pallet. For a long while after her sisters-in-law slept, Eleanor lay awake. She was thinking of the morning's talk with the Maid and it seemed suddenly remote and far away, for life, surely, was about to begin.

Two days later they reached Winchester and in the hall there, with its high-beamed roof, its walls bright with banners and tapestries, her brother was waiting to greet her.

King Henry III had the red-gold hair of the Plantagenets, the same bright blue eyes, his face handsome in a slender, delicate fashion, only a droop to the left eyelid half hiding a slight but unmistakable squint. He loved elegant clothes and jewels and was wearing his favourite colour, green, his gown trimmed with miniver, his tunic of finest velvet, his coronet of gold, an emerald clasp fastening his mantle. There was nothing he enjoyed more than a state occasion when he might be lavish, shower gifts on his friends and show all the trappings of royalty. He was twenty-two years old and had been king for thirteen of them.

Eleanor swept him a deep obeisance but at once he came to her and kissed her cheek, enquiring about her journey. Then it was the turn of her second brother, Richard, Earl of Cornwall, to greet her. He too had the good looks of the family and he was as richly dressed as the King, but his manner was quieter, his talk less volatile – though everyone knew, from a disagreement a year or two ago over a legal point concerning some land, that he could be utterly determined and carry the day even against his own brother and King. Eleanor was devoted to him. She wished her sisters could have been here, but Isabella was now Queen of Scotland while Joan, betrothed to the King of Sicily, was already living at her future husband's court. At least, Eleanor thought, she herself had not to leave England and her brothers for her marriage.

Henry took her hand and beckoned to the tall man waiting a little to his left. A hand was set in hers and Eleanor looked fleetingly up at the husband she had so rarely seen. He smiled down at her, bowing over her fingers in an accomplished manner, though she knew from talk with his sisters that he was more soldier than courtier, that he had spent much of his life fighting in Ireland or France. He was wise in council and well liked by both friends and inferiors, but they had warned her not to expect pretty speeches from him. She had heard nothing frivolous of him and expected a serious man approaching middle age.

But it seemed he was not like that at all for the head bowed over her hand was without grey in the thick brown hair and when he raised himself he was smiling still, his mouth suggesting a natural humour.

'Welcome,' he said and his voice was deep. 'Welcome, my lady. I have waited long for this day.'

'And I,' she said and everyone laughed so that she flushed and lowered her eyes.

'At fourteen it may not have seemed so long,' he said quickly in an endeavour to ease her embarrassment and he led her to the chairs set for them on either side of the King's on the dais. Trestles were being set up and as the barons and knights and ladies of the court scrambled for their places, ushers and serving men hurried to lay the royal cloth, to set out silver goblets and the tall salt cellars. Small bowls of water and white napkins were set by each place at the high table and as the dishes were carried ceremoniously to the King and his guests, minstrels in the gallery began the entertainment.

Eleanor was hungry, yet after a few mouthfuls from a dish of roast peacock, a favourite of hers, she found her nervousness returning and surreptitiously glanced sideways at the stranger who was her husband. She could not see him clearly for he sat on the King's left and was talking to his sister Isabella, but he seemed so big, larger than she remembered. He had been wed before, when he was a boy of eighteen, but she had been told that his bride had died within a year. Since then, apparently, he had shown little interest in women, though she had heard that in the interminable arguing in council about her marriage settlement, he had shown some impatience.

She did not know what to expect from him, and to cover her nervousness, began to talk animatedly to her brother Richard, describing her journey and the crossing of a swollen ford, telling of the discomfiture of a stiff lady who had been toppled in all her finery into the water. She ate a salmon pasty and laughed at the tumblers who were performing in the centre of the hall, with time now to observe the guests come for her bridals.

There were loud-mouthed barons with a reputation for cruelty such as William de Braose and the Earl of Lincoln; others like Gilbert de Clare who ate and drank greedily, concerned mainly with their pride and their stomachs; there were the marcher lords, the Mortimers and Montgomery, who acknowledged the King's authority but paid little heed to it; and at the lower tables a teeming number of knights who owed fees to one or another of the great men and were eager to make their way in the world. The hall rang with talk and laughter, the guests reaching for dishes of meat or whole chickens to tear to with their teeth, while at the King's table the guests were given new-fangled forks to help them spear their food. The Earl of Chester pushed his aside, preferring a knife and his fingers, but the King ate neatly with his silver prongs and called it a civilized tool.

The Justiciar, Hubert de Burgh, sat a few seats beyond her, his eyes tired, his hair grey and receding. For twenty years he had guided the young King, first as his guardian and tutor and then as his chief councilor but men said now that he had feathered his own nest too softly in the process. He had had four brides, the last being the Princess Margaret of Scotland, a plain but elegant lady who had given Eleanor a belt of strangely fashioned silver set with semi-precious stones from her own country. She was inclined to be imperious and Eleanor thought her brother growing tired of both the de Burghs, particularly since Hubert's failure against the incursions of Llewellyn, the Welsh Prince.

Among the older men was Randulph de Blundevill, the ageing Earl of Chester, still blunt and outspoken, his manners leaving much to be desired as he reached for a dish of meat, sucking noisily through broken teeth. Ruling the County Palatine of Chester, he enjoyed great power and had spent his life close to the throne. There was little love lost between him and de Burgh, but on the surface tonight all differences were laid aside. The men were drinking deep, some of the ladies also, and Eva de Braose was seized with a fit of hiccuping. Eleanor could not keep back a giggle as the feasting grew more lively and the music swelled louder, the dancing lost some of its propriety, and it was like a sudden dip into cold water when her brother signed to the Countess of Gloucester that it was time to escort her to the bridal chamber.

She rose and everyone in the hall rose also. Cups and goblets were raised to her and William himself turned with his in his hand, drinking the contents at one draught. For one moment she thought she saw an expression almost of affection in his eyes, but how could it be? What did he know of her, any more than she knew of him?

Then she was hurried away in the midst of a group of ladies and in a chamber above they undressed her, washing her body with water perfumed with oil from the east, rubbing her skin until it glowed. They combed her hair freely about her shoulders, letting it fall in dusky silken strands well below her slender waist. When she shivered in her nakedness, Isabella de Clare said, 'Never mind, child you'll soon be warm enough, I'll warrant,' and the others laughed.

'Too warm, if William is anything like my lord,' Eva de Braose said. 'When I think of my bridal night and the shock of it –'

Sybilla, the elder by several years, broke in, 'Hush, sister, don't alarm the Princess.' She kissed Eleanor and said cheerfully, 'Pay no heed to Eva. She should have been a nun.'

'If Providence should call my lord away, I promise you I would persuade our brother to allow me to seek a holy house,' Eva retorted severely. 'I would not willingly take another man to my bed.'

Isabella began to turn back the covers. 'What nonsense you talk. The nuns are good women for the most part, but chastity is a cold bed-fellow, at least so I think.' She took Eleanor's hand and led her to the bed. 'There, my dear, lean against the pillow thus and let me draw the sheet about your chin. We must be modest when the men bring your bridegroom to you.' She bent to kiss her little sister-in-law and whispered 'There's naught to fear. William is a kind man and he has waited many years for you.'

Eleanor gave her a grateful glance, but it was impossible to still her jumping nerves when there was a knock on the door and Sybilla opened it to admit a crowd of gentlemen, led by the King and his brother. With much laughing and one or two lewd jokes which Eleanor did not fully understand William was led to the bed. He slid in beside her, the cover was drawn up over him and his long gown removed over his head. Hot spiced wine was drunk and Eleanor was glad of it for it warmed her and made her less aware of all the eyes on her. She did not look at William but something in her, pride perhaps, resisted the amused indulgence of the company, kindly though it was. They knew what she did not, and for a moment she wished herself back in Bristol Castle, sewing with the Maid whose life had been so simple.

Henry came to her, kissing her heartily. 'It is time I saw to my own bridal, eh, little sister? Perhaps I shall follow you to this marriage bed. It is fit for a King as well as a King's sister.' He ran his hand down the hangings of the bed, the royal arms embroidered at the head of it, his slender fingers ringed with emeralds appreciating the feel of the material, while his eyes wandered in a satisfied manner over the rich furnishings of the room, the carved chair by the hearth, the solid table, the coffer inlaid with mother-of-pearl.

He had wanted to marry Marjorie, the youngest of the Scottish King's daughters, but as the eldest had wed Hubert de Burgh his council considered it below him to take the younger and he had to look elsewhere. But he had considered himself in love with Marjorie and it added to his resentment against his Justiciar. The recent proposal that he should wed Leopold of Austria's daughter had come to nothing for the bride had been snapped up by the German King before the Bishop of Chichester had so much as broached Henry's suit. Bumbling old fool, Henry thought, but perhaps he was well out of it. They said the girl had buck teeth.

He looked down at Eleanor and was pleased with this match at least. He owed his throne to William Marshal's father and this union would bind the powerful Marshal family more closely to him. He beckoned to the Bishop of Chichester to proclaim the blessing, kneeling devoutly while prayers were said over the bridal couple.

Eleanor had her eyes cast down and did not raise them when with more laughter and talk the company who had crowded the room filed out. The candles were blown out and then she and William were alone in the darkness.

She shivered and he said at once, 'Are you cold, my bird?' and set his arm about her shoulders. 'You are not afraid of me, are you?'

'No, no,' she said. She had never seen a man's body naked, except in a picture in a book concerning the treatment of broken limbs which her governess had hastily removed, and here was this big man lying beside her, about to possess her, and the lie on her lips only added to her fear. She was in his arms now but for a little while he talked, asking her of her doings in the past few years, of the things she liked to occupy her time, drawing her out on the subject of hawking which she loved. She was only half aware that such consideration was rare among hard-living barons with little time for niceties, and it was only as she relaxed a little, responding to his questions, that he turned to kisses instead of words.

He was restrained at first, his mouth gentle, but as his hands passed over her his lips grew more insistent. His body was heavy, overwhelming her and the hurt, utterly unexpected, made her want to cry out. But she bit back the sound, refusing to reveal her pain. Eva had been right, she was not cold now but hot, aware of sweat between their two bodies, his panting breath on her face, the blood drumming in her ears.

And then it seemed it was over. William rolled away from her and though for a moment his hand lingered on her breast, though he kissed her again, his moustache rough against her lips as he murmured an endearment, his breathing grew slow and regular and he slept, his head against her shoulder.

Slow tears gathered and trickled down the side of her face. Was this what the Maid had so longed for, what Isabella seemed to find so satisfying? Her body felt bruised, her head ached, and she wondered why God had chosen so strange a way to bring about the union between man and woman and the new birth that followed it. Perhaps quite soon she would be pregnant and then there would be more pain, more violence to her young body. Holy Mother of God, she prayed, help me to bear it, to understand Eva must be right, no woman surely would ever willingly choose to take a second husband.

At last, exhausted by the long day and its culmination, she slept and was only awakened by a movement beside her. She stirred slowly, aware of daylight, and saw that William, partly dressed, was sitting on the bed beside her.

He smiled and said, 'I always rise early.' He put out a hand to touch her cheek gently. Unwittingly, as the memory of last night came back to her, she shrank from him and the movement, though instantly suppressed, was not lost on him. 'Dear wife,' there was a deep kindliness in his voice, 'be patient a little while. I will teach you to love me.'

And suddenly she knew that despite the years between them, miraculously he understood. She looked into his face as if seeing for the first, time the true quality and character of this man she had married, a man who kept to the ideals of knighthood, a fighting man but without the common brutality, a man unswerving in loyalty. She sat up, hugging the coverlet about her, half hoping he would take her in his arms again, but he merely lifted her hand and put it to his lips, being wiser perhaps than she knew.

'I will send your women to you,' he said and stood up, fastening his mantle about his shoulders. 'Later we will ride together.' With a brief smile he was gone and the room seemed oddly empty without his large presence. She lay back on her pillows and an entirely new sense of well-being came to her.

CHAPTER TWO

Eleanor had shut her eyes upon the shuddering world and lay with her face pressed into a pillow, not wanting to look at her anxious women, Ellen hovering beside her, a hand on her forehead, Megonwy gabbling prayers, Doll as sick as she was. It seemed extraordinary that the sea which had looked so smooth and calm and beautiful yesterday could turn overnight into this grey heaving monster that turned her stomach to water. She had never been on a ship before and in this moment swore she never would again. The ship rolled and, shivering and exhausted, she longed only for dry land, for something beneath her feet that would keep still.

Why did Henry have to decide on this expedition to Brittany, to take William with him, and her because she would not leave William? Even the prospect of seeing her mother, waiting to greet them at St Malo, faded before the present misery.

The door of the cabin opened and she heard low voices, but she kept her eyes tightly shut that she might not see the tilt of the cabin, all her possessions rolling about. However, a moment later another hand, much larger, was laid on her forehead and a loved voice asked how she did.

She opened her eyes and tears spilled out of them. 'My lord - oh, my lord, how long will it be?'

'Before we land?' He bent to kiss her clammy brow. 'Your brother is so concerned for you that we are to put into harbour at Jersey to give you time to recover. My dearest love, you will soon feel better, I promise you. Seasickness passes very quickly once you are on land again, and the next time we go to sea perhaps we shall not have such vile weather.' He looked down at her pale, tear-stained face. 'Poor little bird, it will soon be over now.' He gathered her into his arms and she lay thankfully against his chest, drawing comfort from his most comforting presence.

By now the wind was dropping a little and the ship's pitching eased. William stayed with her and when they made port it was he who carried her, wrapped in his own fur-lined mantle, down the gangplank and on to the shore. She was taken to the house of a knight and his lady and there, to her surprise, within an hour or two she began to feel a great deal better. She drank a little wine which put the warmth back into her limbs and her shivering ceased.

'There,' Ellen said, her rosy face all smiles, 'your lord was right, my lady, you will soon be your own self again, though by'r Lady I feared we'd all be drowned.'

'It must have been a very bad storm.' Eleanor set down the cup and slipped off the bed to look out of the window. The security of a steady floor was a great relief, and the sea had lost its wrath. The April sky was grey still but the wind had died and a gentle rain was falling. She could see the English fleet riding at anchor, her brother's ship with the royal banner hanging limply close by the harbour wall, and she asked if her old nurse knew when they were to sail again, for sail they must. If she had to brave that monster out there again, it would be best to go surely while it was calm.

Ellen said, 'I did hear 'twas not to be until tomorrow's full tide, to give you time to rest. Come back to bed, my chuck.' Eleanor yawned and owned she had become very sleepy since drinking the wine, and when tucked up she fell soundly asleep and did not wake until it was growing dark. Supper that night was taken aboard their ship, now still enough to banish her fears, and she sat between her brother and her husband and ate hungrily, her appetite quite recovered.

Henry teased her for costing them a day's journey, but he was smiling and cheerful. 'We are on the threshold of a great campaign,' he said, 'and one day more or less will not hinder us. This time we will send the French back across their borders and take hold of some of the land my father lost. I must admit I am impatient to see my mother.'

'It is to hoped she will bring adequate forces,' the Earl of Chester said rather glumly. 'We do not have the men or the supplies I would like to have seen.'

'Oh!' Henry gave an expressive shrug. 'That is to be blamed on that old traitor de Burgh. He was against this venture from the start and did all he could to baulk me.'

'Saving your grace's pardon,' Gilbert de Clare broke in, 'if he did so he did it with your grace's welfare at heart. A man may hold opposite views on a matter without being a traitor and my lord Hubert has served you from the day the crown was set on your head, and before.'

'Maybe, maybe.' Henry's tone was petulant. 'But he will not see that I am a man now and it is I who command.' Briefly he recalled how, when he had ridden last year to Portsmouth to set out, he had found such inadequate preparations that he had lost his temper. He had rushed at his chancellor with a drawn sword and only the intervention of the Earl of Chester had prevented bloodshed. He did not like losing his temper, preferring to keep life smooth and pleasant and conducive to his own tastes. He would rather be visiting a cathedral in the building, or a shrine, than sit listening to dreary accounts of demands on the royal treasury. It was up to his chancellor and his exchequer to find money for him, and as it was he had had to wait further months before setting out, all on account of the parsimony of Hubert de Burgh who had become in his eyes too arrogant for comfort.

'Enough of the tiresome fellow,' he said lightly. 'He will sing a different tune when we go home in triumph with my grandfather's lands under my hand again.'

His brother Richard took a long pull at his goblet. 'No easy task. This is poor stuff, Harry. Hubert never did have much of a palate. I shall be glad when we can command better wine.'

'We did not think to be so long at sea,' Henry retorted, smiling at his sister. 'Can you brave the water once more?'

Eleanor suppressed a little shudder, refusing to appear cowardly before all this company. 'I am quite well again now, brother,' she said with dignity, and the thirty hours it took them to reach St Malo were calm enough that she had no more sickness. She stood beside William on the deck as dawn came up on the second morning and, watched the French coast draw near, the gentle breeze barely stirring her hood, the ship moving so smoothly that she actually enjoyed the motion. The beauty of the morning sky, the glittering sea, the green of the coastline stirred her to exclaim at it and remark that there was something to be said for a sea voyage after all.

William was plainly relieved to see the colour back in her face, but then he was always considerate. She thought back over her year of marriage and in a sudden gust of emotion thanked the Blessed Virgin that she had not died on the voyage out, for she adored her husband now and the thought of being without him was horrifying. Her love had grown, deepening with respect for him, for his dignity, his quiet manner, his integrity. His love-making was like the man himself and sometimes she wished for more passion, for some of the fire she had read of in French romances, but William was not, to her fifteen year-old mind, a young man and innocently she supposed she could not expect it. When she lay with him at night it was always with pleasurable anticipation and yet she sensed there was something missing. She tried to talk to her sister-in-law about it but was overcome with embarrassment, and Isabella clearly thought such matters not for discussion.

'Duty and obedience dictate our state,' Isabella had said, 'and if love comes with them then thank God for your good fortune, and do not question too closely.'

Eleanor said no more but one thing she knew, that she was seldom happier than when William was beside her. He was, he must be, the best of husbands, and if there was something undiscovered, if instinctively her body craved something unachieved, she must not complain about that. She slipped her hand into William's and asked how soon there would be fighting.

'Soon, please God,' he said, 'it is what we are come for,' and seeing the expression on her face added, 'My heart, a well-armoured knight can survive many battles and I know what I am about.'

Her fingers tightened on his. 'Will your brother be there to meet us?'

'I fear not. I've not seen Richard these seven years, not since he wed Alain of Dinan's daughter. He is in a difficult position for he holds our father's Norman lands and the King of France is his suzerain. He is Louis's marshal into the bargain.'

She was disappointed. She did not like Gilbert Marshal, William's third brother who was in minor orders and held a living in Suffolk, but who plainly cared little for his calling, preferring to be at court in his brother's shadow. She liked Walter and Anselm well enough, but had wished to meet the Richard of whom William spoke so highly.

'We will come to terms with France in due course, I expect,' William said. 'The regent, Queen Blanche, is a strong-minded woman, as one would expect of a grand-daughter of old King Henry, and she is no fool. When we have filched what we can there will be a truce and then perhaps we will see Richard.'

They stood together watching as the ship drew in, the sailors scrambling in the rigging, throwing ropes to those ashore. The waiting crowds lining the wharf cheered the arrival of the English host enthusiastically while the knights of the Count of Brittany sat in their saddles, spears held erect, to provide an escort for the King of England. Henry came ashore dressed in full armour, a white silk mantle thrown over it, and the crowds yelled themselves hoarse.

He turned to the Earl of Chester. 'You see! We are welcome here. I shall soon rule over all that my father lost.'

In the bustle of landing, while William was supervising the unloading of his gear and Finch, in charge of his lady's boxes, was not aware that she was ready to mount, Eleanor stood momentarily alone beside Mabille, her hand smoothing the palfrey's soft nose.

A knight disengaged himself from a group and appeared suddenly at her side. 'May I assist you, my lady?'

She turned to see a tall slender man with straight dark hair that fell thickly across his forehead. His eyes, set between straight dark brows, were of a deep, cool grey and he had a symmetry of feature that gave him an almost classic beauty, though it was lessened by a habitually grave expression. Only when he smiled, as he did now, did the full effect of his fine features become apparent. He was dressed plainly, almost poorly, and his mantle was fastened with an unadorned clasp. She had seen him before among her brother's knights, but she did not know who he was. A younger son, perhaps, with his way to make.

'Thank you,' she said and prepared to mount in the usual fashion, but to her surprise found herself lifted bodily into the saddle.

She looked down at him somewhat haughtily and he said, 'You are a mere featherweight, lady. I can set my hands to meet about so little a waist.'

'And you have a great impertinence; she retorted. 'A hand for my foot would have sufficed.'

He bowed, a slightly ironic expression on his face that somehow made her feel she had been childish, but she did not expect unknown knights to be familiar with the King's sister. He handed her the reins and would have left her without speaking but that she halted him by asking his name.

He turned back and looked directly up at her. 'Simon de Montfort, my lady.'

'So, daughter.' The Queen mother, now Countess de la Marche, looked her up and down approvingly.

'You are grown into a woman. Do you carry a child under that fine gown?'

Eleanor blushed. 'No, madame, I do not think so.' She found her mother somewhat overwhelming.

'Well, well, there's time yet.' Isabella of Angouleme had grown a little plump but she still had traces of the devastating beauty that had turned men's heads. Ellen had told her mistress, among other tales, that once when the Queen had taken a lover, King John had found out and one morning she had awoken to find the unfortunate man dangling from a rope at the foot of her bed. Eleanor still felt a thrill of horror remembering the story, and though her mother had been happily wed for thirteen years to Hugh de Lusignan and had a brood of growing lads now paying their respects to their half-brother, the King, she still had an air about her that made her daughter believe Ellen's lurid tales.

The whole company mounted up and rode away and as they went, Eleanor asked her brother Richard what he knew of Sir Simon de Montfort.

Richard gave her a surprised glance. 'Have you had speech with him? He is a mere supplicant at the moment, another foreigner trying to find an inheritance in England. But he has a reasonable claim. His great-uncle was Robert de Beamont, Earl of Leicester in our grandfather's day and the Leicester lands should, by default of a male heir, go to the de Montforts of Montfort L'Amaury.'

'Where is that?'

'Some thirty miles south of Paris. Robert's widow, the Countess Loretta, lives in a convent near

Canterbury, a redoubtable old lady, one of the de Braose family, and Sir Simon came ostensibly to visit her, but in fact to ask our brother for the Leicester lands and earldom. The stewardship of England goes with them so it is no small matter.'

Eleanor turned her head but she could no longer see the dark young man from France. 'What did Henry say?'

'Well, Chester has them at present. He's the nephew of old Sir Simon, this Simon's father who's been dead these many years. The Earl was supposed to hold them until Amaury de Montfort came of age, but apparently my lord Amaury has waived his right in favour of his younger brother – only Henry says he will not deprive Earl Randulph of them while he lives.'

Eleanor's lips curled into a little smile. 'So Sir Simon has got nothing for his pains?'

Richard glanced at her. 'That seems to please you. Why?'

'Oh,' she gave a little shrug, 'I thought he was rather arrogant. Where do we lie tonight?'

'We shall probably get no further than Dinan, but we should be at Rennes the day after tomorrow. Our uncle Geoffrey once owned the castle there, and had the drawbridge up more often than down. He and our other uncles were always quarrelling about something.'

'I am glad you and Harry are not like that.'

'No,' he answered soberly, 'but that does not mean that I bow to Henry in everything. You may recall that a few years ago when he gave a manor on my land at Berkhamstead to that upstart German fellow. I got it back and without the use of the sword.'

'I remember. William thought you were right.'

'Henry is too impulsive. I am not.'

She looked sideways at his profile. No, she thought, he was always the coolest member of the family but at the same time not one to cross.

The long columns stretched away behind her and in the excitement of the venture she forgot the insignificant knight from Montfort L'Amaury and enjoyed the Breton countryside. The sun was warm on her face, William had left his serious converse with Gilbert de Clare and come to ride on her other side, and she found herself praying she might soon be able to answer yes to her mother's first question. To bear William a son would be the crowning of her love.

At Nantes Henry entertained his Breton and Norman supporters with various entertainments, jousting and pageants and banquets. Every day there was hunting and hawking, or a display of wrestling or archery. He was in holiday mood and opened his coffers wide to show his allies that the King of England was no skinflint. After two weeks he set off for Bordeaux, seized a castle on the way and convinced of his ability to command entered that city to ringing acclaim.

Eleanor was exultant for him but William said carefully, 'It was a small castle, my love, and the garrison yielded all too easily. I fear that is not enough to make our French foes fear us.'

He was right, for Queen Blanche, though she kept an eye on the English, did little beyond suppressing the beginning of a rising in Normandy. French nobles hurried to her to swear their loyalty and she bided her time, having shrewdly assessed the temper of the young English King.

The weather was halcyon in Guyenne and Eleanor enjoyed the entertainments, the dancing and music in the evenings, and she was hardly aware of the growing discontent, of her husband, Earl Gilbert and the Earl of Chester talking earnestly and uneasily in lowered tones. The soldiers, convinced there was to be no fighting at the moment, began selling their equipment to pay for their lodging, for the King's coffers were being emptied at an alarming rate to feast the local nobility and there was little left for the common man waiting to earn his plunder. The round of pleasure went on. Henry visited Castillion and Perigueux, studying church buildings, going into ecstasies over the new style of vaulting, talking constantly of his determination to rebuild the abbey church at Westminster. He sent for Master Peter of Derham, his master mason, to come all the way from England to see the soaring arches he wanted to adorn his chapel. War seemed to be the furthest thing from his mind.

So the summer drifted on until he fell sick with dysentery. He lay and groaned on his bed, all his self-confidence evaporating, and when he was sufficiently recovered to be on his feet again the expedition now had a sour look. He had little money, discontented barons, and rebellious soldiers.

'I am surrounded by dolts and cowards,' he said in a burst of irritation. 'None of you puts my interests first and if we have failed it is not my fault. I have been badly served from my generals down to the meanest fighting man. I shall go back to England.'

'Brother,' Richard said, 'we can borrow more from the Jews. They sit safe enough in London. If you wish to stay, send your clerk Mansel to find us more funds – he has a smooth enough tongue to do it.'

'I don't wish to stay,' Henry retorted and glowered at his court gathered about him. 'I have had my fill of incompetence. In England I can set my hand to more congenial tasks.'

'Sire,' William Marshal said, 'give me leave then to stay and treat with them. I am sure Earl Randulph and Earl Gilbert will aid me.'

Both earls signified their assent and the King said petulantly, 'Stay if you will, I care not.' His glance fell on his sister. 'Well, do you stay too or will you come back to England with me?'

'With your leave, I will remain with my lord,' she answered with a touch of pride in her voice and Henry stamped off out of the hall, a disgusted young man who had discovered he was no soldier. Richard, with an expressive shrug, followed him.

Isabella de Clare also refused to leave her husband, for Gilbert was plainly unwell. He seemed to have difficulty in breathing and Isabella told Eleanor that she feared his lungs were affected. They stayed in

Bordeaux while their lords went campaigning and but for her anxiety Eleanor would have enjoyed the pleasant days in this sunlit city, riding or hawking by day and listening in the evening to the Provencal troubadours whose songs were enchanting. One lost his heart to her and wrote verses which he proclaimed with emotion trembling in his voice to such an extent that Eleanor laughed at the poor man and sent him away much discomfited.

The three Earls effectively put a stop to the French army which was about to march into Brittany. They recaptured one or two border fortresses and Eleanor and Isabella rode north to meet them at Nantes, prepared for a triumphal feast. But a shadow was cast over their joy at the sight of Gilbert barely able to sit his horse, his chest heaving, his body a mere skeleton. His squires eased him from his saddle and within a few days he was dead. Instead of feasting a watch was kept by his grieving widow and his friends, and as soon as it could be arranged Isabella sailed for England, bearing his corpse home for burial. William and Eleanor stood on the quayside to watch her go and Eleanor thought how like she was to William in the stateliness of her bearing.

A few days later, missing Isabella's company, Eleanor was going down the stair to meet the Countess of Aumale with whom she was to ride, when she encountered the knight from Montfort L'Amaury. He stood aside for her to pass but there was something in his appearance that caused her to pause. He wore a new surcoat emblazoned with a badge showing a fork-tailed lion and there was a ruby ring on one finger.

'Well, messire,' she said, 'my husband told me you had stayed behind in the Earl of Chester's service. It seems you acquitted yourself well in the campaign.'

'I slew a few Frenchmen,' he said lightly.

'Your own countrymen? Your brother is King Louis's liegeman, is he not?'

'There are many men who hold lands of both King Louis and King Henry. And I am King Henry's man,' he retorted, a gleam of triumph in his eyes. 'My lord of Chester is pleased to approve my conduct on the march and he has agreed to yield me the earldom and lands of Leicester. If your brother will be gracious enough to confirm me in them I shall be Earl and Steward by right. I am no longer the landless man I was at St Malo, lady.'

'I rejoice for you,' she said formally. 'But you will find that foreigners are not liked in England.'

'Then I shall have to make myself an Englishman,' he said and as she did not answer stood aside to allow her to continue down the stair. She went on and out into the courtyard, wondering why he always gave her a slightly uncomfortable feeling.

There seemed to be little more to do in France, neither side prepared to move further against the other, and in the New Year Eleanor braved the sea again to return to England. They were more fortunate in the weather this time and on landing at Portsmouth were met with the astonishing news that her brother had asked for the hand of William's widowed sister. The King had approved the match and Richard came to see William to ask his permission, for Isabella's marriage was in her brother's gift.

'Gladly,' William said, 'if my sister is willing. She has not mourned half a year yet.' Richard of Cornwall did not, however, seem to think this was any barrier either to himself or to his proposed bride and Eleanor kissed him heartily, only too happy that he should take Isabella to wife. Everyone liked Richard, she thought, and fond as she was of Henry it was to the sensible, reliable Richard that she gave her private confidences. She was, however a little surprised at the speed with which the match had been arranged.

Isabella was at Gilbert's manor at Marlow and thither William and Eleanor rode. He assured his sister she need consider herself in no way bound to remarry as yet, but she replied calmly that it pleased her well.

Later in the privacy of her bedchamber whence Eleanor had followed her, she said, 'You are shocked? But I do not like my lonely bed. Gilbert was a good husband, a strong man, but he could see no more in life than a day's fighting or hunting, a good dinner and a wife in bed with him. Now your brother is a very different man. He has a mind as keen as any and although he is younger than I am, I think we shall do very well together. My son is eight years old now and as the new Earl of Gloucester he needs guidance. Already he is growing so fond of Richard.

'I thought you cared for Gilbert,' Eleanor murmured.

'Well, so I did, but he is dead, God rest his soul,' Isabel said practically, 'and I am a rich woman. My Lord Richard is heir to the throne until such time as the King marries and begets a son, so it is an advantageous marriage on both sides.' An amused look came into her eyes. 'Your brother can always turn one gold piece into two and will not waste my heritage.'

'If you wish it, that is all William and I are concerned about,' Eleanor agreed, 'and of course I am happy that you should wed my own brother. I do believe,' she paused looking directly at her sister-in-law, 'I do believe it is more than just a good marriage with you?'

Isabella smiled, a slow secret smile, and clapped her bands for her maids to come to undress her. 'You are very observant. I think I would have taken Richard if he had had but one hide of land.'

The wedding took place in April in the church by the river at Marlow, the King and whole court attending, and finding lodgings in the manor or the guesthouse of the Templars at Bisham. The bride, only six months widowed, discarded her mourning and wore a gown of vivid blue, while the groom eclipsed even his own brother in the richness of his dress. Eleanor thought her husband seemed pale and quieter than usual and she wondered if he had doubts about the match, but he gave his sister's hand into that of Richard of Cornwall with smiling goodwill, wishing them a life together as content as his own with his young wife. The celebrations lasted several days, all the knights and tenants from the surrounding countryside feasted and wined, even the peasants were supplied with barrels of ale and an ox to roast. A tourney was held in which all the noble guests took part, and at last at the end of the third day, after a long morning's gallop over the Chiltern hills, an afternoon watching the King's tumblers and some Moorish entertainers who could swallow fire, a final feast was given in the ball. It was late when William and Eleanor sought their bed. They lay in each other's arms, too weary for love-making, and Eleanor was just drifting into sleep when William made a sudden sharp sound.

'What is it?' she asked sleepily. 'Were you dreaming, my love?' And then, as he gave an anguished groan, she sat up sharply. 'William! William, what is wrong?'

He was clutching at his stomach. 'Pain – such pain. It has been there – for some days –'

'Oh, why didn't you tell me?'

'I – I did not want to spoil the wedding. Oh, Jesu!' He rolled over, and was violently sick.

Terrified, Eleanor sprang out of bed, clutching at a night robe and calling out for help. One of the pages who always slept at their door came running, rubbing sleep from his eyes.

'Find a physician,' Eleanor screamed at him. 'Wake my lord's man, get my women – hurry, hurry!' She caught the rush dip from its holder in the wall of the passage and lit the candles by the bed. William was groaning in agony and she grabbed a bowl to hold for him, fear and cold causing her to tremble so that she could scarcely keep it steady. When the spasm passed, she caught his hands and held them to her breast, for he seemed deathly cold. He tried to speak but his eyes were hardly able to fix themselves on her and he seemed only half conscious.'

In a short while the room was full of people in hastily donned gowns, her women bringing extra bedclothes, the King's own physician bending over the sick man. Even the bridal couple had been roused, Isabella's face distorted with horror when she saw how her brother was suffering.

'He must have been poisoned,' she cried out. 'Holy God, who could have done such a thing?'

'He says he has been ill for days,' Eleanor seemed to hear her own voice from a long way off, her mind numbed. One of her women set a furred cloak about her shoulders in an endeavour to stop her shivering.

The physician straightened. 'Lady, I do not think it is poison. I have seen this sort of sickness often before. It is a strange disorder of the belly and I will make a potion that may ease him.'

All through the dark hours William fought his illness. The physician brought medicines but they seemed to give little relief. Once Eleanor cried out to him, 'Can you not do more? God's love, sir, surely you have other remedies to try?'

'I will bleed him, lady. Perhaps that will ease the humours.'

Eleanor watched the operation in a kind of agony herself. It was impossible that William, sturdy as an oak tree, should be lying here sweating and sick, his blood trickling into a bowl, the candlelight flickering on a face drawn and ashen. Afterwards he seemed quieter but much weaker, and towards dawn, in utter weariness, he turned his head a little. He had been lying with his hand in Eleanor's and his fingers tried to hold hers.

'My love.' She could barely hear the words. 'Eleanor, my heart –'

'I'm here.' She flung herself down beside him to be closer to the trailing voice. 'William, I'm here.'

'A priest –' He opened his eyes a little wider. 'Get me the priest. I – I would be shriven.'

'No, no!' she cried out incoherently. 'You need not – this will pass. William! William, don't leave me –'

'Please God, no,' he muttered, 'but if it is His Will – I would not go to Him unshriven.'

The priest came and they all withdrew a little. Eleanor stood in the circle of her brother Richard's arms, unable to believe any of this was really happening, that it must be some nightmare from which she would awake to find herself in bed and William bending over her to kiss her awake. She was vaguely aware of Richard saying something in an endeavour to strengthen her, and he sent a message to the King, lying in the Abbey guesthouse. When the slow, difficult murmuring had ceased and the priest raised his hand in absolution Eleanor burst into tears and stumbled forward to take William's hand again into her own. It was icy cold and she clutched it in her own, rocking backwards and forwards. He had closed his eyes, one final spasm convulsing him before he opened them again. He looked for her and half raised his other hand as if to touch her cheek in the familiar gesture, but it fell to the coverlet again. There was a faint smile on his face and his eyes remained fixed on hers.

The physician bent over him. 'Lady, he is dead.'

Eleanor let out one shriek and pressed the hand she held against her mouth, her eyes dilated, oblivious of Isabella's cry, of Richard crossing himself, the horrified murmurs that went round the room, the priest's praying.

And then merciful darkness flooded over her and her brother caught her as she fell.

CHAPTER THREE

Edmund Rich, scholar, teacher at the university at Oxford, treasurer of Salisbury Cathedral, was thought by many to be half-way to sainthood already. Young men flocked to listen to him when he taught or preached and those in trouble came crowding to his lodgings, for his kindness and wisdom were renowned and he turned no one from his door. At the same time he saw through the sycophant and the hypocrite and sent them packing with sharp words and no time for mere courtesies.

His friendship he gave to the honest, the truly religious, and he recognized one of the latter in the knight who had recently been confirmed in the possession of new lands and revenues. The Earl of Chester had given full approval to the transfer and Edmund Rich, though he disliked the Earl's hard living and blasphemous talk, nevertheless respected his judgement. He met the young man thus honoured at Salisbury where Sir Simon wished to make an offering towards the new building begun by old William Longsword, dead these seven years.

The liking between them was mutual. He had watched Simon at Mass that morning and observed his devotion was more than mere outward form, that he did not occupy half the time chattering to his friends as many men did, but kept his gaze fixed upon the altar and the Host. Afterwards they breakfasted together in Edmund's simple lodging, his guest sharing the plain fare and asking for nothing else.

'You are on your way to Leicester?' he asked and Simon nodded.

'I fear that my lord of Chester has had so much else on his hands that there is much to be done. Leicester castle is in a poor state and the stewards do not appear to have collected all the rents, or else they have lined their own pockets. The knights' fees are overdue and what has happened to the fines in the manorial courts I do not know.'

'The new broom will sweep all clean,' Rich said, smiling gently.

'And doubtless my knights and tenants will not love me for it. They see me as a foreigner, but I will win them over by fair dealing.'

'Nothing could recommend you more.'

'I mean to be just,' Simon said. 'It seems to be a quality about which the Englishman feels strongly. But my income will be small, not much above two hundred and fifty pounds a year and most barons would look down their English noses at that. I'll not be able to keep many spears about me at first, but with God's help I'll mend all that.'

Rich looked into his serious face, the grey eyes determined. 'I believe you will, my son. I will find a good priest to be your chaplain.'

'There will be much for him to do at Kenilworth. The priest there has been slack and grown fat and lazy and I will have him out. A man who abuses God's privileges can expect no mercy from me.'

'And deserves none, but send him to me. I'll see he has work to do and does not starve. Now tell me more of – ' He broke off as there came a knock at the door and in answer to his summons a young monk entered.

'Father, there are two ladies below, the Princess Eleanor and Mistress Cecily de Sanford. They ask if they may speak with you.'

Edmund looked a little surprised. 'I did not expect them but I believe I did notice two veiled ladies in chapel this morning. That poor child, she is broken with grief. To be widowed at sixteen is very hard and she truly loved her husband.'

'He is a great loss,' Simon said formally.

'I wish there were more like him. Perhaps I can give the Princess some spiritual comfort, if little else. I must not keep her waiting.'

Simon de Montfort rose at once. 'I'll leave you then, Master Rich. Thank you for your time and your breakfast.'

Edmund smiled up at him. 'You are always welcome, Sir Simon. God's blessing go with you.'

Simon bowed his head reverentially and went out. The Princess Eleanor was in the small entrance below, a veil hiding her face, accompanied by an angular woman of indefinable age. Both were dressed in mourning. Simon stood aside to allow them to approach the stair and as the Princess passed him, he said, 'God give you grace to bear your grief, lady. I am truly sorry for it.'

She looked up, startled, as if she had not been aware who he was. 'Sir Simon? You are kind, but I do not look for comfort.' He made as if to say more, but she went on up the stair, followed by her companion, and in the room above knelt humbly for Edmund's blessing.

He gave it and then helped her to her feet. 'Come, sit down and tell me how I may serve you. Mistress de Sanford, we have met before, I think?'

'Aye, Master Rich, when my brother studied under you – rhetoric and theology as I recall.' The older woman sat down on the window seat, leaving Simon's vacated stool to her charge. 'As you know the King has placed the Princess in my care. I too am a widow and I know something of grief.'

'Yet I think,' Edmund said gently, 'that you had many years with your husband, that you were not as young as this child when you were bereaved.'

'That is true, sir,' she agreed in a cool voice, and her eyes, set close together, stared at him with an earnestness that he recognized all too clearly. 'The hand of God strikes regardless of time or age and the Princess, fearing He is displeased, wishes to devote the remainder of her life to Him.'

He turned back to the girl. 'Lady? Can it be true that you wish to be a nun?'

Eleanor sat very still, her hands folded in her lap. 'I – I don't know: perhaps. I cannot think just yet. Oh Master Rich,' she looked up at him for the first time and could not keep back the tears, 'why is God so cruel? I loved my lord and he loved me. When there is so much misery in life why could we not have kept our love? Two short years was all we had.'

'It is hard, my daughter, to understand the ways of God, but Christ in His mercy will help you bear it. As to affliction we do not know why it strikes one and not the other. What matters is how we bear it and you have courage.'

'Have I?' She gave him a wan smile. 'All I know is that I would forswear the world. Already my brother considers another husband for me and I cannot think of anyone else in William's place.'

'You are not with child? I did hear – '

'We wondered if it might be so,' Cecily put in, 'but now we know that it is not, so there is no impediment to this child forsaking a cruel world.'

'I see.' He rose and went to stand before Eleanor. 'Do you then wish to enter a holy house? I would have you be sure for you are very young yet, and a Princess of England.'

'I don't know,' she said again. 'I have prayed, I have asked Our Lady to show me what is right.'

'We have both prayed,' Cecily broke in, her face tense with fervour, 'and we wish, widows as we are, to take at least a vow of chastity together, to swear before the Queen of Heaven to keep ourselves pure for as long as it shall please God that we remain in this vale of tears.'

Edmund's tone was surprisingly severe when he answered her. 'Mistress, you may do as you wish, but it is my duty to see that the Princess knows what she undertakes. Child, all life is before you and grief will pass. I assure you of this.'

'What can men know of widowhood?' Cecily demanded and Eleanor looked up through her tears.

'No one can ever replace my lord. I would rather live bound to Christ than wed another. Can I not swear that without entering a holy house – yet? Perhaps one day I may, if my brother permits it.'

'Yes, you may swear it,' he agreed, 'but such an oath is binding and as the King's sister, life must hold great opportunities for you.'

'I know – I know!' she cried out, 'but I can only think of my dear lord. I am utterly lost without him at my side and would run from any greatness apart from him.'

'Why do you try to persuade her back to the world's vanities,' her guardian asked. 'Surely to live as a chaste widow, espoused to Christ, is a higher calling than any other?'

Edmund gave a deep sigh. 'The devil must have an advocate, mistress, and it is a grave step the Princess wishes to take. I would hold no one back from a life devoted to God but it must be taken with a clear mind.'

'She wishes it and I with her. Together, with tears and prayers, we will offer ourselves to Him and it must be done at once before this poor lady is tempted –'

'– To be young?' he interrupted. 'Mistress, I am God's servant first and man's second, but even so I say that chastity without charity is a poor thing.'

'I would have thought,' Cecily said with an odd touch of annoyance, 'that you would have been only too glad to see the Princess settled in a manner where her wealth might benefit Holy Church.'

'Many a priest would say so,' he agreed, 'yet I have a horror of those cages in the market place that keep young and tender birds away from the freedom of the sky.'

His words brought a sudden recollection of William's fondness for calling her his bird and Eleanor's tears ran down her face again.

Mistress de Sanford had flushed and something in Master Rich's manner caused her to be silent. Eleanor too sat without speaking, twisting her hands together and trying to control her weeping. At last she said, 'I do wish it, Master Rich. I would like to wear the ring of one betrothed to Christ. We have brought two for the purpose.'

He gave her a long searching look. 'Very well,' he answered and his tone was gentle again. 'Come to my chapel, dear child of God, and it shall be done.'

Together Eleanor and her guardian knelt before the altar and swore perpetual chastity, receiving their rings from Edmund's hand, and he blessed them. Eleanor looked at a statue of the Virgin and out of her misery prayed desperately for comfort. She had found it nowhere. In the first anguished days she had been half out of her mind with grief, hardly aware of what was being said and done. Of the requiem in the Temple Church where William's body was lowered to rest beside that of his father she recalled nothing but Richard's arm about her to support her.

She had lain for days on her bed, surrounded by her women, fed with broth for she could keep no solid food down. Never had Eleanor so longed for the comfort of her own sisters, but Joanna seldom came south across the border and was pregnant at the moment, while Isabella in far-off Germany was even more inaccessible. Richard spoke highly of the Emperor Frederick, their volatile, magnificent, meteoric brother-in-law, and suggested that Eleanor might benefit from a visit to the German court, but she was too broken to consider it now. He did, however, persuade her she must rise and be herself again, and when she did so she begged Henry to allow her to retire to the quiet of one of William's manors. The King, with the complicated business of her widow's settlement to deal with, enquired for a noble and pious widow. When Mistress Cecily de Sanford was presented to him, he sent his sister in her charge to the Marshal manor of Inkberrow near Worcester.

And there, leaving all her financial affairs in Henry's hands, she had come more and more under the influence of Cecily's religious fervour until she felt that a life of prayer and fasting was necessary for the sake of William's soul and her own salvation. Shattered, lost without his secure presence, all her joy in life gone, she was open to the first strong influence to hand and that was Mistress de Sanford's.

Now the thing was done and she knelt waiting for peace to come. In a measure it did. When she rose to prepare for the return journey it was with a calm born of despair and with the memory of Edmund's kindly blessing hovering over her.

They rode back to Worcester, Finch a yard or two behind her, watchful as ever, but his face wore a somewhat sullen expression. He did not like Mistress de Sanford who had wanted to dismiss him, mainly he thought because he whistled while he was busy in the stables and she did not think it seemly. But he always whistled and his young mistress in happier days had often asked him what song it was that he produced so tunefully. He thought now, in his simple way, that a little less gloom would do his lady no harm, and fortunately she had roused herself to countermand Cecily's orders. Nor did she forbid him to whistle.

Her guardian forswore fine clothes, dressing herself and her charge in peasant russet and occupying the day with hearing Masses, ministering to the poor and the sick, and with much reading from holy books. Cecily was very learned for a woman and for a while dominated their life together, arranging the day to suit her own austere ways. A monk of St Albans and once called to advise them on their study. Eleanor tried to listen to his discourse but found him wearisome.

Heartsick and lonely she moved in a state of dulled acquiescence from one of ·her manors to another, or stayed in convent guesthouses. She could think of nothing but William, remembering every detail of that last night, and then retreating from that to recall all the happy moments when life seemed to stretch endlessly ahead with the hope of children to come. She knew now that she was not pregnant, as she had hoped in the first weeks after his death, but the recollection of all the joy she had had with her middle-aged husband only brought fresh misery, and in this state of wretchedness Cecily imposed on her as she would not have done in normal circumstances.

In the late summer Isabella came to see her and was frankly horrified at what she had done. The Countess of Cornwall turned on the unfortunate Cecily and told her what she thought of one who could influence a grief-stricken girl of sixteen to

Vow herself to perpetual chastity.

Mistress de Sanford flushed but she stood her ground. 'To serve God is of greater value than to serve men, my lady.'

'You must have had a singularly dull marriage bed,' was Isabella's comment. 'Celibacy is all very well for nuns, and if the Princess really wished to vow her life away I would not for the world turn her from God's service, but let it be done when time has passed, not when the child is ill and broken by my brother's death, Jesu rest his soul. In any case I am come to bring you both to court. My next brother Richard is in England. He is now Earl and Marshal in William's place and the King wishes to settle the business of your dower.'

It was a relief to see Isabella again, for the Countess's robust common sense was bracing, and though she had renounced all thought of a second marriage, Isabella's own example proclaimed that a widow re-wed defeated loneliness. But then

Isabella had not loved Gilbert as she had loved William.

The court was assembled at Gloucester, preparing for the Christmas festivities and it was there that Eleanor met Richard Marshal. The first sight of him made her eyes fill for he was very like William. Although he was neither so tall nor so robust he shared the similarity to their father, the old Marshal, and except that Richard was fairer there were moments when in a turn of the head she could have mistaken him for William.

The new Earl of Pembroke, confirmed in that place by the King, greeted his sister-in-law with courtesy but it seemed to her that the smile so often in William's eyes was missing, and his manner was more serious. Men said he was clear-thinking, an honest man, but she did not warm to him nor, she thought, did he to her. She suspected he thought of her as the King's sister rather than as William's wife.

There was a great deal of talk about lands and manors, about monies due. Her marriage portion was hers by right, but the discussion dealt with the division of the great Marshal inheritance. William's debts, and surprisingly there were some, became the new Earl's responsibility, not hers, but a third of his holdings should come to her as her dower, free from debt. Wearied by it all, distressed by the nearness of a man whose very voice reminded her of her grief, yet who seemed to be reducing everything to market bargaining, she left her seal on the table beside the King and went away with

Cecily to pray in the great cathedral under the soaring arches that pointed the way to Heaven. But William was dead and not all her tormented prayers could bring him back again.

It was strange to be once more at court and she listened with a sense of estrangement to the latest gossip. Hubert de Burgh was in trouble it seemed, hounded by the Bishop of Winchester, Peter de Roches. Ridiculous rumours were put about concerning Hubert, one in particular suggesting that he had poisoned

Eleanor's husband.

'What nonsense!' Richard Marshal cried out. 'They were friends always. I'll believe none of it.'

But the King chose to believe some of the accusations, being under the influence of his Poitevin bishop, and Hubert fled to sanctuary, only to be dragged out by de Roches's men. At once the prelates of England demanded that sanctuary be respected and he was allowed to return. Both Richard Marshal and Richard of Cornwall spoke in his defence, but Hubert was forced to hand over his castles and his treasure and when his coffers yielded enormous sums of gold, the King was highly indignant. 'Why should Hubert have all this money when I am constantly in need?' he demanded.

Two of Hubert's friends, who happened to be tenants of the new Earl of Pembroke, rescued Hubert and carried him off to Chepstow castle where the King's writ did not run. The Marshal had ordered his men to side with a traitor, Henry swore, and he seized their lands, urged on by the

Bishop of Winchester. The Earl stood by his men, though he denied having given them any such order, and furthermore continued to defend Hubert.

'Your grace is over-indulgent to foreigners,' he said on one occasion. 'The Bishop is well named Peter for although St Peter was called the Rock by Our Saviour, this man earns the name for very different reasons. The ship of our state will founder on it if your grace continues to yield to him.'

His brother-in-law, Warin de Munchensai, agreed. 'Sire, he leaves too much of your affairs in the hands of his nephew Master des Rievaux – and there, may I say, "nephew" seems to be a misnomer.'

The King went crimson with annoyance. It was rumoured that the Bishop had been overfond of a certain fair girl who had sewn his surplices for him and that the "nephew" was the result, but Henry refused to listen. Des Rievaux was astute in money' matters and Henry needed him. 'That is nothing but idle gossip,' he said and sent the Earl of Pembroke to deal with the rising problem of the incursions of Llewellyn, Prince of Wales, on the marcher lands.

Eleanor had little interest in these affairs, but slowly youth was reasserting itself. She watched the mummers at Christmastide, listened to the minstrels, and surveyed the dancers with a growing hunger.

On Easter Saturday, when William had been dead two years, she attended the solemnities in Salisbury Cathedral, where the beauty of the new building was a tribute to William's father's old friend, Will Longsword. She and Mistress Cecily had fasted all day yesterday and her young stomach was crying out for food. A bowl of soup was all that her guardian had ordered this morning, and catching a glance of herself in the water of her ewer it seemed to Eleanor that she had grown very thin, losing the promise of a well-shaped figure. She had prayed and prayed but no light of zeal lit her face as it did her companion's, and though she believed in God's mercy and trusted William's soul was in His hands, the life she led with Cecily was as dry and empty as a corn husk.

Already offerings were being brought to the church for the Easter Mass, and someone passing nearby to lay flowers at the feet of the carved Virgin had dropped a primrose. Eleanor bent to pick it up. The little delicate flower with its velvety stem seemed to embody all the hope of spring and she held it in her hand, gazing down at it. Tears blurred her eyes and then miraculously they dried. Hardly realizing what she did she put the pale petals to her lips. She seemed to feel William's presence close to her and there came the overwhelming certainty that, though she would never deny her love for him, he would not want her to be as she was now. It was as though life, stifled for a while, was flooding back into her limbs.

 She rose and said to Cecily, 'We will return home now,' in so firm a voice that the astonished Mistress de Sanford followed her from the church.

On the ride back to William's manor at Wexcumb they spoke little but Eleanor's spirits were rising in rebellion with every mile. Reaching the house, small but enough for the two ladies, she immediately ordered a supper of hashed eggs, followed by a custard and raisin tarts.

'But the fast!' exclaimed Cecily in shocked tones. 'My lady, have you forgotten?'

'I have fasted enough,' Eleanor retorted, 'and I am very hungry. Tomorrow is Easter day.' She hurried up to her bed-chamber calling for Doll and Megonwy and began to open chests, rummaging through her clothes. 'Where is my blue gown? Jesu, have I no respectable garments left?'

Cecily had followed her, panting a little, and was staring at her in astonishment. 'Lady, what has happened? You cannot mean to forsake your russet – nor the life we have chosen together?'

'I made a vow,' Eleanor said, 'and I have not broken it, have I? Nor has my brother pressed me to do otherwise, but I am young and William would not wish me to live in this half death.' She was struggling out of the hated russet, Doll helping her while Megonwy, with a certain malicious delight, for she did not like Mistress de Sanford, was pulling out the desired gown, brushing out the creases and finding a white mantle, a jewelled belt, and pretty openwork crespine.

'There, my lady, it will be a joy to see you in such colours again. We all thought 'twas a shame that –'

'Hold your tongue, girl,' Cecily said sharply. 'You are not thinking, my lady. You have given yourself to God and these gew-gaws are not for you.'

'I was a child when I did it.' A new independence born of experience and grief and loneliness was emerging with every word. 'But I am not a child now. And a few new gowns will be delightful, and surely no sin. I intend to go to court.'

'But we said we would not go into vain society again, that we would renounce the world –'

'Oh be still!' Eleanor cried out. 'I tell you again I am not breaking my vow but I will go to my brother. I am still a Princess of England and it is right that I should sometimes be at court.'

'Many high-born ladies have not deemed it hurt their state to live within convent walls,' Cecily said severely, but it was with a certain wavering as if she knew she was losing the argument. 'There is the Countess of Leicester, for one.'

'She is old. I would not mind if I were seventy. Is supper ready?' Eleanor asked with a twist of her head as a page came tapping at the door.

She ate hungrily, talking to Robert Smith, clerk to her small household, and to Sir John Penrose, one of the knights sent by the King to attend her when she travelled from one manor to another. Hitherto Eleanor had taken little notice of any of them but now she asked Smith for an account of the monies in her treasure chest. After supper, sending the huffy Cecily to her bed, she sat for a long time over Smith's account books, a frown gathering on her forehead.

'It seems my brother-in-law is in arrears with my dower payments. And why when I am entitled to a third of my late husband's income do I receive a mere five hundred pounds? I know his income was over two thousand pounds a year.'

The clerk was nonplussed by his mistress's sudden and perceptive interest in her finances. He was an honest man but too much in awe of the great men concerned to query the money supplied. 'The King agreed to this settlement, and I only handle what is sent, my lady.'

'Then I see shall have to take my affairs into my own hands,' she said determinedly. By Wednesday in Easter week she and her small retinue had reached Winchester where her brothers welcomed her warmly. Henry had been somewhat disconcerted by her vow, having it in his mind that a royal widow was a great financial asset, but at the same time his devout nature accepted it and prayed with her in his chapel that she might be strong in her resolve. Richard said little. 'Foolish child!' was his first comment and after that, busy about his own affairs, he did not seem disposed to talk about it. He was plainly glad to see her emerge into court life again.

Eleanor joined, demurely enough, in the Easter feasting and shortly afterwards journeyed into Nottinghamshire with her brothers to watch a great tournament at Blythe.

She sat with Matilda Marshal and watched Matilda's son Roger Bigod, a mere youth of eighteen, distinguish himself against many of his elders. Matilda who, like her sister Isabella, strongly resembled her father, was kind and sympathetic, patted Eleanor's hand and said she could well understand her action in view of the loss of such a man as William. Earl Ferrar, their brother-in-law, carried off another prize while Waiter Marshal beat all corners at the butts on the following day.

Eleanor enjoyed the whole affair, the excitement, the brilliance of the court, the fluttering banners against the blue sky, the shouts of the knights taking sides in the contest, and she was conscious all the while of the disapproval of Cecily, sitting stiffly behind her. After a few days Eleanor told her that she would be happier living pensioned in a convent and dismissed her. Cecily departed, her final injunction to her charge that she expected this incursion into the world to bring down the wrath of heaven on her. She would, however, endeavour to placate the judgement from on high by her prayers.

Impulsively Eleanor kissed her, for the older woman had been her stay during the first lonely, wretched year, and promised to visit her often.

Then she turned her attention to more weighty matters and taxed her brother with her financial situation.

'I do not understand,' she said, 'how you could allow Richard Marshal to deny me my due rights. I have here a list of figures –'

'My dear sister,' the King broke in, 'you agreed to the settlement. Your seal was set to it.'

'My seal was left in your charge as you well know, Harry. I was too grief-stricken to care.'

'Master Mansel here saw to the drawing up of the agreement, did you not, John?'

'I did, sire.' The slight clerk, with his cautious eyes, bowed to Eleanor. 'Lady, I did my best for you, but the Marshal inheritance is large and complicated and there were ten to share it.'

'I am William's widow,' she said sharply, 'and he was the eldest. Now, not only has his brother appropriated all William's furnishings in my absence, but he is refusing me my just dues. There are rents owing from my Irish manors too.'

'They were handed over to my lord of Pembroke in return for a settled income for you. It seemed that this would be more convenient for you.'

'Convenient, yes,' she retorted with spirit, 'if I received it, but I have had no monies this quarter.'

'I will look into it, lady,' Mansel said deferentially but with a covert look at his master.

'And William's debts? It seems they are not paid, and they at least are not my responsibility.'

'Aye.' Her brother Richard had at this moment walked into Henry's chamber to overhear the last words. 'And it is fitting that our sister should have a more noble household. I always thought Mistress de Sanford, virtuous lady though she is, hardly the one to company Eleanor for too long. It is a great pity she made you take a vow of chastity, my dear. You should have taken my lady Isabella for your guide.' He smiled across at her. 'She would have told you that a second marriage is no bad thing.' He saw a tense expression cross his sister's face and went on, 'But no doubt she will speak to her brother for you in the matter of your dues.'

'I hope so,' Eleanor said, 'but as to a second marriage, though I have not taken the veil I am espoused to Christ.' She was conscious that she was repeating Cecily's words and added hastily, avoiding the subject of wedlock, 'Harry, you will help me to regain what I have lost, will you not? God knows Richard Marshal has no right to defraud his brother's widow. I have no clothes fit for my position, nor money to pay my attendants.'

Henry rose and put an arm about her. 'Why, I will see your household increased as befits my sister, and any of my manors where you wish to stay are available to you. And don't leave court yet, you are so newly returned to us. Let me send my tailor to you. I have some fine yellow velvet newly come from Paris which will suit you well, so you shall have it.'

It was good to feel alive again, to have her brothers caring for her once more, and in her own apartment later she stood stretching her arms and twisting her figure about while the tailor tried to take measurements. He proposed various designs, talking of the new fashions, and the little round cap to sit so becomingly on the wimple that would suit her very well. In the middle of all this Isabella walked in with her youngest sister Joanna de Munchensai. They both embraced Eleanor and welcomed her back, but Isabella added, 'I am sorry to hear you are angry with my brother. He is the Earl now and there are great demands upon him.'

Something warned Eleanor to be careful but in her newfound sense of freedom caution was not uppermost in her mind. 'Need has nothing to do with it,' she retorted, 'and William would be very angry that his brother should appropriate what is my due. Two years I've been widowed and already he owes me more than two hundred pounds.'

'I'm sure it is a mistake,' Joanna, always the most timid of the family, was beginning, when Eleanor overrode her.

'I do not think my lord Richard makes such mistakes.'

'He has had much to occupy him since he came from France,' Isabella said. 'There is always trouble in Ireland, and this business over Hubert de Burgh has concerned him greatly.'

'Hubert rose too high and took too much for himself,' Eleanor said. 'A fault all too common, it seems. And Richard is a liegeman of King Louis. I remember William telling me that. It might have been better had he been content to stay in France.'

'You are prejudiced against him, sister.' Isabella's tone was severe for once, 'But you should know how highly William thought of him. He is wise in state affairs and the King would do better to listen to him and to my lord Hubert than to that man, de Roches. He schemes always to be rid of my brothers and other English barons that see through his wily ways. Let him go back to Poitou, I say.'

'Politics are not for us,' Joanna put in. The present Earl was her favourite brother and she tried to change the subject. 'Dear life, how thin you are grown. You will have to get some colour back into your cheeks.'

'Mistress de Sanford must have kept her on a meagre diet,' Isabella suggested.

The criticism, accurate though it was, roused a spurt of annoyance in Eleanor. She was very fond of Isabella but now they were treating her as if she was no more than a poor relation seeking restitution.

'My lord of Pembroke must learn that he cannot escape his commitments to me,' she said haughtily. 'He may be all you say, but to me he is merely a man who defrauds his brother's widow. And when that widow is a Princess of England –'

Isabella gathered up her mantle. 'If you will see it no other way, then we had best not talk of it.'

Thereafter a coolness existed between them for a while. At court it became obvious that the barons were almost wholly in support of Richard Marshal in his claims that the King had taken some of the Marshal inheritance into his own hands, but Henry was utterly under the influence of the Winchester faction and would not listen to his protests. The Earl of Chester, perhaps the one man to keep a balance between the English and the Poitevins, made an attempt to reconcile the two sides and arranged a conference. The Earl of Pembroke agreed and the Bishop of Winchester rubbed his hands with pleasure.

'He is delivering himself up to us,' he said. 'If your grace will be guided by me you will have him confined to the Tower at once and banished the kingdom.'

'Of course,' Henry agreed, snatching at the chance to rid himself of a man he disliked. 'Let him be seized the moment he arrives, and see that there are sufficient men to overcome his retinue. He travels as if he keeps greater state than I do.'

'Is that wise?' his brother asked. 'Pembroke is no fool. It would be better to have him as an ally than an enemy. He has much of the old Marshal in him.'

'You are careful as always, my lord,' the Bishop answered smoothly, 'but perhaps you are influenced in this case by the fact that the Earl is your brother-in-law.'

'Not at all. I am merely using my commonsense.'

'And mine tells me the King would be advised to be rid of a man who bids fair to put himself into the place once occupied by de Burgh.'

This remark brought Henry to his feet. 'It shall be done. I'll be rid of Richard Marshal and the rest of the brood if I can.' For one fleeting moment his mind rebelliously threw up a misty picture of himself as a boy of nine, a gold circlet set on his head and the old Marshal lifting him high to present him to the barons, loyalty itself. But he thrust the image away. 'See to it, my lord Bishop.'

Richard said nothing further, nor did he speak to his wife of it for he misliked the whole affair, but one of the King's attendants who was enamoured of a sewing woman in the Countess of Cornwall's service repeated to her that a trap had been set for the Earl of Pembroke. The girl told her mistress and Isabella sent a warning to her brother not to ride to Woodstock for the meeting. He turned back and raised his standard against a King who could thus plot against his freedom and perhaps his life. He made an alliance with Llewellyn of Wales and though stating he had no desire to quarrel with his liege-lord he did quarrel with the advice given him by foreign advisers. He and his Welsh ally seized certain castles that Henry had purloined and defeated a royal army sent against them.

'I will pay a shilling for every enemy head sent to me in London,' Henry blustered, but he was uneasy. Too many barons, while not involving themselves in active rebellion, nevertheless made it plain that they considered Richard Marshal had been hardly dealt with.

It was finally Edmund Rich who saved the situation, at least for the time being. He had been appointed Archbishop of Canterbury and, little as he wanted to emerge from his quiet retirement, he had felt bound to do so. His first act was to bring about a truce between Pembroke and the King and to persuade the King that the peace of England depended on his dismissing his Poitevin favourites.

Henry sulked for days, but as always when faced with a moral crisis he weakened and both the Bishop of Winchester and his nephew Peter des Rievaux were advised to take up their residence in France for a while. Englishmen breathed again and Henry turned his attention to his building programme, spending more time with his master mason than with his council.

Isabella's part in warning her brother was suspected and she retired for a while to Berkhamstead Castle. She was expecting a child and glad of the excuse to leave court for a while.

'I am very sorry,' she had said to Eleanor when they chanced to meet one morning shortly before her departure. 'Sorry that we should not be friends any more. You think my brother has used you ill and I think yours has used mine worse. No doubt you think too he should have been shut up in the Tower but I'm glad I warned him.'

'You talk as if I wished to rob him,' Eleanor replied. 'I wanted no more than my due and that he would not give me.'

'Perhaps,' Isabella sighed. She seemed suddenly less defensive and saddened by the whole affair. 'It has caused grief between my husband and myself, though,' she laid a hand on her stomach, 'this child has healed that. Dearest Eleanor, we women have so little choice in the business of the world and we can be torn between husbands and brothers, but let us part as sisters.'

Eleanor held back, but only for a moment. It was impossible to forget all Isabella's past kindness. She embraced her. 'God speed then, and may He give you a safe delivery.'

'And you?' Isabella held her away to look at her. 'I hate that vow you made. You are grown so beautiful now. I know you loved William dearly, but

I think you should wed again. I am so happy with Richard.'

'And break my oath?' Eleanor gave an uneasy laugh. 'I am afraid our new Archbishop would be very angry with me if I did.'

'He is a holy man, but I think he does not know what women feel and a barren woman has a sorrow no man can guess at.' She saw a strange look pass over Eleanor's face as if the Princess had not thought of this, and she added hastily, 'Never fear, my love, there will be some answer to your situation, I am sure. In the meantime will you write to me? Tell me if there is any news of my brother? I know Gilbert is at Court but he is no hand with letters and he does not see things coolly.'

'I will write,' Eleanor assured her and kissed her with all the old warmth.

But when she did write it was with the worst possible news.

After Archbishop Edmund's truce, the Earl of Pembroke retired with Henry's permission to Ireland to deal with some rebels stirring up trouble there. But he had not been there long before he was betrayed by men in the pay of the exiled Bishop of Winchester; he was ambushed and wounded, and his wounds so badly cauterized that he died of the treatment.

One of his friends, returning to England, brought letters supposedly signed by the King encouraging his Irish vassals to put an end to the Marshal's life. The English barons were shocked and declared as one man that for such dealing with the son of the old Marshal someone must be made to pay. Like a weathercock Henry's feelings swung round in the opposite direction. He burst into tears, swore Peter des Rievaux had written the letters and used his seal without his knowledge, and declared vengeance on the murderers, calling the dead Earl wise and noble and England the loser by his death.

'Dear God!' Richard of Cornwall exclaimed, 'haven't you been quarrelling with the man these two years?'

Isabella wept bitterly at the loss of a second brother but the birth of a son, named John after her husband's father, revived her spirits until the baby sickened and died.

The sad occasion was made one for a general reconciliation, however, and when Gilbert Marshal, giving up all thought of pursuing his religious career, demanded the earldom and title of Marshal, the King yielded to him. He did not like Gilbert, but as the dead Earl had no heirs he could find no good reason to deny him. Gilbert was knighted and became a peer of England but whenever he appeared at court Henry scowled at him and on one occasion refused him admittance to the Christmas feasting.

Eleanor did not like him either. She thought he tried to ape his elder brothers while having none of their abilities; he was even more tight-fisted than Richard and the arguments over her dower went on.

She found herself now the first lady at court. She spent a great deal of money on her wardrobe and on her household which now consisted of several ladies in waiting, knights to attend her when she rode out, a chaplain, an excellent cook and all the necessary servants. Finch became master of her stables, to his great delight, and she dressed Doll and Megonwy in identical gowns and had them attend her constantly, standing behind her chair when she received guests. The vow of chastity, taken so long ago, faded into the back of her mind, but on one occasion when the Archbishop came to Winchester he sought to remind her of it.

'I fear you have forgotten your promise,' he said, sighing heavily. 'Did you put that away when you laid aside your russet gown? Your dress is very lavish for one dedicated to our Lord.'

'I was beside myself with grief,' she said. 'You are my father in God, you know what was in my heart then. But I have not forgotten my vow.'

'Perhaps not, but for how long will you be faithful in this worldly life at court?'

'How long? I have not thought of forsaking it.'

'There may come a day when you will. Then –'

'Then –' she took his hand and kissed his ring. 'Then I shall fly to you for strength.'

'Please God,' he said. 'I will pray for you, child. Will you come into the chapel with me now?'

'I can't.' She added hastily, 'Forgive me, but Henry is awaiting me. He has given me a new merlin that I am schooling and he does not like to be kept waiting when the birds are ready. I am overdue as it is.'

'Very well.' He sighed again. 'But remember it is well to give more to charity than to your gown-maker.'

She slipped away and a few moments later, in Mabille's saddle with her hawk on her wrist was enjoying the ride out beyond the palace into the countryside.

On this particular day Sir Simon de Montfort ranged himself at her side. He was always in England now, and men said he was rapidly restoring order and prosperity to his Leicestershire lands. Certainly he was very changed from the man of St Malo. He was constantly at the King's side and since the departure of the Bishop of Winchester and his nephew, Henry turned more and more to Simon as his new confidante. There was something in the Norman Earl's cool appraisal of people and affairs that the volatile King appreciated. The fact that Simon at this time was also, to many of the barons, yet another hated foreigner, worried Henry not at all. He called Simon his head and once when they were visiting the work at the abbey he pointed to a carving of a stone griffin.

'There,' he said, 'a noble animal but gentle. That is what I am, a royal griffin, and you shall be the lion at my side.'

Eleanor thought of that remark now. She had the feeling Simon saw through Henry's extravagant phraseology to his inherent weakness. It would have been very different if Richard had been the older brother. On the surface Richard and Simon were friendly enough, but she had heard Richard make a disparaging remark about the new Earl that showed he had not the same feeling towards him as his brother.

Cantering beside her now, Simon began by remarking that it was a good thing for the country that the King was to marry at last. Eleanora of Provence might be a surprising choice but would no doubt prove an excellent wife.

'So my brother Richard says,' Eleanor agreed. 'The lady is called La Belle in her own country where the standard of beauty is high. I hear her sisters are equally lovely.'

'Since her father, the Count, has no money it is as well that they have beauty to commend them,' he observed. 'The Queen Regent of France was quick to engage the eldest for her son. King Louis and our King should be' on good terms now that they are wedded to sisters.'

'Perhaps.' She gave a little shrug. 'I have never noticed it is necessarily so.'

'You are thinking of your Marshal relations,' he said acutely, 'and you are right, of course. Earl Gilbert and your brothers can hardly be called on amiable terms.'

To change a subject which she had no mind to discuss with him she said, 'I believe the Lady Eleanora is a verse-maker. My brother Richard brought home a copy of a poem she had written after he had visited her father. It was clever enough to capture Henry's imagination. I must confess I am eager to see this paragon.'

'And I,' he agreed. 'I am to play my part as Steward for the first time at their wedding.'

'Maybe you will seek a bride of your own soon,' she said and then wondered why she had said it, for he turned to look full at her, the grey eyes holding an expression she found hard to read. To her annoyance she felt her colour rise.

'Perhaps,' was all he said. He looked very striking today in scarlet velvet, a fur mantle about his broad shoulders, a black velvet cap on his dark head, and she was further annoyed to find that he affected her in an odd way. He added, 'I would wish, lady, that you might have a like happiness to your brother's.' Her flush deepened.

'Bridals are no concern of mine,' she retorted and spurred Mabille to join her brother Richard.

CHAPTER FOUR

'Beautiful! Beautiful!' Henry said exultantly. He turned the diadem in his hands, the jewels, emeralds, rubies and diamonds catching the candlelight, all set in gold. 'It is a crown fit for a Queen, do you not think so, Richard?'

His brother was leaning back in a carved chair, a chessboard on the table between them, the game interrupted by the late arrival of the royal goldsmith. 'Indeed. But fifteen hundred marks is a lot of money.'

'Not too much for such a bride as my Queen will be. You have seen her, you have told me of her beauty.' He handed the crown back to the goldsmith. 'You have done well, Master Warewood. Pray take this to my treasurer to be locked away with the rest of my lady's jewels.'

'The man bowed himself out and Henry asked, 'You like the new decorations here brother? The green for my painted chamber, the hangings, the table silver?'

'It is all in the best of taste,' Richard agreed, 'but whether you can afford it is another matter. Our brother-in-law in Germany is still owed a great sum for our sister's marriage portion.'

'Oh, I know you think a great deal of Emperor Frederick, but he is not so poor he cannot wait awhile,' the King retorted. He himself had waited long enough for a bride and he was now twenty-nine years old. He was carrying a little more weight and his complexion had grown ruddier, the curling golden hair on his forehead no longer as thick as he could have wished. But what did that matter when his person would outshine all the others there? Money poured through his fingers and his own wardrobe was lavish in the extreme, but he was well aware that his coffers were singularly empty of coin.

'I don't know how it is,' he said with a touch of petulance, 'that you always seem to have money. Your tin mines and stannaries must yield a high profit.'

Richard had returned to the game and with the careful consideration he gave to all things he moved his bishop. 'Well enough, but that is a mere part of my income. Money will grow if handled well, Harry.'

'Oh, I know you loan your treasure to bishops and barons alike and get a good return on it – '

'I am not a usurer,' Richard broke in, a rare sharpness in his voice. 'I lay out my money to a friend, but only on the safest security and I ask only for a return on it that is reasonable. If a man cannot repay – and I press no one too hard – a manor or a knight's fee will suffice in place of cash.'

'But you never seem to lose any money,' Henry grumbled in such a tone that his brother burst out laughing.

'Of course not, nor need you if you curb your extravagance, and be a little wiser in the advice you listen to.'

'I am King, I must be seen to be King, and as for the crowning of my Queen, should I not let my new Savoyard relations see that England is a great country? Shouldn't London be hung with banners, shouldn't there be trumpeters to greet her and pageants for her pleasure? God's teeth, the city aldermen are rich enough and we must show that we are not so poor as the Count of Provence.'

'If you can make them open their fat purses you are a clever man,' Richard said. 'But I agree with you. If the girl had not been so lovely and so intelligent I would not have urged you to take her without a marriage portion and no dowry at all except a reversion of our mother's in due course. She's healthy enough to live to a ripe old age so God knows when you'll get that.'

'One can't wrest blood from a stone, I know that, but whereas the Count has no money, my landowners have and they are naught but a pack of skinflints.'

'They will do well enough when the day comes. I hear talk of a pageant on the river and other festivities. Your bride will not be shamed.'

'I do not know how you hear all these things.'

'I listen,' Richard said, 'which is sometimes more to the point than talking. Well, I can lend you a thousand pounds, Harry, for' – he paused thoughtfully – 'shall we say the castle of Wallingford?'

'Agreed, agreed. You are a true brother, Richard.'

The Earl of Cornwall smiled. 'Not so true perhaps. I have you in check.'

The King, in high good humour, conceded the game. Any other meaning to his brother's words eluded him.

The wedding was magnificent. Eleanota La Belle had a breath-taking beauty that raised vociferous cheers wherever she went. At the wedding in Canterbury Cathedral she wore a shimmering gown that drew gasps of admiration from all the ladies there. 'Paid for, or not paid for, by our King,' a cynical voice was heard to mutter, but the occasion was too romantic and exciting for the kill-joys to be listened to.

They rode on to London and down flag-hung Chepe and Ludgate Hill towards Westminster and her crowning, a procession of prominent citizens greeting them in finest array led by the King's purveyor of spices who fancied himself as a dancer and a wag in his less serious moments. The banquet that followed the setting of that rich diadem on the young Queen's dark head was perhaps the most spectacular ever seen in St Stephen's Hall, every man who had any part in it rewarded with one gift or another. The London citizens claimed the right to cook the royal food while others passed wine in golden cups and country girls brought in wreaths of holly and ivy to decorate the ball, and at the end, every article used was carried away by some delighted attendant.

Gilbert Marshal, who had further quarrelled with the King by wedding that very Princess Marjorie of Scotland with whom Henry had once imagined himself in love, was permitted, in the general flush of goodwill, to carry out his duties as Marshal while the Earl of Leicester discharged his office of Steward for the first time.

Simon appeared in ceremonial robes carrying a golden ewer, a napkin over his arm, for the King to wash his hands and he supervised the serving of the banquet, seeing that the richest dishes went to the most high-born guests. The choice of these dishes had been his prerogative and as he was keenly interested in food and especially in the choice of wine with a flair for the unusual, the banquet drew exclamations of appreciation from the guests. There were peacocks roasted, and served redressed in their own colourful feathers, swans' flesh sliced in a succulent sauce, sturgeon boiled and decorated with olives, oysters and lampreys, and a concoction of eggs and rice coloured with saffron and spiced with ginger. Pastries of all sorts, bowls of almonds and raisins followed and there was marchpane coloured and formed into the shape of bells and flowers and bridal wreaths. When the Earl sat down in his place beside the Princess Eleanor she congratulated him on the achievement.

'Thank you, lady. I wish only to please his grace.'

'You told me once you would make yourself an Englishman. I think you are succeeding.'

He smiled and she thought how it illuminated his face. 'I have grown to love England, and not just those of my own rank here.' He had slipped easily into an assumption of the position that went with his title, his days of empty pockets forgotten. 'My people at Leicester are greatly to my liking. There is something about English yeoman who loves the land that endears him to me. He is like your sturdy oak trees.'

'I'm glad,' she said and added, glancing along the high table, 'I doubt if the Queen's relations regard England in that way. They seem to look down their noses at our customs – but of course they will be returning to Provence after the celebrations.' Simon followed her gaze and his smile faded. The Queen had brought a vast train with her, not only of servants, chaplains, cooks and grooms, but also three uncles, and in the days that followed it seemed that the King was enchanted by them. Instead of sending her escort home he kept his beautiful bride's entire retinue at court. 'More mouths to feed,' was Richard's practical comment, but Henry refused to listen. One uncle, Peter, he made Earl of Richmond and gave him a piece of land on the river not far from Westminster where he set about building himself a palace which he named the Savoy. Another uncle, Boniface, darkly handsome and with an overbearing manner, had been made a bishop while still a very young man but he seemed to care nothing for this. He had wanted to be a soldier and came to his niece's court to delight her with his bold wit and charming manners and to annoy the King's English courtiers with equal intensity. Henry now did nothing without the advice of the Queen's uncles and filled the lesser offices at court with other hangers-on to the disgust of those dismissed. 'Jesu!' Earl Ferrars remarked to his brother-in-law. 'Is England to be ruled by these improvident Provencals?'

'It seems so,' William de Braose agreed in his harsh voice. 'The King is besotted by them, but they're nothing but a pack of singers and versifiers. I'd send the lot packing.'

Gilbert Marshal was standing with them in the Courtyard waiting to ride out with the King, and on this January day he wrapped his furred mantle closer about his shoulders for the wind was icy, stirring the ragged ivy leaves against the palace wall. 'I would turn every foreigner out of England,' was his comment, 'not just the Queen's train. Did ever a woman have so many uncles and cousins? And I'd include the jumped-up so-called Earl of Leicester.'

'Why?' Earl Ferrars raised his sandy eyebrows. He was not a man of great intelligence but he worried at a matter until he understood it. 'Sir Simon has not made himself obnoxious as they have. True, he has the Beaumont holdings, but after all his aunt was Countess in her day, and old Chester, Jesu rest his soul, thought him worthy of them.'

'I do not like the way he looks at my brother's' widow,' Pembroke said grumpily. 'Have you not noticed how often he sits beside her or brings his horse alongside hers?'

Ferrars shook his head and de Braose said, 'I'd not noticed it either. You are over-suspicious, Gilbert, and choleric since the King quarrelled with your brother.'

'Quarrelled! He had my brother murdered and "then begrudged me my inheritance. It was more than a quarrel, my friend!'

'Hush,' Ferrars broke in, 'or you'll find yourself in a cell in the ground – or under it. I doubt the Princess Eleanor would consider marriage again, and in any case don't make an enemy of Simon de Montfort. He has the King's ear.'

'Another damned foreigner!'

'Not now,' Ferrars said. 'Get yourself an heir, Gilbert, and look to your own affairs instead of worrying about your brother's widow.'

'God, am I not trying?' Gilbert retorted in exasperation. 'I sport myself every night until my wife begs for sleep and still she is not pregnant.' He thought briefly of his elder sisters and their anxiety about that old bishop's curse. What nonsense! He would show them he had a man's loins.

De Ferrars was still thinking about the earlier conversation. 'I wonder what the Princess Eleanor thinks of our new Queen. My lady says La Belle is very proud for a mere penniless count's daughter, and the Princess is put out of countenance.'

'Eleanor does not confide in me,' Gilbert said. 'Perhaps my sister Isabella could tell us, but she is so busy with her new son she thinks of naught else.'

Isabella could indeed have told them had she wished to confide in her turbulent brother and brothers-in-law for Eleanor came to see her and they sat over the babe's cradle, gossiping and playing with him. He was a lusty boy named Henry after the King, and for a while they talked only of him; of the care of babies and the golden future Isabella planned for him.

But presently when she spoke of everyone's hopes for an heir to the throne before too long she asked Eleanor whether she liked her new sister-in-law.

Eleanor lifted her head. 'I do not like to sit on a stool while she sits on a throne beside Henry. Nor do I like that uncle of hers, Boniface. He wormed the story of my vow out of Archbishop Edmund and suggested a nunnery might be more to my taste than court life. If he was not the Queen's uncle I'd have him whipped for that impertinence. The Queen is – oh, pleasing I suppose, but in such a condescending way. One forgets she's as young as I was when I wed William. If he had lived how different it would all have been.'

Isabella settled the baby in his cradle. 'It's a lonely life you've condemned yourself to.'

Eleanor sighed, a sound that seemed to come from deep within, expressing so much. 'I think I shall become like the Maid and I used to pity her.'

'God forbid!'

'Nevertheless I must bear it. And you have known sorrow too.'

'To lose two brothers and two babes?' Isabella looked down at the sleeping infant as if willing him to survive the hazards of childhood. 'And Richard has taken the Cross, did you know? He and a dozen others, including Sir Simon de Montfort. At least it means he won't be forever at Henry's side, for a while anyway.'

'You don't like Sir Simon?'

'A cold man,' Isabella said, 'and set on his own gain. Oh, he has charm enough, I grant you, but though Henry has not confirmed him in his title yet, he calls himself Earl of Leicester.'

'He has the Leicester lands.'

'Do you defend him, another foreigner? I thought you did not like him either?'

Eleanor shrugged. 'I don't think about him one way or another,' she said and at the back of her mind knew that it was a lie. 'You will miss Richard.'

Isabella looked over her head to the window. 'Yes. He will go to fight in the Holy Land and I shall lie in bed at night and fear for him. What it is to love a man so much that to be without him –' she broke off. 'Forgive me, I should not have said that. I would not hurt you for the world.'

'If I had borne a child –' Eleanor began and then stopped for she saw an odd expression on her sister-in-law's face.

'It is strange,' Isabella said. 'William had no child, nor my brother Richard's lady. Did you know that once in Ireland after a quarrel, an old bishop cursed my father and swore none of his sons would have heirs of their body? Neither William nor Richard had seed of their love, nor Gilbert as yet and he has been wed these two years, yet we five sisters have all borne healthy babes; though' – she gave a laugh – 'Sybilla with her five daughters would give much to have a son. Of course Waiter and Anselm are not yet married, but I believe the curse will be on them too. Ireland is a strange country, full of weird prophets, bishops though they may be.'

'William never told me,' Eleanor said.

'I think he'd not want to believe it, nor wish to worry you, but I believe now it is true.'

'At least it did not extend to you,' Eleanor said, surprised at the seriousness with which the practical Isabella took the meanderings of a long-dead old man. 'Henry is as healthy a babe as I have ever seen. What will you do when Richard is away? Will you go to one of your sisters? Or stay at Wallingford?'

'Matilda wants me to spend some time at Norwich with her. She is not well and would welcome my company, but Richard will leave me in charge of so many affairs. He is so clever with business and my head must work for his.'

'I have been meaning to ask the King for an establishment of my own now that the court has a Queen. If he agrees, will you come and help me to put it to rights?'

'Willingly,' Isabella said and added, 'I thought you would soon wish for it. One court, one Queen!'

It was not, however, until after a summer occupied by bridal visits, processions round the country that all might see their new Queen, that Henry gave Eleanor a castle for her sole use. During the summer she had attended the Queen and they were much together but even Henry, besotted as he was, could not fail to observe that there were small frictions between sister and sister-in-law. Eleanor had been too long the first Princess in the land and she found it hard to step down, while the Queen, flushed with the brilliance of her marriage, was too preoccupied and too lacking in tact to be as careful as she might with the King's widowed sister, still so young and beautiful. The observant Richard pointed out to Henry that it would be wise to give Eleanor what she wanted, and the King, daily falling more and more in love, agreed. With a gesture of genuine affection he offered the castle at Odiham with the manor and park and all hunting rights. It was an almost equal distance between Winchester and Windsor.

'Most suitable,' the Queen said and added, 'You will be able to visit us often. But I expect you will be much occupied there, dear sister.'

There was nothing in her words that could be misconstrued but Eleanor sensed a meaning underneath, a hint that her visits need not be too frequent.

'As your grace says,' she agreed. 'I have of course been all my life so much at court, as befits my station, that it will be a pleasant change to be quiet at Odiham.'

The Queen coloured a little. She did not like being reminded that Count Raimond could not compare as a father to a King of England, even if that King were John Lackland. 'Naturally, your position as vowed to perpetual widowhood would make you prefer retirement,' she said. 'You must find our frolics tiresome.'

'Not at all. I have no wish to cast a gloom upon your grace's nuptials.' Eleanor's tone was smooth. 'Especially as our life here is so new to you.'

These barbs passed unnoticed by Henry and he merely added cheerfully, 'Well, do not stay away too long, sister, and when all is set to rights we will come and visit you. I shall give you that fine black palfrey the Archbishop of York sent to me – she is too light for my weight but she will carry you well.'

It was after Christmas when at last Eleanor journeyed to inspect her new home. The frost and snow of the twelve days of Christmas yielded to a milder spell and she and Isabella rode there together accompanied by Isabella's fourteen-year-old son by her first marriage. Richard had not yet departed on his crusade but he was busy about numerous affairs and agreed to part with his wife while he went abroad to visit his brother-in-law the Emperor Frederick.

The young Richard de Clare, temporarily free from his guardian Gilbert Marshal, enjoyed accompanying his mother. He was growing into a slender youth, proud of his looks and his figure, though he overrated the effect of his long angular face and fair hair that would undoubtedly thin with age. He was very much aware of his position as Earl of Gloucester, Clare and Hertford, titles he had held since he was eight years old; he was enormously wealthy and owing to the wise advice of his stepfather and the jealous guardianship of his uncle, money slipped daily into his coffers. He bore himself dutifully towards his mother but Eleanor suspected that a great deal went on under that cultivated charm. She also had a suspicion that there was a slight tension between mother and son, but she had too much else on her mind to dwell on it.

The castle of Odiham was not long built, with an eye to comfort rather than defence. The octagonal keep was near a small meandering river and the moat, so far from being considered an obstacle to would-be besiegers, was used as a fishpond.

'We'll eat well during the Lenten fast,' Eleanor said laughing.

'I can see a great many pike, and roach too, swimming there, and I don't envisage having to hold my castle against marauders!'

The hall was small but of sufficient size for her retinue, many of whom she had sent on ahead under her steward, Sir John Penrose, to see that all was in readiness for her. Craftsmen had glazed the windows of the hall and there was a fireplace set in the centre and a fire burning there against her arrival. She stood warming her hands while an usher hurried to bring hot spiced wine for her and the Countess Isabella.

In the bedroom above there was also a fire, a new chimney set into the wall and a great bed where she would sleep, and Isabella too for as long as she remained a guest there. Doll and Megonwy were in their element unpacking their lady's toiletries, setting her jewel boxes on a table, her gowns in a long chest where the materials would not crush.

Supper was served in the hall, trestles set up for the household, a dozen knights and their ladies attending the Princess, while the young Earl of Gloucester served her and his mother on his knee.

Eleanor's minstrel, whom she and William had brought back from Nantes long ago, sang to them and she sat at the centre of the table on the dais, glad to have her own establishment again.

After a week Gloucester left them, returning to his guardian Gilbert Marshal, and on the afternoon of his departure Isabella sent their ladies out of the room and said abruptly, 'I wished to speak to you privately.'

'I thought something was amiss,' Eleanor nodded. 'I could not help noticing – '

'It is Gloucester.' Isabella never referred to her son other than by his title. 'You know that some years ago, when I first wed your brother, I sent the boy to St Edmund's Bury to study? My lord de Burgh's wife, the Princess Margaret, was there also with her daughter Megotta.'

'I remember. My lord Hubert was shut up in Chepstow then, and sent them both into sanctuary.'

'Well, Gloucester was still technically under their guardianship, although Henry misliked it, and while he was there the Princess, whether on Hubert's orders I know not, arranged that Gloucester and Megotta – indeed I hardly know how to say it, and what your brother will do I cannot imagine!'

'Isabella! What are you trying to tell me? That Princess Margaret betrothed those two children?'

'Worse than that! She had them married by her own chaplain.' Isabella's face was pale with anger as she came out with the plain truth.

'But how could that be, without Hubert's consent, let alone my brother's?'

'Oh, she must have persuaded the priest into it and in Hubert's place she had some authority over the boy. Sometimes I think our way of sending our sons to be brought up by others is a foolish thing to do, albeit they find less softness than at home with a doting mother.' A faint smile crossed her face but disappeared almost at once. 'I am so distressed about the whole affair and I do not know what to do. My son seems not to think it a matter for such concern, but then he does not know what the King's anger can be like.'

'The marriage can be undone, surely?' Eleanor queried. She had a very good idea what Henry might have to say. 'It is not consummated?'

'No, no, Megotta is far too young. Well, thank God for that at least. It must be annulled, for your brother will never permit it. He has no kind thoughts for old Hubert now for all he has restored his lands.'

'Henry has had enough of leading strings.'

'I know. Eleanor, will you speak to him for me? I would rather you did it than Richard. Although he is my husband and your brother, it would come better from a woman, I think. I told him I knew nothing of it, and God knows I want it undone – were William's wife and this is Marshal business.'

'Very well,' Eleanor agreed. 'I'll do what I can when I see Henry. Dearest Isabella, I am so sorry. But try to put it from your mind for a little and let us holiday together.'

During the spring and summer she and Isabella spent long and happy days furnishing and decorating hall and bedroom, setting painters to work to adorn the plain little chapel. Eleanor ordered guest chambers to be built in the courtyard, a falconry to be set up and larger stables erected under Finch's super vision. He was delighted to see his young mistress in her own castle and he and the falconer reported to her that there was excellent hawking to be had in the flat, rather marshy, surroundings. Further afield there was parkland well stocked with deer and wild boar. At last, as there was no sign of the crusaders being able to depart yet, Richard of Cornwall came to claim his wife and little son and to congratulate his sister on all she had achieved in her new home. They spent an enjoyable evening together but late that night when Isabella came to share her bed for the last time, Richard having elected to use one of the half finished guest chambers, Eleanor felt suddenly alone, as if the loss of such a friend's company would mean more than she realized. There were ladies in her household, wives to the knights serving her, but they were not Isabella.

'I wish you had not to go,' she said.

Isabella laughed. 'If I did not I fear your brother would beat me soundly for being so poor a wife.'

Eleanor tried to smile in response. 'Oh, I know Richard loves you too well to beat you or to be too long away from you. He told me the time grew tedious in Germany without you, but –' she paused, looking round the room, at the great bed, at little Henry's cradle where he slept soundly. Tomorrow he would be gone, his toys and little clothes no longer scattered here. She remembered the Maid's bedchamber, and how she had thought it solitary, pitying the ageing captive princess. Jesu, would she become like that? And tears rose and half choked her.

'What is it?' Isabella asked in sudden consternation. Then as Eleanor shook her head and stifled her desire to weep, she added, 'My dear, I know only too well what is the matter. Saintly old men and pious widows should hold their tongues. They would have us all in nunneries and then where would our menfolk be?'

Eleanor gasped out that it was not Archbishop Edmund's fault, that he had tried to dissuade her.

'Then it was that tiresome Cecily de Sanford. I wish the King had never sent her to you. Eleanor, my love, dry your tears and one day, please God, you will take a man to that bed – in wedlock too!'

Eleanor shook her head again. 'How can I? My vow – to our Lord – how can I break it?'

'The Churchmen take too much on themselves when they say they know His will for us,' Isabella returned crisply, 'Did He not break the Sabbath himself and shock the churchmen of His day?'

Eleanor's laugh was a little shaky. 'Dear Isabella, what am I going to do without you? But don't worry for me. I am well enough as I am.'

'Are you?' Isabella looked straightly at her, her eyes wandering over Eleanor's body sheathed in red velvet, her dusky hair freed from her veil and hanging down in silky plaits, at the slender neck, the rounded breasts, the shapely hips. It was not right, she thought, that such womanhood should be wasted, but she said no more, returning to the anxiety on her own mind. 'Forgive me, Eleanor, but you will not forget to speak to the King for me, will you? About Gloucester?'

'No, no, of course not,' Eleanor answered, relieved to have something else to occupy her thoughts. 'As soon as I see him it shall be done.'

About a month after Isabella's departure, she decided she would carry out her promise and visit her brother at Windsor. Most of the work at Odiham was completed except for the decorating of her own bedroom and it seemed best to be away while that was done. And after a whole summer in residence the castle could be cleaned against her return. However, two days before her planned departure she was coming down the spiral stair when she heard a clattering of hooves outside that undoubtedly heralded visitors. The hall door was open to the afternoon sunshine and as a tall figure darkened it she saw to her astonishment a familiar blazon on a surcoat, a familiar black head, the hood of his mantle thrown back.

She came down the last few steps and across the hall, not even sure that this particular visitor was welcome. 'Sir Simon! I did not expect to see you.'

'Your pardon, lady,' he said in his cool voice but with a pleasant smile, 'but your brother has graciously given me a manor near Alton and as I am on my way to take seisin of it he asked me to bring you a cask of Rhenish with his greeting.'

'You are very kind; she said formally. 'My steward will see to its disposal. May I give you some refreshment before you go on your way?'

'Thank you, but I was wondering whether I might beg shelter for the night and proceed in the morning?'

'Willingly,' she agreed, but was aware he could have reached Alton before the late summer darkness. She clapped her hands, however, for an usher to take his mantle, a groom to give orders for the stabling of his horses and the entertaining of his retinue, while she led him to the dais and a page brought wine. For a while they sat and talked of the court and the latest news. He told her he had been to York to the Scottish King Alexander, and that he had been given the custodianship of Kenilworth Castle. He talked of the Archbishop of Canterbury's opposition to the Pope in the matter of 'Peter's Pence', of the grandeur of the growing church at Westminster, and he told her in witty terms of the latest scandal concerning the Queen's uncle Boniface and the daughter of the Seneschal at Winchester. Eleanor began to see why her brother found this man so attractive a companion, for though his conversation was amusing, and though he laughed at the latest gossip, it was when he referred to the saintly Edmund Rich that she glimpsed his true character. As they spoke of the Archbishop she felt the tension she had always been aware of in Simon's presence disappearing. She asked if he must ride on tomorrow or whether he would care to try the hunting in her park.

Gracefully he accepted her invitation and somehow a week of summer weather slipped by. They rode to the forest where he brought down a fine hart, and went hawking in the marshes, Finch leading the way through safe paths. She had always had a talent for handling the birds and as she let her merlin fly, crying out to it to 'Rake off! Rake off!' and then swinging her lure to bring it home to her wrist, the quarry seized, there was undisguised admiration in his eyes.

In the evenings they supped in the hall with the door wide still to the warm August evening and Eleanor discovered him to be well read and informed, a raconteur who kept her amused and whose tales she was often able to cap.

The weather broke at last on the first of September, a sudden storm of rain keeping them within doors and when she suggested a game of backgammon he came to her chamber where the board was set up. Doll arranged the counters and then sat sewing, her head bent over her embroidery, a little smile on her lips, while the two played with desultory talk and the rain beat against the new glass. It grew chill and Eleanor sent Doll to find a servant to light the fire.

For the first time they were alone and as soon as the door closed Simon reached out without hesitation and took her hand.

'Lady,' he said, and then stopped, his eyes fixed on her. At the touch of his fingers a sensation ran through her. It seemed to turn her stomach, to send the blood racing in a manner she did not recall ever having felt before, even in the days of her marriage with William, and a flush ran up under her skin.

He lifted her hand and turning it put his lips into her palm. 'I adore you,' he said.

Some instinct, retreating from a situation rapidly slipping out of her control, made her turn his words with a flippancy she was far from feeling. 'Messire! You, to use a troubadour's tongue!'

His face darkened. 'I am no court fool to indulge in poet's talk. Do you not know me better than that?'

'I do not think I know you at all.'

'But I know you, my lady Eleanor.' He got up and coming round the table that separated them stood above her. He seemed very tall, blocking what light there was from the narrow window, his eyes holding hers. 'I believe I can make you love me.'

'Love you? Until this last week I was not sure I even liked you.'

'No?' He gave a low laugh. 'Liking has very little to do with it. I have desired you for a long time but until recently I was in no position to think I might ever win you.'

'And now?' She had not risen but sat tautly in her chair, every pulse throbbing, feeling utterly defenceless. She knew she had only to call and her page would come running. Yet she did not call.

He said, 'Now I have your brother's friendship, and I have an earldom to offer you. I have been making myself an Englishman as I said I would. I have even been studying your language that I might talk to my own people in their tongue. With you as a wife, and the King's sister into the bargain, what may I not –'

'Oh!' She sprang up and away from him. 'Is that it? Your protestations of love are all sham. You want me only because of who I am not what I am.'

'Eleanor!' He came close but sensing the rigidity of her body he did not touch her, only his voice was charged with the intensity of his feeling. 'Of course it would advance me to be the King's brother-in-law, but that is not what brought me here. I meant only that my position is now such that I dare attempt it. I think I have loved you from the moment when I lifted you into your saddle at St Malo.'

'You have sought other wives. There was the Count of Flanders' daughter, wasn't there?'

He gave a shrug. 'A man must marry and I thought after your lord died and you took that vow that you would retire to a convent. But when you did not do so, when you came back to court, all that was changed.'

'But it did not mean that I would forsake my promise.' Yet she was aware somehow that she was fighting a losing battle, that he was saying to her only what she knew herself.

He was smiling now. 'I have watched you for a long time. I have watched you sing and dance and hawk and enjoy all the pastimes of a great lady. You have your own establishment here now and a retinue fit for a Princess. You were not made for a nunnery, lady, for you have shed your grief and become a woman again. I think chastity is not for you.'

'You know nothing about it,' she fired up.

'I am a man,' he said, 'and when, do you recall, you told me you were not interested in bridals, there was that in your voice that revealed a great deal – to me, at least.'

She was stricken to silence, remembering how short a time ago she had wept in Isabella's arms, from sheer longing, from fear of the lonely path she had chosen. And now this man whom she had known since she was a young bride, yet whom she really knew so little, said he loved her and put an unerring finger on her innermost thoughts.

In a dulled voice she said, 'I cannot break my vow. It was a sacred promise, sworn before Almighty God. Do you not fear Him, His wrath if I should break it?'

'I fear God,' he said with natural reverence, 'but I also trust in His mercy. You were distraught at the time. I think you did not know what you were doing and you have never taken the final step. Do you not feel yourself turning further and further from it?'

'Yes,' she agreed, her voice scarcely above a whisper, 'but I wear this ring – '

He reached out for her hand and with one swift movement took it from her finger. 'I will give you another.'

She gave a startled gasp, but before either he or she could speak again there was a tap on the door and Doll came in with one servant bearing logs and another a torch and kindling. Eleanor turned away to the window and looked out towards the marshes, the tall bulrushes, the reeds swaying in the dying wind. A mallard rose, quacking, and flew out of her sight. The rain had stopped and there were all the signs of a golden sunset. She was too confused, her mind numb. If there was, after all, to be another man in her life, was it credible that it should be this one who hitherto had aroused only annoyance in her? And yet the fact that he had aroused emotion at all, told her something. Of the feelings of the last few minutes she dared not think. When the fire was lit and Doll sat down again to her sewing, joined by Megonwy, she tried to concentrate once more on the game, but after a few careless moves was glad that supper was announced.

In the morning he rode away and when he took farewell of her in the hall he merely bowed over her hand, but his fingers held hers more tightly than was commanded by courtesy. He thanked her for her hospitality and added, 'I trust to see you again very soon, lady,' laying significant emphasis on the words.

She watched him ride away, attended by half a dozen young knights who clearly thought themselves fortunate to be in his service, a line of squires following, his banner of the lion with the forked tail floating over his head. And for the rest of the day she wandered aimlessly about, unable to give her attention to the carpenter who was making a screen to divide the buttery from the hall.

It was some time before she saw Simon again, for Henry kept him busy, and then it was in no degree of privacy. She rode to Windsor as planned and broached the subject of Gloucester's marriage with her brother. The King was angry, as she suspected he would be, swearing vengeance on Hubert de Burgh who stoutly denied any knowledge of the affair as he had been in hiding in Chepstow at the time. It seemed he had to be believed. His wife took full responsibility for the affair, but as she was a daughter of the Scottish King, Henry had no mind to quarrel with his neighbour over the border concerning it. Before, however, anything was decided, Megotta sickened of a fever and died and so the matter ended, but Henry delivered himself of a vitriolic attack on subjects whose rank made it an offence to marry or give in marriage without his consent and his Council's. Isabella was plainly relieved and Gloucester oddly unmoved; within a few months he was hastily married to Maud de Lacy, daughter of the Earl of Lincoln.

Sir Simon and the Princess Eleanor met occasionally at court and his eyes sought hers first among the crowds surrounding her brother, but always there were others present when they spoke. She began to wonder if he had meant what he said and if so why he was playing such a waiting game. He was always with Henry, riding out to hunt, or walking arm-in-arm with him to watch the new abbey church rising on the foundations of the old one, and she began to grow hungry for an answer to her questionings.

The man intrigued her, but he was not for her. No man was for her, yet the more time went by, the more her desire grew. Her vow, taken so ardently, now became a burden she longed to discard and she began to cast about in her mind how it might be done. She lit a candle to the Blessed Virgin and begged for release, for guidance to that end. She wanted to talk to someone, but she did not know whom to confide in. No priest would take her part in this, and Isabella, though she clearly wished to see her wed again, did not like Simon. Did she herself like him? Or did she love him? What was it he had said? 'Liking has little to do with it?' Perhaps he was right, for she knew she desired him, he disturbed her sleep, his face constantly in her mind.

So it was that all her defences were down, her nerves tense, when at Christmas time she went to Westminster where the King was to keep the feast. Her brother Richard, the other would-be crusader, was still in England and the feast was held with all the usual panoply of Christmas. There were mummers and minstrels, tumblers and a man with a performing bear to entertain them, and on Christmas morning, at the Mass of the Nativity, Eleanor kneeling beside her devout brother was more aware than she would have thought proper at this moment, of Simon close by. His hands were clasped together, his attention only on the Holy Sacrifice and she saw that he was not like so many barons who shuffled their feet and whispered, some even laughing at a low-voiced joke throughout Mass or gossiping behind their hands.

She could trust him, she thought suddenly, with her life – her love! A stain of colour rose in her face and as a choir of boys in white surplices sang the

Christmas paean of joy, 'Hodie Christus natus est . . .' she sent up an impassioned plea that she might be absolved from that vow of six years ago.

The day was mild and bright, a pale sun lightening the courtyard as they came from the chapel to prepare for the day's feast. Eleanor walked proudly, her head high. If she chose to re-marry who would dare to throw the first stone at her? If the churchmen called her an adulteress, let them! She had replaced the ring after Simon had gone, unwilling to excite gossip among her household, but what was it he had said? – I will give you another.

Yet he had not spoken and though she did not realize it, by not hurrying to do so he had gone the right way, the only way to win her.

In the evening a troop of acrobats from Hungary were to perform. Amid the laughter and the music and the overflowing of wine and ale, when the company was very merry, several noble gentlemen very drunk, and the noise rising to the roof, the trestles were cleared from the centre of the hall. Eleanor, who had been talking to the aged mother of the Earl of Lincoln, had moved away a little, intending to return to the dais in order to see more clearly, when she found her hand taken and she was drawn to the shelter of a pillar.

Simon released her hand almost at once and leaned negligently against the stone column that no one might think his talk anything but casual. 'Well?' he said and the grey eyes held hers. 'Have I given you time to consider?'

'Too long,' she answered, the words coming out with impulsive force. 'Too long, by the Holy Cross!'

He gave a low laugh. 'Will you quarrel with me for that? At least I will not have urged you to a too hasty decision.'

The tumblers had entered the hall now, a dozen of them in red tunics, leaping and somersaulting to the cheers of the audience. Simon, giving them only a cursory look, went on, his face grave again. 'It is a serious matter between us. I want you, my lady Eleanor, and I will brave the anger of Holy Church to gain you, but what of you? Do you care enough for me to do the same?'

And then, contrarily because she had longed for him to speak, she held him off for one more moment. The acrobats were jumping from the cupped hands of one to the shoulders of another and she clapped her hands. 'Oh, see! They are clever, these fellows.'

'Eleanor, don't play with me.' He put a hand to her face, turning it forcibly so that she must look at him. In the hall every eye was on the Hungarians, now climbing one upon the other until they formed a living pyramid. Eleanor gave an uncertain laugh and all pretence left her.

'You said at Odiham that I loved you. I think you read me better than I knew myself.'

'Then?' His voice shook with a passion she had never heard from any man.

'I will dare it for you, my lord. I believe I would dare anything for you.' She was amazed at her own words and as he reached out, taking both her hands, drawing her further from the crowded hall, she felt a tremor of sheer joy run through her, a desire she had never known before. Behind a screen now, hidden from the excited courtiers, everyone cheering the acrobats, he took her in his arms and for the first time put his mouth to hers. His lips, parting hers, sent shivers of sensation through her and his hands, passing over her, awakened feelings unknown to her, so that her arms went up about his neck.

But only for a moment. Instinctively they drew apart and he said, 'I would not compromise you, beloved. You will wed me, will you not? As soon as I can get your brother's consent? You will not fear nor hold by that foolish vow?'

'God will forgive us,' she said. 'Such love as ours must come from Him. I knew it this morning. But I do not know what Henry will say. He is so – so careful in such matters.'

'Then I will carry you away and wed you in secret.'

'And lose all you have gained?' She saw the smile on his face and went on, 'My dear lord, don't you recall bow angry Henry was about Gloucester's secret marriage? We cannot do that.'

'I know,' he said soberly. 'Well, we will be open with him, win him over. I think he loves us both well enough to listen to us.'

'He does, I'm sure of it, but if he should not think it right – ' she broke off.

He held her closely again, breast to breast, looking down into her face. 'Have faith, my love. Perhaps in his own new happiness he will be gentle with us. If not, we must dare his anger. Will you face it with me? It is not conceivable that we should part.'

She reached up to touch his cheek. 'I do not think, now, I could live without you.'

His mouth came down on hers once more in a swift hard kiss and then they slipped back into the ball where the acrobats had just reached the climax of their performance. Eleanor was sure they had not been observed.

But John Mansel, the King's clerk, had seen them leave and return and his eyes narrowed. He was a man who stored up scraps of information against the day when they might be useful.

It seemed at the moment that Simon could do no wrong and it so happened that he approached the King when Henry was annoyed with his Council. They were baulking at his demands for funds for his new building schemes and he was weary with being taken to task for having spent so much on his new Queen's adornment and for being so generous to her relatives. The Exchequer was low, Henry's ideas of what was fitting for his two loves, his wife and his abbey church, extremely high. He was tired of having the Earl of Lincoln glower at him, of bumbling old Chichester's quotations from the great Lanfranc's maxims. The Bishop of Winchester, quietly restored to his see, was dying and the barons wanted to force Ralph Neville into his place but he'd not have him, not Chichester by God! Simon de Montfort's strength of personality was a weapon on his side and it never occurred to

Henry that the very attributes he admired might mean that he could not manipulate Simon as he wished. At the moment he only saw that his friend had fallen in love with his sister and was providing him with an opportunity to flout his Council and assert his own mastery.

'Nothing would pleasure me more than to see you wed,' he told them, 'but it shall be done quietly for your sake, my dearest Eleanor. My Council will only be tiresome and protracted. They argued for months, nay years, about your marriage to William and I'll not have that.'

'I thought,' Eleanor said tentatively, 'after Gloucester's affair you might not –'

'I was not consulted then,' he retorted. 'That was the offence. Am I not King? You did right to come to me. I can overrule my Council and show them who is master in this palace.'

'And – and my vow?'

'Oh, as to that –' he made an airy gesture, 'I do not consider it so binding under the circumstances. If necessary Simon must go to the Pope, but the churchmen must make the best of it, and I will pray for you.'

If Simon had scruples he did not voice them, but inclined his head, a faint smile on his lips at the King's confidence in the power of his own intercession with the Almighty. The glittering prospect of marriage with one higher in rank than he had ever dreamed of winning combined with the love and desire that was consuming him was such heady stuff that no other consideration could weigh with him.

'When, sire?' he asked. 'When shall it be?'

Henry sat fingering his chin. They were in his bedchamber after dinner on St Stephen's day. Through an archway was his private chapel; he had even had a hole made in the wall that he might hear Mass from his bed, for he was accustomed to hear two or three in the day.

'It shall be here,' he pronounced, 'on the morning of Epiphany, when most of my guests will be going to their own homes after our festivities – a busy morning when what is done here will be unnoticed.'

Eleanor and Simon exchanged startled glances. 'Only a few days,' she said, 'so little time to prepare.'

'You must not prepare,' Henry told her. 'Would you betray our secret?' He rubbed his hands delightedly and Simon, still looking down at his bride, added, 'Your brother is right, my heart. Do we want to wait, maybe for years, while they haggle over the business, councillors and churchmen alike? You know if we go to the Pope first how long it will take, whereas when the thing is done – ' He broke off. 'If you want me, my love–'

'If?' She could think of nothing but this man beside her and she had, after all, a new gown as yet unworn that would serve as a wedding gown. But she gave her brother one last doubtful look. 'Harry, you are so good to us, you will do what is right, but will the Queen understand? Are we to tell her now?'

He paused and then a secret smile came over his face. 'My beloved wife trusts me in all things. If I do not tell her first, it is only because she is free in her talk with her own people; one of them might let slip our intention. I am determined, Simon, to have you for my brother and none shall know until it is done.'

'Sire!' Simon knelt and put Henry's hand to his lips, and in a rush of warm affection Eleanor knelt with him.

The King looked down at their radiant faces, and leaning forward embraced them both. He had a sense of power, of pleasure in acting in defiance of the tedious men who clamoured to advise him, to argue every point. This time it was he who should have his way. 'Be careful coming here,' he advised. 'Come separately and before the palace is astir.'

'My lord,' Simon said, 'the words alone will not be sufficiently binding. Words can be annulled. Before the world is told Eleanor must be the wife of my body.'

Henry's smile widened. Utterly happy himself with his own young bride, he had already thought of this. 'After Master Walter has done his work, I must go down to speed my departing guests. I will leave a guard at my door with instructions to admit no one until I return – and I shall not return until dusk. There will be wine and cold meats here for you, and my own bed and all the day before you.' He touched his sister's cheek lightly. 'I can trust the rest to you, can I not, Simon – so soon to be my brother?'

CHAPTER FIVE

Long afterwards, when so much had gone wrong, Eleanor remembered his words and the warmth and happiness between the three of them on that winter afternoon. Nor did she forget Epiphany, that day when 'the rest was left to Simon'. After Henry himself had given her hand into Simon's and Simon's ring was set in the place of that other one, even as he said it would be, Walter the chaplain pronounced the words over them and said Mass. Henry gave them his blessing as if he was a hoary patriarch instead of a young man newly wed himself, and then he and Walter departed.

It was a dark morning with heavy rain clouds driving across the sky. Eleanor remembered the day when they had played backgammon at Odiham because the rain kept them indoors, with such portentous results.

'Bad weather is our good fortune,' Simon said. 'It is dark enough today for it to be night.'

In the afternoon they ate in the light of the fire which he had replenished himself from the pile of logs by the hearth. Sitting in the King's chair with Eleanor half dressed on cushions at his feet, the glow of the firelight on their faces, they talked in low lover's tones, although there was no one to hear. Simon spoke of Kenilworth and how he would joy to have her sharing the great bedchamber with him, of his hope of children to fill the hall with their games and laughter.

'I would bear you sons,' Eleanor said, her head against his knee. Her dark hair was unbound and he stroked it, occasionally twisting his fingers in the shining strands, the firelight catching the ruby ring that was her own wedding gift to him.

'And daughters,' he added. 'Beautiful daughters to be wed in the highest courts in Europe. We will found a dynasty, dear heart, that will spread out over the centuries, God willing.' She was silent for a moment, remembering briefly those two short years with William. She had borne him no child and there was a sudden momentary fear that she might be barren, that she might fail Simon in something he desired so ardently. And then she recalled that strange curse said to lie over the Marshal men. Gilbert Marshal was childless too, and Walter had now been married a year or more and his wife showed no sign of being pregnant. It was clearly no fault of hers that she had borne no child. She thrust the fear away and echoed her lover's words: 'God willing.'

'As a thank-offering for this day,' he said, 'we will make a gift to the abbey at Kenilworth, a chalice perhaps, or a fine cope for the abbot, for nothing, nothing now can unmake us man and wife.'

'Nothing,' she said and sliding to her knees entwined her arms about him. His lovemaking all through the dark January morning had been an ecstasy beyond anything she had ever known or imagined, and William and his gentleness faded into the background like a quiet wraith. She felt a deep respect still for his memory, for all he had been, but their nights together had barely stirred her and she remembered the feelings of unfulfilment, the odd longings that were not satisfied. Now she knew what love could be, what fire and delight and satisfaction, for Simon had awakened her body into life, his mouth, his hands, his whole self demanding a response that she found she could give and long to give again and again.

She gazed now into the dark face above hers and put her mouth to his so urgently that in his swift response, he rose and lifting her carried her back to the bed.

As the dark day faded they slept, wrapped in each other's arms, and only when the curfew bell rang did they stir.

'It is nearly the supper hour,' Simon said in her ear. 'We must dress, my heart, and face the world again.'

'Henry says we will not tell them yet,' she murmured drowsily.

'But it must be soon. You are my wife and I must have you before all men, my countess, the mistress of my home.'

'Yes, yes,' she whispered ardently. 'Oh soon, soon!'

He had pushed back the covers and she moved her hands over his strong well-made body, recalling how once she had been afraid of William's nakedness. Now she gloried in Simon's and in her own beauty as he kissed the white skin of her breasts. And as he raised his face she wondered how she could ever have thought the deep-set grey eyes were cold.

The storm broke, as it had to do. It would soon have been observed that the Princess Eleanor no longer kept any of her maidens in her bedchamber at night; some small incident would set tongues wagging, and Henry told them that he would announce the marriage to his Council.

At first he remained impervious to the explosion of a dozen voices.

'Great God!' his brother exclaimed. 'Without reference to us, your Council? This was not wise of you, Henry. All marriages of any importance are referred to us, and to give our own sister, without a word to me, to – to a commoner, a damned foreigner, a man who has not been in England more than a few years –' He paused momentarily, lost for words and the Earl of Pembroke broke in, his face flushed with annoyance.

'By the Rood, sire, I certainly should have been informed. The disposal in marriage of my brother's widow is very much my concern.'

'And mine,' Earl Ferrars muttered. He was in a bad temper for his wife Sybilla had just presented him with yet another daughter. 'I too have a share in Marshal affairs.'

The Earl of Lincoln, very stooped these days, hunched his mantle over stiff shoulders. 'It has always been agreed that no royal marriage should take place without consultation. Your grace has chosen to offend us all in this matter. And I thought the Princess was vowed to Holy Church?'

'Aye,' de Bohun, Earl of Hereford, interrupted sharply. He was, as always, jealous over matters of precedent and disliked the thought of Simon de Montfort's newly acquired position. 'Or can one make and break such vows at will?'

His sarcasm stirred the elderly Bishop of Chichester out of his usual timidity. 'No, no! I cannot believe this, that the Countess should do such a thing. Surely –'

The Abbot of St Albans' comment came far more sharply. 'Of course it is a sin, a great sin. A sacred plight ring is as binding as the veil. Sir Simon and the Princess have committed a sacrilege.' He swung round to face the Archbishop of Canterbury. 'Is not the marriage invalid then, my lord?'

Edmund Rich had been sitting silently through this exchange, his head bowed, the first stunned horror giving place to priestly determination. He raised his head to look at the King, seated at the head of the table, his fingers tapping ominously on the carved arms of his chair. 'I fear you acted on impulse in this matter, sire. Your Council say, rightly, that you should have consulted them, but even more, you should have consulted your spiritual advisers. You are so true a son of Holy Church I am astonished that you did not do so.'

'I have some authority in my own kingdom,' Henry retorted, 'and over my own family or do you all wish to deny me that?'

No one answered this and the Archbishop went on, 'My brother of St Albans is right. Of course the marriage is a sacrilege. I myself heard the Princess take her vow, I myself set the ring on her finger.'

'And that upstart from Normandy took it off, with your good will,' Richard exploded. 'Henry, King you may be but there are indeed limits to what you can do.'

Henry's face had flushed, the colour running up into his high forehead. He had not reckoned on such opposition from his brother who had always seemed on friendly terms with their new brother-in-law. 'Aye, I am King, a fact you are all forgetting. There is not a man here who would not consider it his right to bestow his womenfolk where he wished.'

'But not against God's law.' Rich's voice was stern. 'I believed you had respect for that.'

'So I have, but Eleanor did not take the veil. You know, my lord, she has not intended to do that these many years. The vow was a mistaken impulse, taken by a grief-stricken girl. I will not have her happiness destroyed because of that.'

'Well, if she wanted to marry, we would not argue over that,' Richard said, 'but the Archbishop should have been consulted and a dispensation could have been applied for from the Pope himself if necessary.' Richard looked round for agreement and the Bishop of Chichester added that he could not imagine what the Papal Legate would have to say to the affair.

'It is not his business,' Gilbert Marshal retorted. 'I would have thought that you, my lord Archbishop, could have dispensed the lady from her vow – which of course is the Church's business.'

'Could and would are two different things.' Edmund Rich shook his head. 'Even if I could I would not – not without his Holiness's permission. As for the Legate, he cannot be ignored.'

'I could ignore him,' Gilbert muttered. 'God's death, we have enough of him poking his nose into our affairs. What concerns me is that my sister-in-law's marriage portion has been handed over without a word to anyone to Simon de Montfort. What has he done to deserve a Princess of England for a bride? Nothing, I say!'

'Aye,' de Bohun put in. 'He is well enough for a knight, but he has no place among your barons, sire.'

'He is Earl of Leicester,' Henry flashed back. 'I have given him a place and will confirm him in it tomorrow. And then, whether you like it or not, he will be one of you and have a seat on my Council.'

'Words can't make him one of us,' Pembroke persisted, 'though he may sit on old Leicester's lands. Nor can you force us to like it, sire.'

There was a low muttering agreement among the other lords and the Earl of Oxford added superciliously, 'I do not like the cold way the man has of looking down his nose at us as if his blood were as good as ours.'

'Sir Simon is my friend.' Henry glared angrily from one to the other. 'Hold your tongues, all of you. My sister's affairs shall be dealt with correctly, but Sir

Simon is now her husband and entitled to his place here. I insist that you receive him as such.'

'Oh aye,' Gilbert Marshal grumbled, 'now that it is too late to do anything about it. Yet I suppose the Pope could undo the marriage – unless it is too late?'

Earl Ferrars gave him a warning look but it was unheeded and the Queen's uncle spoke for the first time. Being a foreigner himself he had wisely held his tongue till then, but now he felt that as Earl of Richmond he could join in the argument.

'You go too far, my lords,' he said severely. 'It is incredible to me that you should all thus condemn a man who has done you no harm, and even more incredible that you should take your King to task in this manner. He has the right to bestow his sister's hand where he will.'

'It may seem incredible to you' – the Earl of Oxford swivelled round to face him – 'but that is because you do not understand our laws, nor, it seems the purpose of the King's Council. I suppose such civilized proceedings are unknown in Provence.'

Richmond coloured angrily. 'You Englishmen think you know better about everything than anyone else. Believe me, you are not so highly thought of in France.'

'Uncle! If you please,' Henry held up his hand. He turned to the one man present who had not yet spoken but whose views he had sounded beforehand. 'My lord bishop, what is your opinion? You know the law of the Church as well as anyone.'

Robert Grosseteste, Bishop of Lincoln, was in something of a dilemma. A man of immense intelligence, single-minded and of sound judgement, he was devoted to the Church and to his spiritual superior the Archbishop, but he fought constantly against the encroachments of the Papal Legate and wanted to see English affairs settled by Englishmen. He had also, during the years that Simon had held the Leicester lands, become a close friend to the Earl. He turned in appeal to Edmund Rich. 'My father-in-God, you know Earl Simon as well as I do. You know his true devotion; you know he would do nothing to flout God's law. He does not believe, in contracting this marriage, that he has done so but if we consider he has, then he is prepared to go to the Pope, to ask for the matter to be set right.'

The Archbishop shook his head sadly. 'Is that not a case of bolting the stable door when the horse has fled? I am horrified that he and the Princess could so blind themselves as to what they have done. The very stealthiness of the marriage betrays their hidden guilt, whatever they may say. It is invalid – they live in sin.'

'Aye, it is the secrecy that stinks,' Pembroke muttered and half a dozen other voices joined in the protest. 'Without even consultation with us!'

'And why should the richest prize in England be given to a foreigner?'

'The marriage is no marriage, the Church says so.'

'Simon de Montfort should be sent back to Normandy. '

'Dismiss him, sire. He has betrayed you, all of us, by his wicked scheming.'

'Aye, to seduce our Princess!'

The chorus of angry voices rose until Earl Richard banged on the table for silence, summing all up by saying that at best it was a piece of ill-advised plotting that reflected no good on any of those concerned.

This brought Henry to his feet, his fair skin mottled. He hated argument, hated trouble, whether brought about by his own folly or not, and he bellowed at them, 'By Our Lady, I will not have this! I have done what I have done and you shall not argue with me. My lord of Leicester' – deliberately giving Simon his title – 'shall go to Rome. I myself will give him letters to the Holy Father who, I doubt not, will absolve my sister. And you, all of you,' his eyes went ominously in the direction of Gilbert Marshal, 'especially you, my lord of Pembroke, will incur my deepest displeasure if you are discourteous to either the Earl or the Countess of Leicester.'

Archbishop Edmund rose. 'The Countess of Pembroke is her title, sire, until such time as we hear from His Holiness. And may I suggest – '

But Henry was already striding away from the table. He was fully aware that Richard was not following him, that his brother was standing, in a manner that spoke louder than words, among the other angry barons and prelate.

'My dear sister,' the Queen said smoothly, 'how very romantic! Quite like one of my own poems. But may I say it was not perhaps a wise thing to do.' She had heard the news only half an hour before the stormy Council meeting and had gone at once to the Princess's bedchamber.

'Nevertheless I did it,' Eleanor said quietly. In the new found strength of her love she would have dared anything for Simon.

The Queen picked up a fringe she had been working on and fingered the silk. 'Pretty stuff. If you had consulted me, as indeed a true sister would have done, I might have advised you more carefully.'

'You, madame?' Eleanor raised an eyebrow. 'I had my own brother to advise me. You are new to our country and you do not understand us very well as yet.'

'New? I have been here these two years.'

'Perhaps,' Eleanor said with calculated carelessness, 'but then your time is spent among your own people, is it not?'

'Yet you have wed a foreigner like myself. Your argument carries no weight there, my dear.'

'I am not arguing,' Eleanor said. She was well aware that her sister-in-law was annoyed because she had not been made privy to the secret wedding. Eleanora of Provence was young and very proud, but Eleanor of England was her equal in pride. 'I am merely saying that it was my brother's wish that the matter should be handled as it was.'

The Queen gave an elaborate sigh. 'Yes, it is hard for one to understand the ways of a different people. In my country a vow of chastity would be considered so binding that one would not dare to break it for fear of God's wrath.'

Eleanor felt her colour rising. 'Perhaps God is more understanding of the circumstances than you, madame. We are no less devout in England than you in Provence.'

The Queen laughed. 'You cannot tell me you mean to keep your vow! I am sure Sir Simon is not the man to emulate your King Edward whom you call the Confessor. I read the other day – you see I am studying your history – that he never so much as entered his wife's bed.'

'Your reading of our history may be accurate, madame, but hardly applicable to my lord and myself.'

'No?' The Queen's eyes went coolly over her. 'No, I do not imagine Sir Simon to be of that stamp. He has a look of coldness but any woman can see that there is passion beneath the surface – as I am sure you have found out. Well, at least now you can be open about it.'

'It was never intended that we would be otherwise for more than a short time.'

'As I said, like a French romance, but of course many people will put a different construction on the secrecy and the haste.'

'Then they will find they are mistaken,' Eleanor retorted angrily. 'I am not with child.'

'I am relieved to hear it. That would have embarrassed your brother. But of course one cannot be sure –'

Eleanor seized the fringe that the Queen was still fingering and storming across to the door flung it open. 'Madame, you have no cause to doubt my virtue. I think it best that we do not discuss this any more.'

Eleanora of Provence did not move. 'My dear, it is not for you to dismiss me. But there, I must return to my apartments anyway.' She crossed the room and patted Eleanor's cheek in a condescending manner that sent an even deeper colour into it. 'I do not envy you the wrath that is likely to fall on you now. And I don't mean God's but that of the King's barons and their ladies. Sir Simon is not well liked. But I will stand by you.' She gave her sister-in-law a faint smile and went from the room.

Eleanor in sheer vexation flung the fringe on the floor and ground her foot on it.

That night Simon came openly to her chamber and when she told him of the Queen's insinuations he laughed outright. 'A moment of spite, my heart, that's all, because Henry did not tell her. And she is jealous of you.'

'Jealous?'

'Of course. You are more to the people here than she is.'

'Naturally,' Eleanor said. 'If she did not keep all those Provencal hangers-on around her she would be better liked, only Henry will not send them away. He can deny her nothing.'

'And he has been good to us,' Simon said against her hair. 'You must win the Queen over for his sake, and I must do my best with your brother Richard.'

She gave a little sigh. 'I am sorry he is so offended.'

'I know how much you care for him. I will talk to him tomorrow.'

'Were they all so angry, at the Council meeting?' she asked. 'Did anyone tell you of it?'

'Yes, my lord of Richmond. He spoke for me, but the air was hot, he said, and not one Englishman there approved what the King had done.'

'Perhaps it was wrong,' she said in a low voice, her head against his shoulder. 'Perhaps in breaking my vow I have done a terrible thing.'

'No!' He caught her closely in his arms. 'Eleanor, we have talked and talked of this. We have prayed, and God has not struck us down. It is right that we should be man and wife – do you doubt that? Do you?'

On the last words his mouth came down on hers and when she could speak again she whispered, 'Oh no, no.' And as his hands took possession of her and his love-making drove all compunction, any last lingering doubt from her mind she hoped, ardently, that the Queen's insinuation might soon become a truth.

The whole of England, it seemed, was in a turmoil. With one voice the clerics condemned the marriage, refusing to refer to the Princess as the Countess of Leicester. The barons were furious, their self-importance slighted, their anger directed as much towards the willful King as towards the Norman who had stolen their Princess in so underhand a manner.

Earl Richard and Gilbert Marshal were loudest in their protests and Simon, with his usual ability to appraise a situation betook himself to Berkhamstead Castle where Earl Richard was residing since the Council meeting. Eleanor accompanied him and was shown at once into Isabella's apartments.

'Well!' the Countess said and laughed. 'You have taken my advice at last but, my dear, I never imagined it would be in so dramatic a way, nor that you would set the country by the ears. Nothing else is talked of and Richard is very angry.'

'I know,' Eleanor said. 'I wish he was not, though I care nothing for the mouthings of ill-tempered men like your brother Gilbert. Forgive me, Isabella, but I think he would have preferred to keep me a pensioner all my days.'

'Gilbert is not on good terms with the King and is using this affair to vent his own hurt,' Isabella agreed calmly. Gilbert had never been her favourite brother. She looked her sister-in-law up and down. 'God knows how it will be resolved but I can see that you are happy. You look very different from the days when we talked at Odiham.'

A swift smile broke over Eleanor's face. 'Of course I am happy, as you are with Richard, but I had a very sharp letter from Cecily de Sanford. She is so shocked at what I have done. She still lives in a convent.'

'And wears out her knees praying. Thank God you freed yourself from her, my love. To be a nun if one wants to is one thing, but that life was not for you, nor would William have wished you to cut yourself off from the world. I'm sure he would approve of your marrying again, though the manner of it –'

'Don't you see?' Eleanor interrupted passionately 'Simon is not liked by the barons. The Council would have wrangled on and on and as for the churchmen, they would not have listened for one moment to our plea. And even my dear friend the Archbishop, who was so kind to me when William died, has turned against me.'

'I suppose it is understandable as you took the vow in front of him. I always said it was foolishness, but I think he is right; you should have asked for a dispensation before you wed Sir Simon.'

'And wait, maybe for years. Oh no.' Eleanor sat down on some cushions on a window ledge where she could look out on the large and busy courtyard. 'Isabella, there was too much fire in us for that. Surely you know –'

'I know, as you did not with William perhaps,' her sister-in-law said with sadness in her voice. 'Passion makes women of us, that is what I see in you now, but sometimes it takes away our sense.'

'I would do it again. Isabella, none of you appreciate Simon, what he is, what he can do. He has more to offer Henry than all the Council put together. He is wise like Richard and if we are reconciled with Richard it will be much better for everyone. I did not think you would be against us.'

'Against you?' Isabella came to the window seat and kissed her cheek lightly. 'Dearest Eleanor, I have talked myself hoarse trying to persuade my lord to accept what in any case cannot now be undone.'

'And has be? Will he receive Simon kindly?'

'I can't tell. Richard is very good at listening and saying little in return. Only he does truly love you and so I hope for the best.'

'If he does not, what shall we do?' Eleanor cried out.

'If Richard is with the Council and the barons it will be very hard for Henry and Simon to stand out against them. And you know Henry – he may change his mind, especially if the Pope is angered. But Simon says he will go to the Holy Father himself.'

'The Curia can no doubt be persuaded,' Isabella agreed drily. 'Sometimes I think gold is the only thing that counts in Rome. He would be wise to go with his pockets well lined.'

Simon had in fact come to Berkhamstead with that piece of advice already in his head, for Richard, like the Curia, was open to similar persuasion. In fact Simon was managing a great deal better than either he or Eleanor suspected that he would.

He presented himself at the Earl of Cornwall's private chamber and met the first frosty glance in an open and frank manner that in his judgement was the right approach.

'My lord Richard,' he began, 'I can see that we have offended you greatly and for that I am sorry. We should have confided in you.' There was something immutable about the way Richard was sitting in his great carved chair, his feet on a stool, one ringed hand held out to the blazing logs in the hearth.

For one moment Simon wondered if he had been mistaken, if the King's brother was more upset by the affront to the Church than that to himself, but he went on, 'All I can do now is to appeal to you on the grounds of your sister's happiness.

Are you aware, when you look at her, that she is happy? It may sound foolish but love has come to us, so great a love that I believe with all my heart that it must come from God Himself. That is what made us strong enough to face all that the breaking of Eleanor's vow would entail – and we did not underestimate that.' He paused. The last words were only partly true for he had not expected such violent opposition, nor that he should receive cold looks and resentful mutterings in the streets, as he had last week when he rode down Ludgate Hill. Someone had actually thrown a rotten fish head at the feet of his horse and it had required considerable self control not to lash out with his whip at the offender. But the citizens, poor fellows, were influenced by councillors and aldermen whose pride was hurt and he kept his temper, determined that he should be seen as a man of dignity with no need for shame in the affair.

'Well, you certainly stirred up a hornet's nest,' Richard said. He was aware that he was keeping the suppliant standing, that he had not offered wine, but this business had to be settled first, one way or another. 'As for Eleanor, of course I can see that she is happy, but our friend the Archbishop would tell you that right comes before personal pleasure.'

'I doubt if the Archbishop has ever been in love.'

An appreciative flicker of a smile crept briefly into Richard's eyes. 'A saint is expected to be holier than other men – though St Augustine came late to chastity. No one expected you to be chaste, my friend, neither did I think Eleanor would be content forever in the state she chose for herself. Better to be in a convent than in the world yet cut off from the pleasuring that is natural. It was the manner of your union that offended. And that vow – at least it would have been wise to try to free her from it first.'

Simon said earnestly, 'Earl Richard, I have the deepest respect for the Archbishop, yet for so gentle a man he can be inflexible where the Church is concerned. I must admit I was governed by the fear that even if we went to the Pope I might not win Eleanor.' He paused. Richard's expression was hard to read. 'My lord, the thing is done, whatever the rights, or the wrongs which I have admitted. We are brothers now and in the past you have been good enough to give me your friendship, as the King has done.'

Richard made a gesture. 'Friendship presupposes trust.'

'What would you have said to us, my lord, had we come to you?'

Richard's brows, darker than his hair, drew together. 'You have me there. I think I would not have been as precipitate as my brother.'

'A King's privilege, perhaps?'

'You are adept at words, Sir Simon.'

'I am being honest, which I think you appreciate.'

'A rare quality,' was the Earl's comment. 'I hope that you will find it pays.'

'In your case, I am sure that it will,' Simon said swiftly, 'for I know how much you love your sister. For her sake I ask you to forgive us for not consulting you, to give us your blessing. I will prove myself a good husband and loyal to the realm, for England is now unalterably my home.' He saw a spark of response to this speech and waiting for just the right amount of time, he opened a canvas bag that he carried over his arm and brought out a magnificent gold cup. 'This is a gift, from one brother to another, and here is a platter to match. The ornamentation is superbly wrought, isn't it? The work of Master Stephen of Chepe, whom I'm sure you know. It was my wife who thought you would enjoy such a gift – to show our desire for your forgiveness.'

Richard said nothing, but he picked up the gold cup and turned it in his fingers, tracing the elegant work, appreciating the costliness and the beauty at the same time. The smile that had showed briefly in his eyes spread to his mouth.

'Your arguments are as well turned as this cup,' he said at last. 'Well, you are right in one thing – I care very much for Eleanor's happiness and no one can look at her and deny that you have made a woman of her. She was always beautiful but now –' he broke off. 'It seems I cannot deny her what is perhaps best in life, certainly better than cold chastity.'

He stood up at last, his hand held out. 'Welcome, brother. We are, after all, to be crusaders together and there must be no animosity between us. I will do what I can to reconcile you to my fellow barons and I think they will follow where I lead.'

Simon took his hand firmly. He had a great liking for Richard of Cornwall and for a fleeting moment wished that it was this man, with his careful judgement, his many abilities, who sat on the throne of England.

Richard was as good as his word. When he ceased to condemn the secret marriage and showed himself openly reconciled to his new brother-in-law, the opposition disappeared. There were grumblings, chiefly from the Earl of Pembroke and his particular cronies, and the clergy stood firm, but the battle was half won.

Simon took Eleanor to Leicester and set about raising money.

'That is what speaks in the Curia, or so I'm told,' he said with a touch of cynicism, 'and it is all-important to give gifts in the right places to persuade the Holy Father to a quick decision.'

'I wish I could come with you,' she said but he shook his head.

'This is man's work and I'll travel faster alone. Besides, to show ourselves together would not forward matters. We must seem humble, parted and awaiting his Holiness's decision.'

'Very well,' she agreed, 'but I wish you did not have to sell those woods at Leicester. It is not good to part with land.'

'I must raise money. There are some debts I can call in, but it is tiresome that Henry has never seen fit to settle your dower properly. He signed away your rights for a paltry sum far less than you should have had, and even that my lord of Pembroke is slow to pay.'

'Gilbert Marshal is as tight-fisted as he can be,' she said tartly. 'William was not like that.'

'Well, we will see what can be done about it when I come home. At least you will be able to keep my affairs in order while I am gone.'

He wanted her to see Kenilworth where he had completed Henry's building plans and took her there a few days before he must leave.

The great castle, built in local sandstone of a pinkish-brown colour, stood imposingly on a knoll, surrounded on three sides by water, by a mere and a pool, and on the fourth by the moat. As they rode over the drawbridge Eleanor knew why he talked so much of it. There was a beauty here, a strength, that was to make it her favourite home.

Together they toured the keep, tall and defensive, the more comfortable hall with its bedchamber above. They heard Mass in the newly finished chapel and Eleanor inspected the kitchens while Simon took Finch to the stables.

She made herself familiar with every detail of the place and they dined with the Abbot whose convent was close by the outer wall. She tried to forget that

Simon must leave her so soon, that she would be sitting in solitary dignity at the high table in the hall, looking along the trestle tables at their retinue. She would be alone once more. When the last night came she clung to him as they lay together in their great bed, the bed which Henry had installed for himself and his Queen when they visited Kenilworth.

Simon soothed her, stroking her hair, as unwilling as she for the separation.

'I don't know how long it will take,' he said, 'and I thought it might be politic to pay a visit to the Emperor Frederick and present myself to him. He would be a valuable ally, and I can take messages to your sister.'

'Oh, take her my dear love, and tell her' – she paused, twining her arms about him. 'Tell her I am with child.'

'Eleanor!' he cried out, 'My dear, my love, are you sure?'

'Quite sure now. I wanted so much for it to be so before you went.'

His mouth sought hers and found it. 'I am so glad, so glad. It is a sign of God's forgiveness, I'm sure of it. And it will be a boy, it must be a boy. Please God I will be home long before the birth.'

Her time was nearly come, however, when at last he rode once more under the barbican and into the great court of Kenilworth Castle. He had the Pope's absolution in his pocket, the papal blessing on their union, and the good wishes of the Emperor

Frederick. He had had the luck to arrive in time to distinguish himself at the siege of Brescia and had won Frederick's approval. One of the Queen's uncles, Count Thomas of Savoy, entertained Simon on his way home, and reminded his guest that there was the small matter of an outstanding debt which Simon had owed old Randulph of Chester and which on Randulph's death had, by various means, been transferred to himself.

'Two thousand marks?' Simon queried with rare carelessness. 'A small sum, my lord, and my brother-in-law the King will stand surety for it.'

'I'm glad to hear it,' the Count said. 'My wife's father left Flanders poor enough and I have need of money.'

'Who has not?' Simon agreed, having emptied his pockets in Rome, and promptly forgot the matter. He had no liking for the Queen's relatives and when he reached Kenilworth no thoughts for anyone but his wife.

He laid his hand on her swollen body and felt the child move. 'Beloved,' he said, 'you carry our son proudly.'

On a dark November afternoon he was proved right, for the baby was a boy and seemed strong and well made, with dark hair and Eleanor's blue eyes. Simon stood by the bed while her women bustled about attending to the child, rubbing his little limbs with salt, putting a tiny amount of wine into his mouth and wrapping him carefully before laying him in the wooden cradle awaiting him.

He kissed his wife, smoothing the hair from her damp forehead, his deeply passionate nature stirred by this crowning of their love.

It had been a difficult birth and she was exhausted, but she smiled up at him, his hand held tightly in hers. 'My lord – a boy – as you wished.'

'A fine boy,' he agreed. 'Shall he be called Henry for your brother?'

'A good notion.' Her eyes closed. 'I am so tired, Simon.'

'Then sleep,' he said, 'sleep, my heart. You have done well.'

He bent over the cradle, looking down at the little puckered face and then went out to climb to the roof above their chamber. The afternoon was dank and cheerless, an eerie mist lying over the water, the last wet leaves fallen from the trees, and he remembered how they had said that bad weather had always proved their good fortune. Standing there in the raw cold, the dampness in the air clinging to his hair and eyebrows and silently crying out his Deo Gratias, it seemed to him that the world had never been so filled with light and hope and promise.

CHAPTER SIX

In June the Queen was safely delivered of a son also who was named Edward because of the King's devotion to Saint Edward the Confessor. There was general rejoicing that after two years the Queen had proved not to be barren and Henry was beside himself with pride. He demanded costly gifts for his heir, certain that every liegeman in the country would wish to commemorate the birth of a future king and one disgruntled lord was heard to mutter that though God had given England the infant, the King was selling him.

The christening, in Henry's usual manner, was to be an extravagant feast and it was distinguished by the attendance of all the nobility. Among the godfathers were the boy's two uncles, the Earls of Cornwall and Leicester and together Richard and Simon lifted him from the font, all animosity long gone. There were still odd remarks made, which Simon and his wife ignored, while those who had murmured that there must have been some reason for the haste of the marriage had been confounded when no child appeared until eleven months after that January day. Only Matthew Paris, writing with his pen dipped in sarcasm, maintained that the ways of the Curia were too subtle for mere Englishmen.

A few weeks later, for the ceremony of the Queen's churching, the Earl and Countess of Leicester were offered the fine house of the Bishop of Winchester on the banks of the river not far from Westminster. They arrived there on a summer afternoon with their retinue, their eight-month-old son and his nurses, and all the baggage with which Eleanor found it necessary to travel. She was not going to be outdone in the matter of dress, even by the Queen.

The Bishop's house was built of stone with a high vaulted hall, several chapels, and every comfort possible was supplied. 'We shall do very well here,' Eleanor said. 'I shall be interested to see how my new nephew has grown. Our son was a lusty boy from the day of his birth.'

Simon smiled. 'Will you take a measure and scales to court?'

They arrived at the palace of Westminster just before the supper hour to find the ball filling up with guests and among them Count Thomas. Simon bowed to him in a courteous manner and was about to make some welcoming remark when he received only a cold inclination of the head as the Count passed by without pausing.

Simon was pardonably annoyed. 'What in God's name is the matter with him?' he muttered to his wife. 'I can't conceive I have offended him in any way, barring the – matter of that debt which God knows is trifling enough between men of our rank.'

'He is a tiresome, stupid man, puffed up because his niece is a Queen,' Eleanor said indignantly. 'Let us go and find my brother.'

Henry was in his chamber with his lady, two of her other uncles, Peter Earl of Richmond and Bishop Boniface, and the Abbots of Westminster and St

Albans attending him with a number of other lords. The Earl and Countess were announced by a page and entered, Eleanor sweeping her brother a deep obeisance before coming forward, her hands held out for the customary embrace, while Simon bowed, a step behind his royal wife.

To their utter astonishment Henry's face was dark with anger, the mottling creeping up into his hair as it did when he was in a temper. He turned on them with a stream of vituperation. 'I wonder you dare to show your faces here,' he burst out. 'I wonder God does not strike you down for the way you have violated all the laws of Holy Church. I swear I did not know what a devil I was taking as a friend when you came to England with your grasping schemes.'

There was sudden and utter silence. Simon and Eleanor both stood aghast, stunned by this torrent of words so completely unexpected and unheralded. Only a few weeks ago Simon had been so highly honoured as to stand godfather to the young prince. Henry had walked arm-in-arm with them both in the palace gardens, yet here he was turning on Simon as if they were the bitterest of enemies.

Eleanor stood transfixed, glancing round the faces there and seeing little to encourage her, only Isabella trying to convey some sort of warning from her place behind the Queen's chair.

Simon found his voice first. 'Sire, what can we possibly have done to offend your grace. I cannot recall –'

'Cannot recall?' Henry's voice rose to a higher pitch. 'Jesu, your memory is short when only eighteen months ago in this very chapel here you entered into an illicit union with my sister.'

Simon gasped and Eleanor cried out, 'With your consent!' She felt a sudden trembling in her knee. She had always been Henry's favourite sister, who had never had a cross word from him, and to be the object of such a vicious tirade, seemingly without reason, bewildered her. She looked round for Richard, that voice of sanity, but he was not there.

'Harry – Harry, for God's sake what are you saying?'

'Do not name God,' he stormed. 'It is He whom you have offended most. And you, Sir Simon, you have dared to corrupt the Holy Curia with your filthy money, buying my sister's absolution when my Archbishop refused it.'

Simon was staggered. 'But, sire, since the Pope's absolution Archbishop Edmund has signified that he will bow to his Holiness's decision.'

'I think you may be counting too much upon that;' Bishop Boniface said in his silky voice. 'You cannot be unaware that the Archbishop is always the first to insist on the laws of the Church being upheld. England is a long way from Rome.'

'You, my lord, know little of England.' Simon swung round. 'I was once a stranger too, but I have been here a great deal longer than you and I think I can count on Archbishop Edmund's charity.'

'You may not!' Henry interposed. 'You should be excommunicated for what you have done and my

Archbishop will not be unwilling to carry that out, I promise you.'

Simon had become very pale, his pallor accentuated in contrast with the darkness of his hair. 'My lord, you astound me. You yourself set your sister's hand in mine, you yourself gave me letters to the Pope asking him to look favourably on us, you gave us your blessing.'

'Blessing!' The word became almost a screech. Don't you dare take me to task. I didn't know what advantage you would take of my goodwill.'

'I took no advantage other than that you gave me. And all this happened last year. You gave us no cause then, nor since, to think that anything was amiss between us. You have treated me as a brother, named me godfather to your son.'

'A mistake,' the Queen said with studied negligence. 'I said at the time, Henry, but you would not have it.'

'Aye,' the King agreed, 'fool that I was. I did not know then what you had done. You owe a great sum to my wife's uncle Thomas, a sum the Pope ordered you to pay, and you've done naught about it except swear I'll stand surety for it, and for other debts. And in Rome you had the effrontery to use my name to aid you with the Holy Father himself.'

'Is all this because of a trifle of money owed to Count Thomas?' Simon demanded. 'If so it is very ill-judged, sire. My debts will be paid in time and who better could I call on to vouch for my good intentions than my new brother-in-law?'

'Oh aye,' Henry retorted. 'You would use me all you can, I don't doubt, but I'll not have it. Great God, are there no lengths to which your ambition will not drive you?'

'Harry!' Eleanor took a step forward. 'How can you accuse my lord of such things. You know well how we love you, bow grateful we have been for your care for us.'

'And how ill I've been repaid! I see I can trust no one but my dear Queen, my uncles. Oh, get out of my sight, both of you, I do not want you at my court.' A brief malicious smile crossed the King's face. 'You had best get back to the Bishop's house.

It is no longer at your disposal. I have sent my guards to eject your people and your possessions into the street.'

At that Eleanor flung herself at his feet and gazed imploringly up at him and then at the circle of faces about him. The Queen looked oddly satisfied, the Provencal uncles smug, and the Abbot of Westminster wore a hard look, his opinion wholly on the side of the Church. Only Isabella appeared near rare tears. 'Harry,' Eleanor cried again, 'have you forgotten who I am? Your sister whom you love! We have always been so much to each other. Oh, where is Richard, he would tell you –'

'I have the facts before me,' he said brutally, 'and protestations can't deny them. You have cheated me, cheated Holy Church. Go, I say, go.'

Simon came forward and helped Eleanor to her feet, his hands shaking with the effort to control the tide of rage and injured pride that was sweeping over him. 'Come,' he said in a tight hard voice. 'We do no good here.'

'None!' Henry jeered. He clapped his hands for an attendant. 'Escort the Earl and Countess to their barge.'

There was nothing for it but to withdraw and they went, Simon's hand holding Eleanor's fast, hers trembling in his, and they did not speak until they were in the boat and the oarsmen rowing them down river.

Eleanor was too stunned even to weep. 'Why, Simon, why has he changed so?'

'By the arm of St James,' Simon swore his favourite oath, 'I wish I knew.' But then he shut his mouth hard, aware of the curiosity of the oarsmen summoned so soon to return the Earl and Countess to their lodging. Simon felt his anger rising with the rhythmic sweep of the oars. If his people and goods were really in the street the news of their dismissal would be all over London by nightfall.

The boatman pulled in by the steps leading to the Bishop's palace and there Simon helped his wife out of the boat. There was no sign of anyone here except four guards at the door. Simon gave them no more than a cursory glance and led the way through an archway to the front of the building; a small courtyard giving on to the road that ran from Westminster to the city. And here indeed were all their people, standing about and waiting for them or sitting on loaded chests. Several men were still heaving packages into a wagon while the maid-servants, pale and frightened, stood in a huddle whispering together. The baby's nurse was holding him in her arms and rocking him gently while the Earl's steward, Walter, seemed to be having a vociferous argument with one of the guards at the main door.

It was Finch who came forward to tell how the King's men had come and turned them all out under the astonished eyes of the bishop's own servants. How it had seemed best to obey for he had no idea what his master and mistress would wish. He was bewildered but in his stolid way merely asked what was to be done now. He had the horses saddled and ready and dusk was beginning to fall. Walter came hurrying over and added his indignant voice to Finch's.

'We must go to an inn, at least for tonight,' Simon said. His mouth was drawn down hard. 'There is the Wolf and Duck or the Bell further along. Between the two we should find rooms enough.'

'Oh, lady,' Doll cried out. 'Thank God you are come, we did not know what to do.'

'We'd scarcely time to pack your gowns,' Megonwy said, 'but I've your jewels safe. We've had no supper.'

'We will all have supper soon,' her lord said. 'Finch, get them all ready to go. Are the wagons loaded?'

Finch nodded and while he assembled the anxious servants, Simon himself lifted Eleanor into her saddle. She was shaking, not with cold for the evening was warm but with shock and distress and, desperately anxious as he was, he held her for a moment.

'Take heart, my love. You know Henry – his anger will pass and we will get to the bottom of this affair.'

'But why?' she said again. 'He was so merry with us that day in his own chamber, so happy for us, why should he turn against us now. Can it be that the money, the debts, weigh so heavy with him?'

Simon gave a little shrug but he said nothing for there seemed to be no explanation. The baby began to cry, instinctively unsettled by the disturbance about him, and his father gave him a swift glance between tenderness and anger that he should be 'We must find shelter for him and all our people.'

He led his little cavalcade to the first inn where the landlord, astonished by the unexpected arrival of such company, hastily ejected a merchant from the best bedchamber and found accommodation for the Countess's ladies, her son and his nurses. The rest of their knights and squires and servants found space where they could, but the smoky ill-lit tavern rooms and the plain boiled meats for supper were no exchange for the luxury of the Bishop's palace.

Finch stabled the horses and then entered the back part of the inn where he found the Countess's maids, his lord's barber, Peter, and other servants gathered. The landlord's wife was bustling about trying to find food for all these mouths and she had sent her son to rouse the pastry cook and demand more pies. 'Out of my way,' she demanded as Finch came in with two young squires. 'God's life, not more of you? Yes, there will be supper but not if you get under my feet.' She darted to the great hearth where there was a suspicious smell of burning and ordered one of the Countess's pages to turn the spit. Seeing the lad's indignation at being given a task he considered below him

Finch grinned. 'We'll all have cause to remember this night, I'm thinking, boy, 'he said but there was not much mirth in his voice.

Neither Simon or Eleanor felt able to eat and as soon as their retinue were settled, he said, 'I cannot seek our bed such as it is without some explanation. Rest you, Eleanor, while I return to Westminster. I will not be so dismissed. Some answers Henry must give me. King he may be but he is also your brother and he has no right to treat us in such a manner.'

'I cannot rest while you are gone.' Eleanor roused herself into fresh indignation. 'I will come with you, my lord, for we are together in this. And I too will have the truth from Harry.'

Somberly he looked down into her pale face. 'You are truly the wife I have always desired. I thought perhaps as you are so fond of him –'

'Fond!' she exclaimed. 'It is you who are my flesh and bone now.' Their embrace was swift and passionate and then she added, 'I know Harry so well. We must throw ourselves on his mercy, beg for forgiveness.'

'I do not find begging easy. And forgiveness for what? For owing money to Count Thomas? He can find little else I have done amiss. Nor did we do anything without his consent.'

'Nevertheless,' she said wretchedly, 'we must ask it. And then he will throw his arm about me and call me his little sister as he has done so often after a temper. You will be his brother again and all will come right.'

'I will not grovel for what I have not done.'

'I would not want you to, but we did bribe the papal court, I did break my vow, we did go against all the Archbishop's wishes. Perhaps I should have gone to a nunnery, perhaps this is a judgement on us.'

'For Christ's sake!' He felt his temper rising once more. 'Surely we need not go over all that again? Or do you no longer think I am worth the sacrifice of your conscience, God save the mark!'

'Simon!' A wave of fury shook her. 'You! To say such things to me. Have I not dared the anger of God and His Church for you?'

'And now must face it yet again.'

'So I will. How can you doubt me?'

He caught his breath and then took her by the shoulders. 'Forgive me, forgive me, my heart. I am distraught and Henry has triumphed indeed if he can set us against each other. I wish I had not brought all this trouble on you.'

She gave a little sob and sank against his chest. 'Simon, I love you. I cannot bear it if we quarrel.'

'It is only because we are distressed, dear one. We will go to Henry together and show him how united we are. I will even kneel with you and ask his mercy.'

'He changes his mind so quickly,' she said. 'By this this time tomorrow all may be forgotten.'

'Perhaps. Yet I think there is more to it than we yet know. Will you brave what is to come with me?'

There was a knock on the door and Walter came in with Doll, carrying bedclothes from one of the wagons to replace the fusty covers the inn provided, and Simon wrapped Eleanor in her cloak, leaving Walter to supervise the household's shelter. Then with only Sir John Penrose, two squires and Finch attending them they rode along the dark way back to Westminster.

Henry was in the hall, supper over and the trestles cleared, when they entered. He was talking to Humphrey de Bohun and stroking one of his falcons on its stand near his chair, but he paused, stiffening, as he saw them enter. It was clear in that first moment that they had not acted wisely in returning without his permission but Simon approached the dais and asked for a few words in private.

A hush had fallen on those who had eaten at the King's table for there was no one there who had not heard what had happened earlier, the tale embellished in the telling, and the ring of faces normally so eager to welcome the King's popular sister, even her Norman husband, were cautious, withdrawn.

Henry flung himself down in his chair and scowled at them. Trouble! Why must there always be trouble? He hated it and as always said the first thing that came into his head. 'In private? I have no secrets from my Council, nor my court either in matters that affect them all. If I have a grievance against a subject, however high-born, it shall be heard.'

Despite her further indignation at this public airing of a family matter, Eleanor knelt and Simon with her. 'Whatever we have done,' she said clearly, 'we ask you pardon, Harry.'

She tried to smile at him, relying on the old warmth between them, and Simon took her hand, holding it in his.

'I too,' he said.

The gesture and the words seemed to be fuel to a fire that had not even begun to die, sending sparks upwards with twice the fury.

'You? Ask my pardon? Never!' All restraint seemed to leave the King. 'I tell you again I will not have you here and if you value your necks you will not dare to attend the Queen's churching tomorrow. It would defile my abbey if such as you should enter it.' He ignored gasps from several of the ladies gathered about the Queen, and leaned forward, his hands tensed on the arms of his chair, his vivid blue eyes fixed on Simon. 'You – you seduced my sister, you forced me to give her to you. Why should I forgive that?'

Eleanor gave a sharp cry, her hand to her mouth, and Simon, dropping her other hand, sprang to his feet, his face dark with anger.

'God in heaven! Am I hearing aright? You cannot believe so vile a thing. Not of me and certainly not of your most virtuous sister. In Christ's name, sire, what makes you accuse me of –' He would not speak the word. 'You have never had cause to think we could so betray you.'

'Oh, but I know,' Henry shouted. 'I have heard tales.' He cast a quick glance at John Mansel, his closest and most secret clerk, for although Mansel had reported no more than seeing Sir Simon kissing the Lady Eleanor behind the buttery screen, Henry put the construction he chose upon that innocent encounter. 'Seducer! Liar! I had to give her to you to avoid a scandal. And I knew no good would come of it.'

'None indeed,' the Queen agreed. She laid her hand in a soothing gesture over her husband's. 'My dear, do not distress yourself so. Those who offend God He punishes himself.'

Furiously Eleanor turned to face her. 'Oh, I know you would like to think me unchaste, madame, but it is a lie – a lie!' She could no longer keep back the tears of rage and shame and she turned to her brother. 'Harry – think what you are saying. I can't deny I broke my vow, but it was only for love. Never – never till we were wed did Simon – ' she broke off, utterly crushed by the shame, the insult of such an accusation made before the whole court. She gazed towards Richard, seeing his figure blindly through her tears. 'Richard, tell him. Surely you cannot believe I would be so base?'

The Earl of Cornwall leaned forward and said something in a low tone to his brother, but the King was far too carried away by his own emotions to listen.

'It is all as I said. Why should I be burdened with such trouble, why should I pay the debts of a man who defiled my sister, used my name?' He had worked himself into such a pass now that all sense had left him. 'They should be clapped up, the pair of them. Guards! Escort the Earl and Countess to the Tower. Have them secured in separate quarters.'

Richard caught his brother's arm, his own voice stern. 'Harry, you cannot do this. Let them go while the matter is sifted, but don't imprison them, for the love of God. This is Eleanor, our own sister!'

The King snatched up a glass of wine and drank it hastily and in that moment Simon took the opportunity to help his shattered and weeping wife to her feet. He was ashen, a proud man humbled before all this assembly of people, aware of the smug looks, the sly faces of those who did not like him, the Queen sitting demurely with downcast eyes, but only too glad to see the fall of one who criticized her relatives. His friends were stunned but helpless and as Simon looked round the circle of faces, the Earls of Oxford and Norfolk, de Bohun of Hereford, young Richard de Clare of Gloucester, Earl Ferrars and the aged Earl of Lincoln, he saw doubt, incredulity, the expressions varying but none, in the King's present mood, daring to speak for him. Only Richard of Cornwall reiterated his request.

'With your grace's leave,' Simon said, 'we will go.' Without waiting to hear more he led Eleanor through the gaping crowd, for the unbridled language and wild accusations had been heard in every part of the hall.

Henry's voice followed them. 'Yes, go, go! I never want to see either of you again.'

They went, but Simon would not forget, nor would he ever forgive the man who had said such things to him, who had without cause sullied forever his wife's good name.

There was no rest for them that night. They had barely reached the inn when a breathless messenger arrived from Richard begging them to leave London at once, to go abroad at least for a while for the King was reconsidering the alternative of shutting them in the Tower. It was not in Richard's nature to send so urgent a message without cause and with this shadow hanging over them Simon roused the entire household, ordered some to return to Leicester or Kenilworth at first light, and packing the rest into several boats set off down river towards the sea and a ship for France.

'We will go to my brother,' he said to Eleanor as two days later they stood together on board, watching the dawn come up, the land slipping away from them. 'My poor love, you are so tired. Try to sleep now.'

'Yes, I will.' But for a moment she laid her head against him. 'My lord, I think I am pregnant again.'

'My dearest!' There was his old smile, his swift kiss to send life flooding back into her stiffened limbs, but his second reaction was another wave of indignation. 'That you should be put through such a scene at such a time. Great God, if your brother were not King he would not live after the insults he laid upon us! Sometimes I think he is not entirely sane.'

'He is unpredictable,' she admitted, 'but in the past he has always been more kind than not. I don't understand why he turned against us so long after our wedding.'

'Don't you?' he queried bitterly. 'I do, by heaven. I see it all now. It was the money. He never has any because it slips through his fingers into gold and jewels and fine stone for his abbey, and he thought I meant to force him to pay my debts. Jesu, we all have debts! But gold has always been his flea in the shirt. I should have known. I should have expected it. Why, he has never even given you a marriage portion!'

'When we were wed I cared only for you,' she said. 'No other thought but his consent was in my head. But Richard will talk to him, make him see reason. Oh, my lord,' she strained her eyes towards the diminishing coastline, the cliffs white in the brilliant light of the dawn. 'I don't want to stay away from England. I want to go back to Kenilworth where we were so happy.'

'So you shall, my heart. You are right, we can leave Richard to set matters right. In the meantime we will go to my brother and his wife at Montfort L'Amaury. They will make us welcome and you will like it there.'

Simon's brother received his unexpected guests warmly, a pleasant unpretentious man who was shocked at the story they told him. His wife fussed over Eleanor who was utterly worn out by all she had undergone. As summer passed into autumn the child in her womb quickened, her spirits revived and she and the lady of the house spent much of their time sewing small garments and talking of the rearing of children, but it was not like home. She longed for Kenilworth, for Odibam and Gloucester, Winchester and Westminster and all the familiar places. She longed to see her dear Harry smiling again, calling her his little sister as he had always done until this last dreadful August day. She was still bewildered, aghast at his extraordinary behaviour, unable to believe he could accuse Simon of seducing her, her of taking him for her lover before wedlock. It was as if Henry had been bewitched and she began seriously to consider the possibility, for the Provencals were a strangely volatile people, prone to much superstition and there were several people among the Queen's retinue who might dabble in such things.

Letters came from Richard, assuring them that Henry's anger was evaporating as quickly as it had arisen. Richard himself was preparing for the projected crusade and he suggested that Simon should return and raise what money he could for the expedition. He was sure Henry would receive them both favourably now, and Isabella wrote too, assuring Eleanor of her affection and her desire to see them both safe home again.

'You must go,' Eleanor said. 'Richard would not suggest it if it were not right. But I am too near my time to face the sea and that journey. Go, my love, and write to me soon. If Henry has truly forgotten the quarrel then we must try to forget it too, and then when our child is born I can go home again.'

Simon agreed to this, and leaving her in the capable care of his sister-in-law, returned to England. There Henry greeted him in a friendly manner as if nothing had happened. He gave Simon five hundred marks towards his debt and Simon raised the rest from his estates. If his manner was cool towards the King, withdrawn as it had not been before, Henry did not appear to notice, for he had a habit of not seeing what he did not want to see. To Simon's dismay the Earl of Cornwall was in deep mourning, for Isabella had died in childbed and her baby with her. She was buried in the Abbey of Beaulieu which Richard had founded and Simon stood beside his brother-in-law as the coffin was lowered, knowing how Eleanor would grieve for this, her closest of friends.

Richard did not turn back, however, from the expedition. He buried his grief in a flurry of preparations and Simon spent a good deal of time with him, able at last to thank him for his support.

'Harry lets his feelings run away with him,' Richard said calmly. 'It only needs time and a cooler atmosphere to bring him to a better frame of mind. You see how changed he is.'

Aye, Simon thought, like the weathercock on Paul's church, and God alone knew which way the wind would blow next. But the insult had been so great, the taking away of his wife's virtue so unforgiveable, that no amount of friendliness now could wash it away. 'I fear,' he said and his voice was harsh, 'that the King's change of heart, welcome as it is, will not erase suspicions roused in the minds of other men.'

'A storm in a wine cup,' Richard shrugged, 'and soon forgotten. There is always some fresh gossip to intrigue the foolish, and none of your friends believed it of you. I beg you to forget it, Simon.'

Simon said no more and they rode to the coast together as companionable brothers. He had barely set foot on shore at Calais when a messenger on the way to England came up with him to say that the Countess had been safely delivered of a son, baptized Simon after his father.

Richard shook his hand warmly and suggested that Eleanor should return to England as soon as she was fit to travel. Eleanor, however, had other ideas. The loss of Isabella grieved her deeply, reminding her of William's death, and she recalled all the pleasant hours she and his sister had spent together. She did not want now to go home without Simon and he was only too happy that she should come part at least of the way with him.

Taking their time they travelled south through Italy with their two sons, followed by half the English contingent, the other half marching through France under Richard's leadership, recruiting on the way.

At Brindisi Eleanor set up her household in a palace lent to her by her brother-in-law, the Emperor

Frederick and she was able to visit her pregnant sister. After a pleasant month Richard joined them and when Simon sailed with him to Cyprus,

Eleanor stood watching the flotilla make for the open sea.

Young Harry's hand was held tightly in his mother's. The boy was two and half years old now and advanced for his age. 'Where is father going?' he asked. Eleanor smiled down at him, despite the anxiety she could not entirely subdue.

'To fight wicked people,' she said and forgot for a moment she was speaking to a child. 'To do God's work, but oh Queen of Heaven, mother of God, bring him safely back to me.'

She watched until her eyes were aching from the glare. Nothing mattered but Simon. How long would it be before she would feel his arms about her again, his hands caressing her? How many lonely nights must pass before he would lie with her again, his body possessing hers, love a great fire between them? She thought of England, of Henry with his Queen who had borne him a second son, Edmund, surrounded by minstrels and craftsmen, by goldsmiths and weavers who filled his court. Yet King though he was, he was but half a man compared to Simon and if it ever came to another quarrel between them, she knew she would cleave even more closely to her husband. She saw all Henry's weaknesses now, his instability, his ineptness when it came to government. Though affection remained it was now of a different nature.

And when she went home, nothing could be the same, nothing after what he had said of her. Richard had made her believe that he did not mean it, that he regretted it, but nothing could alter the fact that he had said it and all England knew he had. There were tears on her cheeks now, both for that past insult, for the injustice and degradation of it, and for the parting with Simon. He was far away now, the white sails no more than specks on the horizon. Her thoughts turned to memories of the Maid of Brittany who had died this last year. At least she, Eleanor, had lived, had been loved, borne children.

She turned away from the empty sea, blue and sparkling. Harry's nurse was hovering by the open door and Eleanor straightened her back, her head high. She took his small hand in hers. 'Come,' she said, 'I see it is your dinner time. I wonder how big you will have grown by the time your father comes back to us?'

PART TWO

SIMON'S WIFE

1258-1265

CHAPTER SEVEN

'My dear aunt, your hospitality is delightful, as always.' The Lord Edward, heir to the throne, was now in his twentieth year and so tall that folk were calling him Longshanks. He leaned against the stone window of the Countess of Leicester's bower and looked out across the mere where he could see a cockleboat and a man with a rod.

'Is your lake full of fish? I thought it was more a pleasure place for sailing. It is a formidable defence and I should not care to assault this place.'

Eleanor laughed. 'I can't conceive that you should ever have to besiege me.' But the moment she had spoken the words she wished them unsaid for she felt a curious chill as if they were prophetic.

Edward clearly had no such intuition for he was smiling amiably, still watching the fisherman. 'Nor I. I do believe that is Simon swimming. God defend us, what an occupation!'

She roused herself at once. What nonsense put such a thought into her head? 'Yes, he is a strong swimmer, though I cannot imagine anything pleasurable about it. Edward, will you not sit for a while? I cannot converse happily with a poplar tree.'

He laughed and sprawled his long limbs on a stool, his eyes wandering at the same time to the girl sitting beside his aunt Eleanor. She was young and extremely pretty and when she raised her head just enough from her embroidery to return his gaze there was a coquettish expression on her face.

'I wish I had not to leave you so soon,' he said. 'The company is so pleasant here.'

Eleanor gave him a sharp look, intercepting that exchange of glances. 'I know you find it so. Sadly I shall also lose Alice's company when her husband comes to fetch her at the end of the week.'

He yawned. 'I had forgotten. Gilbert has a bad habit of turning up too soon. I hope you are happy with him, cousin Alice.'

'You should not ask such questions,' Eleanor interposed before her niece could answer. Eleanor had a shrewd suspicion that her nephew, married for some years to another Eleanor, the King of Castile's daughter, was only too happy to flirt with Alice. His bride was too young to be bedded yet and was still under the care of the Queen Regent of France. It was only natural, Eleanor supposed, that Edward should amuse himself for a while. She hoped, however, he did not intend to carry matters too far.

'Alice, my dear,' she said, 'pray go and find your cousin. The Demoiselle would no doubt be glad of your company since we are to lose you so soon.'

'Very well, madame.' Alice laid down her sewing, curtseyed, smiled provocatively at Edward and withdrew.

'If you must seek your pleasure,' Eleanor remarked amusedly when the door closed, 'pray, Edward, seek it elsewhere than with Alice. She could be a dangerous conquest.'

'Do you think I am afraid of Gilbert the Red – or old Gloucester?'

'Gloucester is younger than I am,' she retorted, 'and no mean adversary if you annoy him. You would do well to respect him, though I'm sure you are more than a match for his son. I hear you unseated Gilbert at the Nottingham tourney.'

Edward grinned like the boy he still was. 'Yes, and very satisfying that was. But I promise you, aunt, I would not behave myself so badly under your roof. I've too much care for you and my uncle for that.'

'I'm glad to hear it. Sometimes I wonder why you go about with such a rapscallion crew. That knight of yours, Roger Leyburn, is unprincipled and a lecher. If there is mischief afoot he is bound to have started it, and Roger Mortimer, for all he is my sister-in-law's grandson, is no better than a brigand. It is a blessing Eva did not live to see her daughter bring up such a boy.'

'My Rogers are not all bad,' he said. 'Mortimer is sowing wild oats – we all are – but I suppose we'll come to more serious matters soon. Something will make us, no doubt. In the meantime they are good company and I'd trust Leyburn with my life. We are off to France tomorrow to some jousting and to pay our respects to my aunt Marguerite. My mother wishes her sister to be reassured of our friendship.'

'Then pray don't cause a scandal in Paris,' Eleanor said smiling. 'You don't wish to grieve your father.'

'Never,' Edward said firmly. 'He may be in trouble with his barons and sometimes I think he does not understand what kingship is, but he's the best father in the world.'

There was, Eleanor thought, even more truth in what Edward said than he, at his age, could realize. But it seemed that with the years Henry had not only not learned wiser ways but was even more inclined to say and do rash things.

When he welcomed their mother's second family, the Lusignans, to England, it had proved a most unwise move. The eldest, William de Valence, had married Joan, the daughter of another of Eleanor's sisters-in-law, Joanna Marshal, and now called himself Earl of Pembroke. Eleanor thought his long features effeminate yet with a hint of viciousness in the thin mouth, and she hated his undoubted influence over Henry. He was milking the Marshal inheritance while she was still owed money from her dower and Henry would do nothing about it. Aymer de Valence became Bishop of Winchester and Guy and Geoffrey were loaded with gifts of land and gold and jewels. They were as disliked as the Queen's uncles had been in the early days and Simon had no time for them.

Simon's position was vastly changed. He was greatly respected, and it seemed that Englishmen looked to him as a natural leader. Even this boy idolized his godfather.

He said now, 'Madame, when do you expect my uncle home? I would like to see him.'

'In a few days, I hope. Why do you not wait until then, Edward?'

'I wish I could,' he answered restlessly and got to his feet, 'but I am promised with my knights to the tourney at Evreux and I would not have the French think we dare not face them. They say they have a new champion even greater than Renault de Nevers. But tell my uncle – I don't know – tell him I would talk with him soon. I shall be King one day and he has ideas that would turn England into a kingdom fit for all states of men.'

Eleanor rose and reached up to kiss him. The lad had grown so tall and handsome with his ash-blond hair and blue eyes, and she really was so fond of him, and to find him so in sympathy with his godfather warmed her doubly to him. 'I wish your father could see it.'

'He is set in his ways,' Edward said smiling, with the confidence of youth to improve on what the previous generation had done. He put her hand to his lips, bowing. 'But time is running away. Have I your leave to go and find my cousins? Harry promised to show me his new destrier and then we are all to go to the butts for an hour before supper.'

'Of course,' she said. 'Come again soon, Edward.'

'How could I not? My dear aunt, you are as charming and as lovely as ever and if you were not my aunt I would flirt with you instead of Alice.'

He went out, leaving her laughing. A trifle wild he might be but he had more than his share of the family charm with which he credited her without the temper and instability that so often destroyed the good qualities of the Plantagenets. When as he said, 'something would make him' mature out of his youthful high spirits, she thought he would sit well in his father's place.

 The years had brought much of joy and some sorrow. After the crusade, which achieved nothing but to establish Simon with the reputation of a fine soldier, they came home to a genuine welcome from Henry. For a while there was peace. Henry seemed only too willing to forget the past, though neither Simon nor she could ever entirely banish that spiteful and unjust slur on her virtue; in a burst of generosity he gave them Kenilworth Castle as an outright gift and showered them with lesser presents, rich materials for clothes, silver and gold for their table, casks of wine and tubs of dates and almonds and figs which reminded Eleanor of her visit to Bristol so long ago.

She was proud of her sons, Harry, Simon, Guy and Amaury now growing into tall lads. Six years ago she had given birth to a second daughter after losing the first in childbed, and the girl was baptized Eleanor. But the boys nicknamed their sister the Demoiselle and the name stuck so that she was never called anything else. She was a happy child with the promise of her mother's beauty, that beauty which, in her forties, Eleanor still possessed with the added poise of maturity.

For a long time after Simon's return all had gone well. Then Henry sent Simon to Gascony as seneschal, for the Gascon nobles had got out of hand and become, as Simon said, mere bands of robbers, pillaging and slaying and not behaving as responsible Christian men should. His hand was heavy on them. The worst offenders he shut in prison and when one elderly knight died in his cell a screech of protest went up. Wild accusations were flung at the new seneschal and a deputation sent to London. As usual Henry listened too easily and was too easily persuaded. He was already annoyed by Simon's pressing demands for money to carry out his commission and ordered him home to answer a list of charges.

Eleanor's face burned at the memory of that trial in St Stephen's Hall. That Simon should be put to such indignity had infuriated her, but he came out of it well. He proved himself to have done no more than keep order in a country not given to obedience, and showed that he had emptied his own pockets to pay the King's soldiers. The lords sitting in judgement cleared Simon of all guilt and a furious Henry had gone off to Gascony himself, certain that his presence would settle the quarrels there for good. He found he was sadly mistaken. Inept as always where military skill was concerned, and lacking all judgement, he gave up and sent for his seneschal, told him to complete his seven-year term of office, and returned home.

Eleanor could never resist recalling that return with a touch of the old malicious resentment of her namesake, the Queen. Eleanora of Provence had taken it into her head, during her husband's absence, to revive the old law of Queen-geld. She had demanded payment of this money from the citizens of London, imprisoned those who refused and made herself hated in that most independent city. When Eleanor had tried to warn her that she was going too far, the Queen looked down her elegant nose and said, 'The impertinent fellows need a lesson. Who are they to defy their King?'

Eleanor felt like saying that it was not their King they were defying but his Queen who was exceeding her rights, but she said no more. Henry came back and pacified the protesting Mayor and aldermen, but if there was one thing he understood it was the need of money and he was far too devoted to his Queen to blame her.

Eleanor understood it equally well for she maintained almost royal estate at Kenilworth, entertained lavishly, and it was seldom that there were not important guests at Kenilworth or Odiham or Leicester.

The years had robbed her of a number of friends. Archbishop Edmund had died and been succeeded at the King's insistence by Bishop Boniface, a choice approved by no one. Bishop Grosseteste too, Simon's great friend, had also died and was sadly missed for he had educated their boys and had always been a voice of wisdom at court. A little smile flickered across Eleanor's face as she recalled how he had once asked if he might borrow her excellent head cook, John, for a particular function and had kept him for six years. But there was sadness in her face too, for the Bishop had been spiritual adviser to her and to Simon for so long and not even his friend, the friar Adam Marsh, was a real substitute for him.

Other faces were gone too. Gilbert Marshal had died in a jousting accident and two years later both Waiter and Anselm, his brothers, were dead too. Strangely none of them had an heir and the office of Marshal went to Roger Bigod, Matilda Marshal's son. Amaury de Montfort had succumbed to a fever, his son ruling Montfort L'Amaury in his place. Eleanor remembered him with affection for his kindness to her and to Simon when they were in need. And not only death had robbed her, for Richard of Cornwall had accepted a crown as King of the Romans and had been absent from England for some time. But their great affection for each other remained, and Eleanor was fond of Richard's second wife Sanchia.

In her own household Doll had married and brought up two children and when she died last year Eleanor took her daughter Mary as a waiting woman and her son Philip as a page. Megonwy was elderly now and ruled the sewing women, a girl named Dionysia having taken her place. Finch, rather grizzled but as tough and sturdy as ever, remained as her chief groom with his son serving under him. She and Simon had been fortunate in their servants; the marshal of their household and their steward, both trustworthy men, kept their establishment, under Eleanor's own keen eye, running smoothly.

She rose now and glanced out of the window. The young men were coming back from the butts and she could see Edward and Harry walking together arm-in-arm. Harry was nearly as tall as Edward, smiling as always, a cheerful friendly lad. Simon, walking alongside, his bow in his hand, was shorter and darker than his brother, less handsome, less talkative, but she sometimes thought he was the most reliable, his mood seldom varying. Guy had more of the true Plantagenet colouring, with hair the colour, so old John of Lincoln told her, of her long dead uncle, Richard called the Lionheart. Guy also had the Plantagenet temper. He would flare up into a rage over nothing and though it would die as quickly, nevertheless she foresaw that he would always be in the thick of some trouble or another. Amaury at fourteen was the quietest member of the family, his head always in a book or scribbling poems which he refused to show to anyone, but when it was suggested he should enter the Church he refused with surprising vehemence. He wanted, he said, to remain with his father and brothers and become a knight in due course, but Eleanor guessed that even more he did not want to leave her. They spent a great deal of time together; he was a master of the lute and often sang to her the lovely Provencal songs which Simon had once drily remarked were the only good thing to come out of that country.

She gave a little sigh. She wished life was easier for Simon but he had a new cause, one that he would not forsake as long as he lived and which, she thought, might indeed drain the lifeblood from him. Yet she admired that very tenacity so much. She wished he would come home, then perhaps she could make him rest a little.

Edward departed in the morning after an evening spent enjoying Eleanor's rich supper at which the cook excelled himself, serving cranes in a spicy sauce, salmon pasties made with mouth-watering pastry, almond tarts and sweet coloured jellies. Gallons of beer were provided and both red and white Gascon wines and Edward drank a great deal. Afterwards he led his cousins into hilarious games, dancing and flirting again with Alice. Eleanor watched him go in the morning, amused by the obvious regret on Alice's face and the resignation with which she accompanied her husband Gilbert when he strode into the hall a few days later to claim her. Eleanor liked neither Gloucester nor his impetuous son, but as both supported Simon's ideas she tried not to show her mistrust of them.

The day after Alice's departure the Earl of Leicester came home. After the first greeting in the hall with his large following of knights and squires, some hundred and fifty of them, filling the place, be followed his wife upstairs to their bedchamber. There he embraced her and enquired for her health.

'I am well,' she said, 'but you – my lord, you look so tired.'

She gazed up at the hollows beneath the dark eyes, the gauntness of his face. He was so thin these days, carrying too heavy a burden of responsibility, but this time, with her perception sharpened where he was concerned, she saw that he was greatly disturbed. She drew him to their bed and sat down, her hand in his. 'My dearest, I can see that something is wrong. What is it?'

But he would not sit still and loosing her hand began to pace, his long mantle brushing the floor, slapping his gloves from one hand to the other. 'Sometimes I think Henry should be locked up, like Charles the Simple. Jesu, there are iron bound doors at Windsor that could hold him!'

Something contracted within her. 'What has he done now?'

Simon's mouth was a thin hard line. 'He heaps folly on folly. He will do nothing to curb his spending, and as for this new Chapter House he has added to the Abbey at Westminster, it is wild, wanton extravagance with money he does not have. His tomb for the Confessor's bones would make that saint shudder, and he demands and demands more and more money. He twists everything to suit himself and one would think the Great Charter had never been written for he tramples on each sentence one by one. I tell you, Eleanor, it is past bearing!'

'I think he should not have been a King,' she said slowly and thought of Edward's words of a few days ago. 'Richard would not have been so foolish.'

'Richard has sense, nothing shows it more clearly than his handling of his own kingdom in Germany. As for Henry's last piece of nonsense, it has tried us all to the limit. Why he thought it would benefit his younger son to be King of Sicily I can't imagine. Now the whole affair has become ridiculous with Henry in debt to the Pope for God knows how much money for an enterprise that has failed lamentably. All we of his council can do is to try and extricate England somehow from what he has done. Dear God!' His exasperation seemed to shake his thin frame. 'How is it that a man can be so stable and loving a husband and father and so insane outside in the world. Sometimes I think he is insane.'

Eleanor listened to this outburst in silence. She felt no great partisanship for Henry, her thoughts were all for Simon. 'Is this all, my lord? It is not new and I think my nephew Edmund well out of that Sicilian business. I feel something further has happened to distress you.'

He paused to look down at her. 'You are the heart of my heart. You know what I care for most. No, it is not all. William de Valence has been causing trouble again. I'll not call him Pembroke for he has no right to the title. I'm sorry, for I know he is your half-brother, but I loathe the man and I'd like to see him shackled in the Tower.'

'I don't care a snap of my fingers for him,' she retorted.

'What has he done now?'

'He and his hunting party chanced to ride across the Bishop of Ely's land two weeks ago and bethought themselves that they were thirsty. The Bishop was away but they entered his palace and when the servants brought beer, as any honest Englishman would find satisfying, they demanded wine. William let his fellows smash open the casks and get drunk on the best wine. They broke off the bungs and the wine was still running when they rode off, hardly able to sit in their saddles. By the arm of St James, I'd have the lot flogged.'

'And then the Bishop found out?'

'Good man that he is, he said they might have had the wine for the asking without damaging the casks and wasting it all. And that's not the end of it. One of de Valence's brigands got into a fight with a miller of ours and beat the fellow up and set the place on fire. Wicked, vicious behaviour and needing sharp punishment – and so I told de Valence at the council meeting.'

'What did he say?'

'Say?' Simon's eyes blazed. 'Christ, I'll not repeat it! But he dared to take me to task, to call me a traitor and rake up old sores, saying I had no right to what I had won by –' he broke off abruptly.

Eleanor felt her stomach turn. 'Oh, my dear, will men never forget? Surely Henry did not stand by and allow this?'

Simon gave a harsh laugh. 'He would have done, but by then both de Valence and I had our swords out. I'd have killed him if I could, but Henry came between us.'

'Thank God, he did,' she cried out. 'Simon, if you had been slain –'

'Slain?' he echoed. 'I could have dealt with that young fool with one hand.' He paused by the window, his eyes on the sunset sky, the sun well down now, vivid gold and pink reflected in the still water of the mere. 'I tell you, wife, we have had enough.'

'We?'

'Gloucester, Norfolk, de Bohun, Oxford, some others. We will not stand by any longer and watch the Lusignans ruin this country, for that is what their greed and rapaciousness will do combined with their evil influence over the King. I tell you' – his dark face was alive with a burning passion now – 'I will not keep silence when I see good laws trampled on by such men. What had our miller done that he should be so ill treated? And in any case on my land it is I who administer justice. But Henry will not listen, he gives them everything they want and pardons all their excesses. I don't suppose you have heard the latest of these. It seems that Geoffrey was so annoyed with one of Henry's cooks who spoiled a sauce that he liked, that he carried the fellow off, hung him up naked and upside down, pulling out his hair until he died. Holy Cross, hell must have been made for men like that!'

She gave a little shudder. 'There was always bad blood in the Lusignans. I wish my mother had never married Hugh. But surely Henry punished Geoffrey for this?'

'The master of the cooks complained to him and do you know what Henry did? He pulled a face, sent the man back to the kitchen and went on with his supper. I saw it! He would not even reprimand Geoffrey, yet it was murder, plain murder.' She was silent, horrified that Henry should be so weak, Geoffrey so cruel, and she watched Simon pacing again, restless, possessed by one idea.

'I will never rest,' he went on, 'never until the rights of humble men are protected. That is what we have pledged ourselves to, to care for the people, to have the country governed not at the whim of one man but by a well chosen council, and perhaps even a gathering of the people, men from all over the land to represent their own needs. It is the only way.'

Bewildered she said, 'But the King is the King, anointed, the highest authority, consecrated by God.'

'But he is not above the law, certainly not above God's law. For all Henry's pious ways sometimes I think he does not know what Christian principles are. I wonder what he admits to his confessor, if he knows what wild folly he indulges in? The higher the office, the greater the responsibility and he does not seem to understand that.'

'What are you going to do?' she asked uneasily.

'I am going soon to Oxford, and you with me if you will. The hoketide parleying meets there and we mean to confront Henry, to force him to swear again to the Charter. We will have reforms so that he can't put underlings of his own choosing into high places. That fellow Mansel, a nobody, has the King's ear more than Gloucester or myself, but we mean to make an end to that situation, to have a great meeting where all men can be heard.'

'You care for them, don't you?' she said. 'I don't mean just those of our own rank, but people like that wretched cook and our poor miller.'

'Yes.' he said. He came back and sat down beside her. 'I think it was living here at Kenilworth that made me care. We know all our own people, down to the woman who brews the beer, and Dobbe looking after our sheep. I rule them, but they trust me. Who can trust the King, let alone his foreign favourites who care nothing for England but what they can steal from her?'

She remembered how, so long ago, he had been looked on as a Norman adventurer himself. Now no one thought of him except as a true peer of the realm and he was fast becoming a champion of ordinary folk, so that men came from all walks of life to ask him to redress their grievances. The hypocrite and whiner got short shrift from him, but a man with a genuine grievance never failed to get a hearing.

'Yes,' he said again, as if proving his own mind out loud, as he so often did with her, 'I think that business of the cook, minor as it was, finally fixed my intention. There will always be cruelty and injustice, but by the living God we should punish it, not go on eating our supper!'

That night he lay in her arms, too tired for sleep, his head against her shoulder, talking of his plans, his hopes for a better order, the things that must be done to achieve his vision. He was over fifty now and saw the time growing shorter, and there was an urgency in his voice that betrayed nervous exhaustion.

'You must sleep,' she said at last. 'My love, you can do nothing if you do not rest.'

'I find it hard to rest when there is so much to be done.' She tried to soothe him, passing her hands over his shoulders and back, pushing her fingers through his hair, but he was in such a state of tension that there seemed to be only one way to release it. She set her mouth to his, knowing the old magic would work, but she was hardly prepared for the intensity, the sudden flaring of wild passion, exhausted though he was. He took her as if it was that dark wedding morning once again, his body thin and hard, hers a little plumper and softer, and after a while she gasped out thinking his possessing of her would never cease, as if he must pour all his frustration and anger, his love and hate into one outflowing of physical need. And then as suddenly he relaxed and lay sprawled across her, asleep almost at once.

She did not move, uncomfortable though she was, for not for anything in the world would she rouse him from that blessed sleep. She set her lips against his hair, more deeply in love than ever she had been at the beginning, great though their passion had been then. Let Henry do what he will, this man lying here was more to her than anyone in the world. Whatever he chose to do she would be with him to whatever end God chose for them.

In Oxford they lodged at Beaumont House and the first meeting of the barons took place at the castle at the beginning of April. The banks were bright with spring flowers, blossom was breaking out on the trees and the sky was a soft blue full of the promise of spring.

Roger Bigod, Earl of Norfolk and Marshal of England, spoke for the barons, setting before the

King the list of demands, those demands so close to Simon's heart, that he had enumerated to Eleanor.

Henry listened in irritable silence. He was hard pushed for money, especially since the Sicilian disaster. He wondered now why he had ever thought of it for young Edmund, his especial darling, that bright-haired boy with his winning smile and slightly hunched shoulder. He wanted something for Edmund as a second son, but he had been trapped into reaching out for what had proved to be a nettle in his hand, a hollow crown that had embroiled him in debt and had now been seized successfully by another claimant. So much trouble! And now these stiff-necked barons led by Gloucester and his own brother-in-law Simon were demanding, not asking, things of him such as the barons at Running Meade had demanded of his father on a June day more than forty years ago.

John Mansel urged him to play a waiting game, to seem to yield, to hold off for better times, but looking at these stern faces he wondered if he could do it. Why could they not leave him alone to enjoy his family, his love of art, his joy in building? He could be so magnificent a King if only they would give him the means to do it.

April was almost out and they were still talking when he came one day into the great hall to take his seat on the throne. The doors opened and the leading barons came in, dressed in full armour.

He felt the colour leave his face, a sickness in his stomach.

'What – what are you at, my lords 'Why do you confront your King in battle harness? Am I your captive?'

'No, sire,' Roger Bigod said in his clear resounding voice. He was an open-faced man in his thirties, popular, an accomplished knight, and he believed in his cause. 'No harm is intended, but we want you to see we mean what we say. We will have the reforms laid out. We will have each office of the crown filled by men of worth; we will have a Parliament and a Council to discuss the affairs of the realm, and we will have no more ventures abroad that end to the detriment of this country. Nor will we have foreigners ordering affairs within our borders.'

'Aye.' Simon stepped forward. 'We have had enough of such interference. We have decided that no men of foreign birth should hold castles in their own right. I, as one born abroad, willingly place Kenilworth and Leicester at the disposal of the Council.'

'Agreed, agreed,' the other barons broke in loudly but William de Valence, standing beside the King, shouted out that he would never yield Pembroke to men who betrayed their King.

Simon faced his enemy yet again. 'Understand this, de Valence. Either you yield your castle, or – it will be your head that you lose.'

There was immediate uproar, the Lusignans and others of the Queen's men adding to William's defiance. Henry for once acted wisely. He seized his half-brother's arm and held him in check. 'Be silent,' he hissed. 'Would you undo me altogether?'

De Valence subsided, glaring at the Earl of Lincoln. Henry looked helplessly from one to the other of his determined barons. He saw the Marshal's eager, earnest face, too honest to compromise; the Earl of Lincoln, wrinkled and grey, his mouth set grimly; the Earl of Oxford with the usual cynical expression in his eyes as if the whole business, so humiliating to his King, was a mere amusement. Gilbert the Red sat beside his father, his freckled face set in harsh lines while Gloucester's uneven features were cold and relentless. The Earl had broken a nose during a tourney: he loved jousting but seldom did well and now, not yet forty, he had lost what looks he once had. If his enormous wealth and influence were on the enemy's side, Henry thought, it was the greatest blow against him. As for his brother-in-law, he saw nothing in that stern dark countenance to give him any cause for hope.

At last he said, 'I cannot fight you all. So be it. Have your way – and may God reward you all!'

That night Simon told Eleanor it had been a momentous day for England, and in the weeks that followed he and a number of others including Gloucester, Roger Bigod and the Bishop of Worcester sat down as a committee to work out the necessary Reforms. These 'Provisions' the King reluctantly signed. A few weeks later, beaten down by public opinion and their own inflammatory behaviour, the Lusignan brothers left England.

'You think you have won,' Henry cried out to Simon. 'You take away my brothers; my dearest friends, you undermine my rights as King – do you expect me to love you for it?'

'No, sire,' Simon said grimly, 'but I expect you to abide by your promises.'

The court returned to London and the Earl and Countess of Leicester lodged at Durham House. Simon was constantly at work with the Council, implementing the reforms, and Eleanor had to endure harsh words from the Queen who roundly called them both traitors. 'In that case, madame,' she retorted, 'half my brother's kingdom might be called the same. My lord is not alone in this.'

'I am surprised at you,' the Queen snapped. 'You cannot remember, of course, but someone must have told you what your father suffered at the hands of unruly barons. A few heads would fall if I had my way.'

'Thank God you have not,' Eleanor said sharply. 'Henry is unwise enough as it is. At least he has seen that he must now defer in some measure to his council.'

'Ruled by your husband.'

'Better than by your uncles – or my half-brothers.'

It was the end of any pretence of friendship between them.

'You are no sister to Henry, nor to me,' was the Queen's parting shot as she swept out of the room and Eleanor was glad enough to see her go. After that they met only at court functions when Simon chose to attend, though on one occasion Henry wept openly to see his wife and his sister on such frigid terms.

On a warm afternoon in May when Simon had come early from Westminster and his deliberations, a sudden thunderstorm broke over their heads, to be followed by torrential rain. A fire burned in the centre of the hall and they went to sit by it, Eleanor and the Demoiselle busy on a piece of embroidery while Simon dozed in his chair. He looked very worn still and Eleanor was glad to see him resting. Harry and young Simon had gone to visit Gilbert the Red, but Guy and Amaury were playing a game of chess, Guy intently absorbed, Amaury listening dreamily to the sound of the storm.

'Wake up, brother,' Guy said. 'If we are going to play, for God's sake, play.'

'Very well,' his brother answered amusedly. 'I am not so lost as you imagine. There, you are in check.'

'But not beaten.' Guy moved a piece. 'You did not see that, did you?'

'Oh no. But I'll have you yet. What was that?' as there was a sudden thumping sound.

'Only thunder,' Guy said, but his mother raised her head from her sewing.

'I think someone is knocking,' she said and nodded to an usher to open the door.

Outside the rain was still streaming down and on the steps that led up from the river stood half a dozen men. They were all soaking wet, water dripping from their hats and among them was the King himself.

He stood in a puddle and said, 'I was on my way to the Tower when the storm came up. I must ask shelter, though I'd rather it was in any house but this.'

Eleanor sprang up, ignoring the last remark. Simon woke from his doze, startled, and seeing the party huddled by the door, rose and came forward:

'So you are come to us for shelter, sire?' he queried in an edged voice. 'You are welcome. You will find only hospitality in this house.'

For a moment they confronted each other, the sodden King, rain dripping off his mantle on to the floor, and the tall gaunt man whom he now saw as the enemy of all he held most dear.

Reluctantly he came into the hall and Simon called to his sons to attend the King. They sprang forward to take his hat, his cloak, and he gave them an odd glance, as if his distrust extended to them, young as they were.

'Do you assure me so, Sir Simon? I am glad to hear it, for I think I fear you more than the storm.'

He came forward to the fire, warming his cold hands at the blaze, while his sister and her husband stood silently watching him.

CHAPTER EIGHT

The Lord Edward had come home from France and was riding into London followed by a stream of young knights and squires. On London Bridge he was cheered and a girl ran forward with a nosegay for him, a delicate blending of flowers and herbs to keep away the oppressive smells of the city. He leaned down to kiss her soundly on the mouth before tucking the flowers into his tabard and the cheers redoubled, but his face wore a graver expression than it would once have done. He had enjoyed himself abroad but Roger Leyburn, who had been to England on business for him, had returned with such an account of the doings there that Edward felt obliged to return. It ceased to be amusing to wander through France and Flanders and Germany jousting and drinking and wenching when grave matters affecting his own future were taking place at home. He rode to the Tower and dined there with the two Rogers and a number of his knights and then took a boat up the river to the steps of Durham House where, he was told, he would find his aunt and uncle.

The river as always was busy with shipping of all sorts, merchantmen bringing wine from Gascony, spices and dried fruit from the east, and loading in return with bales of wool. All the wharves were bustling with trade. Barges and smaller craft ferried all manner of folk up and down river and across from one bank to the other, and to Edward on this hot August afternoon London was the greatest city in the world.

The boat drew up at the steps of Durham House and he sprang out lightly where the water lapped the stone. He was wearing a blue gown and over it a magnificent tabard with the leopards of his house embroidered upon it, a black velvet cap on his fair head, and as he glanced up at the walls he saw another figure as tall and as richly dressed as himself. His uncle was standing on one of the turrets, looking out at the river, lost in thought until he seemed to become aware of the boat below and the arrival of his nephew. He turned and disappeared down the steps.

Eleanor welcomed their unexpected visitor warmly.

'I swear you are taller every time I see you,' she said as he bent to kiss her. 'You must be above your uncle now. Ah, here he is. Simon, Edward is come to visit us.'

'So I see. Welcome, nephew. We did not know you were in London.'

'I only rode in this morning.' Edward accepted wine and for a while the talk was desultory. They listened to his account of his travels but it was clear that that particular light-hearted sojourn was something he was prepared to consign to a youthful past. Graver matters were on his mind.

Eleanor sensed that he wanted to talk to Simon and left them to speak to her steward about supper for her guest, while Simon took Edward to the private chamber where he conducted his business. There he sent his clerk away and offered the Prince the only chair, but Edward with a pleasant gesture indicated that his godfather should take it and sat himself down on a stool.

'Well,' Simon said, 'what has brought you home? Your father is in Paris.'

'I know. But I have heard that my uncle Richard intends to come home to swear to the Provisions you set out at Oxford and I would see him. He knows that I have sworn.'

Simon regarded him gravely for a moment. 'Reluctantly I think. Do you mean to adhere to them? Do you understand our aims? I thought you too frivolous to care.'

The words were hard but the tone not unpleasant, and Edward leaned forward eagerly. 'Perhaps I was, but I have had time to think. My lord, I do believe in your plans for the better governing of this country. England is the best place in the world, that much I have learned on my travels, and I mean to be the kind of king such a country needs. When my time comes, which, God being merciful to my father, will not be for many years yet, I mean to rule rightly, to have a council about me of the best men in the kingdom.'

'And the lesser men? Will you see justice done to them too? Will you care for your merchants and yeomen, your knights of little substance?' Before Edward could answer Simon asked a different question. 'Did you know I had quarrelled with Gloucester?'

'Aye, he came running to my father and a sorry mess he looked. He has lost his teeth and his skin is horrid to behold. Nothing King Louis's most skilled physicians could do was able to cure him. I thought at first he had had some strange fever, but he told us he had been poisoned.'

'So we all heard. I would not have put it past him to accuse me of it, only it seems suspicion fell in another direction for his steward was in receipt of a large and un-explained sum from Sir William de Valence.'

'That man!' Edward exclaimed. 'I don't like him but he stays loyal to my father whereas Gloucester blows hot and cold. Do you trust him?'

'Not I, but for good or ill at the moment we are reconciled.' Simon gave his nephew a faint smile; the new earnestness of Edward's conversation appealed to him. 'Well, the Earl hanged his steward for the poisoning, so I suppose he feels justice has been done.'

'Why did you quarrel?'

Simon flung out his hands in a gesture that betrayed his deeply felt resentment. 'Because he did not seem to understand what our reforms meant. He insisted that the King must deal justly and according to the law with us, his lords, but he sees no necessity to show the same consideration to those below him. He would brook no interference in his dealings with those he rules and he rules more than most of us. God in heaven!' Simon's voice rose. 'What are we fighting for, if not for those very reforms we set out at Oxford?' His eyes grew sombre. It seemed to him that the Earl had gone back on the very heart of their cause, the cause that had become the whole of life to him, and which Gloucester was trying to manipulate so that he lost none of his own autocratic power. His mind went back to that ugly scene. The barons, pledged to him, resented Gloucester's rudeness, his speaking as if to an underling, but they were also in some awe of the senior peer of the realm and were slow to take sides.

Simon himself was in no doubt as to Richard de Clare's untrustworthiness, however, and he had cried out that he would be a traitor to all he held dear if he was to work with one so fickle. If Gloucester would not hold by the Provisions he was the traitor! He had hurled the words at his one-time comrade and storming out had gone to France, immersing himself for some months in family affairs. But his Oxford party wanted him back, begged him to return. Gloucester was with the King apparently on friendly terms, and Simon came home.

'We are well rid of him,' he said now. 'Let us hope he finds Paris too attractive to come back to England at least until matters are quieter.'

'I never cared for him,' Edward said, 'but Gilbert is not such a bad fellow.'

'One of your young bloods,' Simon agreed, 'but not yet proved. Edward, you have not really told me why you have come. You know that your father is against all that I am doing, that he is in France to win the French King to his side, signing away

Normandy and Angouleme into the bargain, I've no doubt. Only Gascony and Poitou will be left to England and your aunt's rights are being ignored.'

Edward shrugged. 'It is a move in the game, I suppose.'

'It is no game.'

The Prince looked up and saw the stern expression on his godfather's face. 'I did not mean that I look on it lightly, only that what is lost by one move may be won by another.'

'I've no doubt the King's closest advisers think so. I hear John Mansel has gone to Rome.'

'Tiresome fellow. He creeps about like a weasel. Uncle, I love my father dearly and I know you mean him no harm, at least – you do not, do you?'

'None,' Simon said at once.' He is the King and I will adhere to him in that office until I die. But he must be brought to see that he has done things even a King should not do.'

'I have often wondered –' Edward paused. 'You could have been his right hand, you could have ousted all the Savoyards and Provencals, made yourself the second man in the kingdom. Why did you not do it?' '

Simon leaned back in his chair, the hollow eyes thoughtful.

'Perhaps because I would have had to cheat my conscience. Yes, I could have done it, but my desire lay not that way.' His eyes seemed to his nephew to burn with a fervour that grew each time he saw him. 'Please God, I'll not die until I see at least part of that desire put into practice.'

Edward got up. 'Please God you've years to give us all,' he echoed, with the ability of youth to see only what he wanted to see. It did not seem to him that a man could burn himself out for a cause without the triumph restoring him. 'Will you and my aunt dine with me tomorrow?'

When he had gone Simon returned to the turret. He stood there often these days, a prey to depression such as he had never known in his younger days, a melancholy overwhelming him at times like a black cloud. Gloucester's defection wounded him deeply, for that the Earl had defected to the King he had no doubt. The rest were loyal enough but the future looked dark. If Henry won the Pope's backing, the King of France's support, Gloucester's aid, and if Richard came home with his shrewd advice, who could say what confrontation that might bring? It was not only the barons whose grievances against the King were plain; the seething simmering discontent of the citizens of London was growing. And in anguish he wondered why others could not see what was so clear to him.

It was growing dark, and Simon looked up at the clear sky, a crescent hanging low, a myriad stars above. The night was so calm and peaceful, and his spirit so restless and oppressed that he clasped his hands together, praying for reassurance, for some of that to enter his soul. For a moment it seemed to him that God was indeed with him, that he need not fear the future, nor quail at whatever struggle lay before him.

A voice broke into his absorption. It was Philip, his wife's page, to inform him that supper was laid in her bower. They sometimes supped alone when she thought he was tired, and as he went down the narrow stair he found himself longing for some of his nephew's youthful optimism. He was weary when he entered the bower, but it seemed Eleanor was waiting to speak urgently with him for as soon as he entered she began. 'Well? Did you talk with Edward? What does Henry mean by this pact with Louis? Is he going to ignore my claim to my mother's holdings?'

Simon sat down, his hands hanging over the arms of his chair. 'We only touched briefly on that. There are other, greater concerns –'

'My lord!' she broke in. 'What is of more concern than my rights in my ancestral lands? Oh, I have been so cheated, all my life. I have never had the monies due to me from William's estates and now it seems I am to lose all that my grandfather won for our family. Is Plantagenet to be no more than a name from the past?'

'I cannot say. Of course it is wrong, but it is England that matters.'

'Simon! Will you do nothing about it?'

He gave a heavy sigh. 'What can I do? Henry will not listen to me. If you are so disturbed about it, journey to Paris and see both your brother and King Louis yourself.'

She felt a flush rising in her face. 'You would send me alone?'

'Harry or young Simon could go with you, but I do not want to leave England, especially now that Edward is back. Richard may arrive at any moment and it is vital that –'

'Vital that your Parliament is called?' she queried. 'And I shall be robbed in the meantime.'

'I am sorry for that. God knows we never have enough money and you should receive some dues from France.'

'I will never sign any agreement with Louis until I do, but we may lose all because you will not go to Paris on my behalf.'

There was a discreet knock on the open door and several servants entered bearing dishes, to be followed by the friar, Adam Marsh, to say grace over the meal.

When the servants had gone he said gravely, 'My children, did I hear you quarrelling? It is not right that you should do so, you who are set up as an example to so many.' His face was pale above his plain brown gown, a thin man fervent in his devotion to the founder of his order, Brother Francis, his fingers holding the crucifix at his belt, sandals on his rather grubby bare feet.

Eleanor caught at her temper, aware that it was strained these days. If it had been anyone but the Franciscan who so reproved them she would have turned roundly on the culprit, but she had too much respect for this holy man to do so and he was in a particular position, being both her confessor and Simon's. 'No, Brother Adam,' she said, 'I do not quarrel with my lord. A slight disagreement, that is all.'

She gave Simon a swift warm look and to her surprise saw a hint of tears in his eyes. She wished then that Brother Adam would say grace and go, that they could eat their supper. Perhaps the hot food and the wine would refresh Simon, take that strained look from his face. She was angry and hurt at the bartering away of her status as one of the inheritors of her grandfather's empire, but when it came to the point only Simon mattered.

At last, when they were alone, the supper cleared, she came to him and knelt by his chair. His hands seemed cold and she wrapped them in her own.

'My dear, my lord, forgive my hasty words. You are doing so much, all you can.'

He gave her a long searching stare. 'Not enough, not enough. Will there ever be enough time for all that must be done?'

She put her arms about him and he lowered his head to let it rest on her shoulder.

In the weeks that followed Edward spent most of his time with his uncle. They were seen riding in and out of the city together, hawking in the open country north of Moor Gate, in conference in the Tower or hearing Mass at Westminster. Some unkind tongue whispered that perhaps the tall dark Earl wanted to set the young Prince on the throne, seeing in him, as many did, a hope for the future. But neither contemplated such a thing. Simon held by his oath of fealty to the anointed King, regardless of his contempt for the man, and Edward loved his father far too well for such treachery.

They talked instead of warfare. Edward had no experience other than a foray against the Welsh and he was an eager pupil, listening to the older man's clear-headed views on siege works, assaults and open battle.

Winter closed in and after Christmas the time approached for the Candlemas meeting of Parliament, called for by the Provisions. Henry was ready to sign his agreement with King Louis but Louis refused to ratify any treaty that had loose ends. Finally in return for fifteen thousand marks out of the sum the French King would pay for the ceding of northern France, Eleanor agreed to waive her claims. It was a fair amount of money and she felt only relief that at least one of Simon's problems was settled.

King Louis took King Henry's hand in his and proclaimed that henceforth there would be only love and peace between them, and England awaited the return of her King. But still he lingered in France, admiring buildings, listening to the choir of Notre Dame, enjoying the ritual of the great cathedral and the luxury of the French court.

'What shall we do?' Edward asked. 'Only my father can summon the lords to Westminster.'

Simon stood with his arms folded, deep in thought. 'So it has always been, but he has agreed – as have we all – on three meetings a year, and this is the time.'

'I have sent messengers,' Edward said. 'I have begged him to come but I've had no word.'

Simon became even more depressed as the dark days of January passed. At last a letter arrived bearing the royal seal.

Henry would not return as yet, and therefore the meeting must be postponed.

Wild arguments broke out in the baronial party. Gilbert the Red said loudly that as his father was also with the King, a Parliament was not possible; the Earl of Oxford thought it would be better to leave it until after Easter as he had pressing affairs of his own; the Marshal, Roger Bigod, was troubled by the idea of such an unprecedented step as calling a great meeting without the King and threw in his lot with those who accepted the postponement. Finally all agreed except Simon. The Lord Edward considered that his presence would suffice and he supported his uncle, but he was young and untried and his voice carried little weight. Nevertheless the two of them announced that the postponement would be short and if the King still did not come his son would summon the barons in his place.

'At last,' Simon said to Eleanor, 'at last we are showing a strong hand. I believe now the rest will obey. I have made it plain that no hurt is intended to the King but the business of the realm must go forward.'

Edward was triumphant, the taste of power in his mouth.

'Dearest aunt,' he said warmly to Eleanor, 'my uncle is the wisest man I know and I will bring my father to see he is worth all his other advisers put together.'

He clapped his cousins Harry and Simon on the shoulder and promised them places about him when he should be in a position to give them. With their father's approval he knighted both the young men, all of them dining afterwards in William Rufus's great hall at Westminster.

Harry de Montfort was full of enthusiasm for his cousin Edward's optimism, but the younger Simon though his adherence to their cause was as firm, confided to his mother that he thought his father believed they were all too sanguine, that nothing was going to turn out quite so easily as Harry foretold.

'Your father is probably right,' Eleanor said. 'Simon, promise me – '

He came to her and took her hand, his dark eyes on her anxious face. 'Anything, mother, anything.'

'Promise me whatever happens you will never leave your father's side. I cannot always be with him and he needs you and Harry, both of you. His spirits are often low.'

'He could have my life for the asking, you know that, and Harry's too.'

'You are good sons,' she said. 'I never thought it would come to this – my brother and your father so far opposed to each other. There were times when we were all so happy.'

Simon was silent, sensing she was lost in a past he knew nothing of but after a moment she thrust away the memories and pressed his hand, owning that she knew she could trust him.

Some weeks later she was sitting with the Demoiselle and her women, Mary and Dionysia, in her bower at Durham House. The shutters were closed against the cold of a March wind, the fire burning unsteadily and occasionally filling the room with smoke, when Simon entered, followed by his two elder sons. Neither was as tall but they were well-built young men and she thought they were a trio to be proud of.

Abruptly Simon said, 'Your brother Richard has arrived in London with Gloucester.' He saw the momentary warmth light her face and heavily he added, 'They have closed the gates.'

She stifled a gasp. 'Against you! Richard has shut them against you!'

'Yes. They are summoning all the men they think loyal to them to be prepared to take up arms. It will come to war yet.'

Eleanor threw down her sewing and came to him, her hands laid on his arms. 'Richard could not fight you, my lord – nor me, for it is the same thing. There has always been love between us.'

'I fear it has given place to something else,' he said harshly, 'and I suppose it was inevitable. We have defied the King and Richard is loyal to his brother. Neither does he like any departure from convention, you know that. That is why he took issue with Henry over the matter of our marriage.

Now we have dared to break with convention again and I do not think we will win him to us this time.'

'Oh.' Eleanor let him go, twisting her fingers together. 'If only I could see him, talk to him, tell him what this means to us. But Edward will perhaps be able to see him, persuade him.'

'The gates are shut against Longshanks too.'

'Then we still have that in our favour,' Harry said cheerfully. 'Edward will hold by you, my lord.'

But would he? Eleanor wondered, and she waited in growing unhappiness, watching the lines deepening on Simon's face. Edward dined with them and did not seem in the least cast down, certain that his uncle and Gloucester would come to Parliament and understand that they were only trying to ensure order.

But a week or so later the news broke that King Henry had arrived and overnight everything was changed. He rode into the city, accompanied by his half-brother Sir William de Valence and with some three hundred spears at his back and lodged in the Tower. When Edward appeared at Ludgate asking to see his father he was refused entrance and in stunned amazement turned and rode back to Westminster.

The news had also reached Durham House and Eleanor, knowing her brother, was aware of a prick of fear that she took good care not to show. Only in her nephew did she see a cause for hope; to be shut from his father's presence might throw him wholeheartedly into their camp.

The younger Simon remarked – shrewdly that he thought it more likely to send Edward begging for pardon.

'He won't do that.' Harry scoffed at the idea. 'He cares too much for our father to do that.'

'You don't see further than your own nose,' Guy told him.

He was still chewing over his resentment that he had not been knighted with his two elder brothers when the Prince conferred that honour on them. 'Cousin Edward is the King's heir. Do you think he will forget that?'

'No, but neither will he forget his promises, the plans he made with father that concern him closely.'

And in the morning when the Lord Edward was announced Harry flashed his mother a glowing smile. It died, however, when they saw Edward's face.

He came across the vaulted chamber, his embroidered tabard over a mail tunic. His sword hung from his side and his young face was taut.

'Well, nephew?' Simon surveyed him, adding, 'I can see you are come to tell us something.'

'Yes.' Edward looked from one to the other, his distress patent, but he hardly paused before going on. 'I have come to say that though I believe with all my heart in your cause, I cannot oppose my father any longer. I sent Roger Leyburn to him last night on my behalf and he will see me today, providing I forswear all other allegiances and do homage to him.'

There was a moment's silence. Then Harry cried out, 'Cousin! After all your promises! How can you?' Simon folded his arms across his chest, facing the unhappy young man. 'Edward, you gave me your word. Is it worth so little?'

Before Edward could answer Guy had his sword half out. 'Traitor! Prince you may be, but you are betraying my father and you will answer for that.'

'Not willingly,' Edward retorted, 'never willingly. My uncle's hopes are mine still, but other ties are more binding when it comes to life or death.'

'Traitor!' Guy shouted again. 'Oath-breaker!' and his sword came fully out of the scabbard.

Edward stepped back involuntarily, feeling for his own hilt.

The Demoiselle gave a smothered cry, frightened by the angry words and the scraping of steel, and she caught at her mother's arm. Already she adored her cousin Edward and for a moment thought Guy would indeed kill him, but her father's hand had shot out and come down hard on her brother's wrist.

'No, Guy, I'll not have that. Edward, you are man enough to make your own decisions. If this is what you wish to do then do it. At least you had the courage to come and tell me. But leave my house now – you'll not be molested. Only I will not call you nephew again.'

Eleanor had been listening in horror to the quick exchange of angry words threatening to turn to worse deeds. Now, disengaging herself with a sharp admonition from her daughter's clutches, she came to stand between Edward and her sons.

'Stop, I beg of you. Edward, think – oh, think. You have always cared so much for what your uncle thought.'

'I still do,' he said. Ignoring a snort from Guy he took her hand and put it to his lips. She could see that he was very pale.

'But I must go to my father. I cannot be shut away from him or from my mother.'

He went, a disappointed young man forced to sacrifice youthful ideals, activated not so much by expediency, though he never lost sight of his destiny, but by a genuine love that was proving stronger than he knew.

Spring came, a fresh bright spring reminding Eleanor of the April days in Oxford. She and Simon felt isolated, the barons uneasy. A large force of mercenary soldiers arrived from France and marched into London. A week later they escorted the royal family to Winchester and no one moved to prevent them. In June Henry announced that a papal bull had been issued releasing him from the oath he had sworn to the Provisions at Oxford.

'I am King again,' he told his astonished court and thought himself the shrewdest of men. He had outmanoeuvered his enemies, he had King Louis and the Pope behind him, and in his self-satisfaction he entirely overlooked the effect his action would have on his lords and people. He saw as a victory what they saw as a temporary setback, and confused their present capitulation with total surrender.

He was very pleased with himself on this June day and sent a messenger to Scotland bearing a letter inviting his daughter Margaret and her husband King Alexander to pay him a visit. Margaret was his favourite child and he wanted her to share his triumph.

His Queen was already scheming how to be rid of the de Montforts, aided by William de Valence and her uncles, while Thomas of Savoy had crossed the channel solely in the hope of seeing the Earl of Leicester brought low.

The barons were utterly taken aback by the Pope's decision, shocked at the total disregard of a binding oath, and disgusted by the King's perfidy, but for the moment there seemed to be nothing to be done and one by one they trickled back to court.

In black despair at such weakness Simon ordered Eleanor to have their belongings packed. 'Take the boys and our Demoiselle and go back to Kenilworth,' he said, 'before the King takes away that which we have. He will not harm you but it will be better if I am away for a while. My nephew writes that there are affairs needing me at Montfort L'Amaury.'

'Oh no.' Eleanor caught at his hands. 'Not another parting, my dear lord. You need me, you are not well.'

'I am not ill,' he said with a slight smile, 'except in spirit. Keep a good heart, watch over my affairs at

Kenilworth, and I will come back when the time is right.'

'And if it is too long, I will come to you. You cannot keep me from you. I would rather lose all than be parted from you.'

His mouth came down hard on hers, and they held each other as if all their distress was pouring itself into that passionate embrace. She glanced up at him when he released her, at the sad disillusioned expression on his face, longing for any other solution but this. But she knew he was right and set about gathering her household, her sons, and the Demoiselle who cried bitterly at saying farewell to her father.

And as the cavalcade left Durham House, their lord ready to take the opposite direction, Eleanor knew she hated Henry for his silliness, his petty scheming, his greed. It was Simon who had the larger vision, Simon who had more in his head than the shape of a flying buttress or the design of a silver cup.

For a last moment their horses stood side by side, their tails swishing at the flies, and Eleanor said impetuously, 'Don't grieve, my heart. They're not worth it, not any of them.'

Unexpectedly he answered, 'I was thinking of Arnold of Ashaw. When we were last at Kenilworth he brought in his dues and more as a gift to me, his lord. He and his like are worth the struggle – and it's not over yet.'

No, she thought, as she took the road north, every movement of her horse's hooves bearing her further from him, not over yet, but where would it all end? Would he wear his life away in this hard struggle?

CHAPTER NINE

Queen Eleanora did not feel well, had not been in good health for some time. She was subject to a burning sensation in the chest, to occasional fever that prostrated her on her bed in acute discomfort, and her physician seemed unable to ease it. But the attacks passed and her impetuous spirit was unimpaired.

One morning when just such an attack had eased she left herbed, had her maids dress her and went down the spiral stair in one corner of the White Tower, past the beautiful chapel where she and Henry heard Mass when they were in residence, to the hall below.

Henry was standing in one of the deep window embrasures, his hands clasped nervously together, his expression hovering between fear and anger.

'What is it?' she asked. 'What has that devil done now?'

'It is not Leicester,' he answered, 'though I don't doubt he's incited them, but the mob has gone wild. Look at the flames! Half London is burning. Dear God, is all the world gone mad?'

Bishop Boniface said, 'Those clowns out there need a sharp lesson. If I had a few more men at my back I'd show them that a man of God can mete out justice.'

'And I would hang the cowards who have deserted us,' Eleanora flashed. 'I thought at least John Mansel could be trusted.'

'I told him to go,' the King said. 'He has done too much for me to be safe here. None of my friends will be safe, not even you, my lord Boniface. I charge you to leave at once.'

The Queen's uncle made a graceful gesture. 'If it is your wish, sire. In France I can work on your behalf.' He bowed and would have put his niece's hand to his lips but for once she snatched it away. 'Yes, go, go!' she said. 'I'll not desert my lord.'

He bowed. 'I but carry out the King's will. God keep you, sire.'

He withdrew, only too glad of the excuse to be away from the mob of whose hatred he was well aware. When he had first been appointed Archbishop he had ridden roughshod over his monks and people at Canterbury and no one had forgotten this. Within ten minutes, in the plain robe of a lay brother, he had slipped out of a postern gate.

Eleanora looked after him with contempt. 'If I were but half the man he is I'd not act so. I never thought to call my uncle coward.'

Henry reached out his hand for hers. 'But I want you to leave too. One of Sir William's men has just come in and he says the mob has slain all the foreigners they could find in the city, and the Jews too for lending us money, poor wretches. It is Jewry you can see burning. A yellow robe will not be safe in the streets this day.'

She gave a shudder. 'They are mad, mad! And it is all Leicester's fault. If he had not come back from France –'

'Do you think I would not have prevented that if I could? My fickle scheming barons sent for him and I suspect young Gloucester of being at the root of it. Truly I think Almighty God did me a great disservice when he took the Earl his father from this world. Richard de Clare held by me last year, but Gilbert has had his head turned by Simon, as have half the young fools who owe allegiance to me. Even Richard's boy, young Almaine, has gone to serve under him and put their cursed cross on the shoulder of his surcoat. De Warenne too, and Edward's friend Roger Leyburn. And John de Vescy. I remember how his father opposed mine at Running Meade – like father like son. Oh!' He shook with frustration. 'Why – why should they not live at peace with their King? Why should I be forced to yield my power to them? Am I not God's anointed ruler?' He paused for breath. 'I will not, I say will not! But I fear for your safety, my dearest, and that is why tonight want you to take our barge and go up the river to Windsor. You will be secure there.'

She raised her head proudly. 'I will not run away from the scum of London. They are the clowns you call them and I've dealt with them before.'

'And that is the very reason why you are in danger,' he said. 'I must command this of you.' His eyes filled suddenly and he cried out, 'All ever wanted was you and our children and beauty all about us, and these hard men have robbed us of it.'

'We have been happy together,' she said, 'and no one can take that from us.'

An hour later under cover of darkness, the royal barge slipped out bearing the Queen and her ladies. She was wrapped in a dark cloak; a hood over her head, and the royal standard was not in its usual place. Nevertheless as they approached the bridge with its thirteen solid piers, a sharp-sighted pedlar recognized both boat and occupant, too familiar to Londoners to be mistaken, and yelled to his fellows that the foreign bitch was escaping.

The citizens were drunk this night on stolen wine, inebriated by the sight of foreign blood flowing in the gutters, the hated Jews lying dead in mounds, their houses looted and burned. None of them had forgotten the matter of the Queen-geld, nor Eleanora's behaviour to the Mayor and leading citizens. A wild struggling mob streamed to the gaps between the crowded houses on the bridge and screeched their fury at her.

'Stone her! Drown the bitch!'

'Sink the boat and send the witch to hell!'

The abuse went on and there was a dash for rotten eggs, mud, stones, cabbages and any filth they could lay their hands on. The barge was pelted, an egg broke on the Queen's cloak causing her to recoil from the stench, while other missiles hit her ladies. They were all crying with fright and one screamed as a stone struck an oarsman and he fell in the water to be sucked under where the river rushed between two piers.

'Turn the boat,' the Queen ordered fiercely. 'Oh, Blessed Lady, protect us! Turn the boat, I say, we cannot go on.'

Never, she thought, had any Queen been so treated, and bitter hatred rose in her for those vulgar, yelling, unwashed faces above her. The terrified oarsmen had a hard struggle to bring the barge round against the pull of the waters, but they did it and brought her back safely to the Tower.

There in a state of collapse she was carried to her bed, while her husband, sick with fear, sent a messenger to his brother-in-law asking for terms.

Simon was at Oxford when the King's knight reached him and he acted with the swiftness that always bewildered Henry. He had returned from France at the insistence of his friends, Gilbert the Red now Earl in his father's place, the Earls of Norfolk, Oxford and Hereford, and a number of others adding their voices. Henry, after his assumption of power, had returned to his old ways, ignoring the law, doing exactly what he wanted to do, and Simon found the country seething, earls, batons, knights, yeomen and merchants, all ready to prepare for war. He too was certain that combat was now the only way to bring Henry to his senses.

He did not even pause to go to Kenilworth, only sending his greeting to Eleanor and summoning his two eldest sons to attend him. He was surrounded now by young men, and he knew himself to be the pivot of their ideals. To have Richard of Cornwall's son among them was a triumph indeed. He kept these young men about him, entrusting much to the hot-tempered Gilbert the Red who was eager for personal triumph but with the sense to realize who was the best, the only leader for the campaign.

A good army to command, Simon thought, with some older heads to keep the young in check, but it had not yet come to a fight.

In a panic Henry announced his wish to talk and met his brother-in-law at Windsor, in the meadow below the castle walls. The encounter was brief, for neither had any intention of conceding cherished ideals to the other. At last Henry rounded on Eleanor who had accompanied her husband.

'I do not understand you,' he said petulantly. 'I gave you so much and yet you look at me as if I were your enemy. Are you not still my sister?'

'I am my lord Simon's wife,' she retorted and they stared at each other, a great gulf between them. There seemed nothing more to be said.

Both sides retired to endeavour to find some terms for a truce, but before anything was done an unexpected blow was struck for the King. The Lord Edward, now wholly committed to his father's cause and far from sharing his fears, raided the new Temple where his mother's money and jewels were kept. He forced doors and locks and seized the entire treasure. With this he paid the force of Welsh mercenaries that he commanded and lured both his cousin de Warenne and Roger Leyburn back to the case. He also worked on Henry of Almaine, until that honest young man went to Simon and said that as his father was with the King he did not feel able to take up arms against him. But neither, he added ingenuously, would he draw his sword against his uncle of Leicester.

Simon gave him a sardonic smile. 'Do you think I fear your untried sword, pup? It is your inconstancy that will make men distrust you.'

Almaine departed, crestfallen and red in the face, and Simon, bitterly disappointed at the defections, agreed to the King's suggestion that the whole affair of the Provisions and the oaths taken should be laid before the King of France who was willing to listen to both points of view. It was a last throw for peace.

The Earl and Countess spent Christmas at Kenilworth with all the seasonal festivities but Simon knew himself to be morose and unable to share in his sons' enjoyment of the feasting.

Before Twelfth Night he had further cause for depression. A bedraggled brewer arrived from the Welsh marches and poured out a miserable story. It seemed that the King, who had a genius for doing the wrong thing at the wrong moment, had given three of Simon's manors to Roger Mortimer to keep that young man to heel. Mortimer, instead of investing them sensibly, seized what he could, burned the houses, and was now holding the Earl's bailiff to ransom. Simon was, with reason, furiously angry. He dismissed Henry's excuse that these manors had been merely a holding for the crown, and told Eleanor this was yet another item to lay before King Louis. It would show him how little any subject in England could depend on their sovereign's word. He would have thundered straight to London if he did not now that Henry was probably well on his way to France.

The next morning Simon set out to ride to the coast. It was a bitter day with ice on the ponds and puddles, the ground like iron, frost crackling on the trees. He rode in silence, brooding on the turn of events and the best way to present his case to King Louis. He had faith in his ability to make that saintly monarch see his point of view, understand that a King who constantly broke his word and who ran to the Pope for absolution from any vow that displeased him, was not a man who could be trusted. Englishmen needed some sort of restraint put upon their royal griffin, he thought, remembering Henry's silly remark about himself during the building of the abbey. He kept up a good pace, Sir Roger Foliot bearing his banner over his head, his knights streaming behind him, his squires wearing his livery of the fork-tailed lion, his elder sons beside him.

'We'll reach Northampton by nightfall,' Harry said. 'A hot meal and a warm bed won't be amiss after this ride. Jesu, but it's cold.'

'Who cares a fig for the weather?' Guy's tone was sharp. 'I'd rather we were warming ourselves by turning our steel on our cousin Edward than words on the King of France. Why we did not deal with Edward before we left I do not know.'

'He'll not break the truce while we're gone,' the younger Simon told him. 'We all liked Longshanks. Do you want to see him dead?' ·

'Yes!' Guy flashed, 'and all enemies of our father.'

The Earl turned on him. 'Do you think I want the King's heir slain? Do you think that would enhance my standing in the world? No, by God.' He swung round again, and in that moment his horse put an unwary hoof into an iced pot-hole and came down, throwing his rider over his head on to the hard ground.

For a moment Simon lay stunned, sick with pain, vivid colours flashing before his eyes. He seemed to hear someone cry out and became aware of confusion, men dismounting, Harry holding his head, Simon bending over him. There seemed to be blood trickling down his forehead. On one knee beside him Guy said urgently, 'Are you badly hurt, my lord? Can you get up?' He had some cloth and was wiping away the blood. 'This cut's not deep.'

A frightened squire had brought a costrel of wine and Guy seized it, holding it to his father's lips. Simon drank a little, his head clearing. His horse seemed unhurt, on its feet again, but as he struggled to rise a sharp pain made him catch his breath. 'My leg,' he said and was surprised to hear his voice so calm. 'I think it is broken.'

Harry called for a litter to be made at once, two men cutting saplings for poles and stretching a mantle over them, while Guy found a firm stick and bound it to his father's leg. The pain was excruciating but Simon bore it without comment, nor did he speak while he was lifted on to the hastily made litter though he could not repress one groan.

They were no more than twenty miles from Kenilworth and he ordered Simon and several knights to bear him back. It was too late to reach the castle tonight, but they could take him to Dunchurch and home on the morrow. Harry he commanded to proceed to join others of their party in London.

'You must speak for me,' he said faintly. 'You and de Bohun and the Bishop of Worcester must put our case as well as you can.' But, oh God, he thought as the litter jerked uncomfortably over the uneven road, that this should happen now! It was the worst of blows for he knew well he was the heart and soul of the baronial cause and only he could have brought full pressure to bear on King Louis. Was it a punishment from God? Was he the one at fault? No, he did not believe that, would never believe it.

He began to feel faint and nauseated, every movement causing him agony and when at last they got him back through the gates of Kenilworth Castle he had lost consciousness.

When he woke again it was to find himself lying on his own bed surrounded by worried attendants, Eleanor by his side, her face creased with anxiety. She slipped one hand under his head. 'My love! Thank God you are come to your senses. Try to drink a little wine.'

His barber, Peter, held a cup to his lips and he swallowed some. His physician was there, touching the leg with careful fingers and as Simon glanced at him questioningly he said, 'The bone will knit, my lord, but it will take time. You are not at the age when bones heal quickly, and you have bruised your shoulder badly as well as cutting your head. But as I say, in time –'

'Time!' Simon broke in as he had done once before. 'Time is what I do not have.'

The leg was set, the physician complimenting Guy on his initial bandaging, while the chaplain murmured prayers and anxious knights gathered in the chamber whispered among themselves, shocked at this blow.

Simon's hand tightened on Eleanor's. 'Send them away, all of them. I would be alone with you.'

The room emptied and she sat beside him, one cool hand on his forehead. 'Does your leg pain you much, dear heart?'

He made a grimace that was sufficient answer. 'And my head aches damnably. Your hand is healing in itself. Eleanor, it is the most cruel trick of fate, or the Devil, to lay me on my bed at such a time.'

'I know, I know. You must trust to Harry and the rest to do their best for you.'

'They will, but they are none of them as versed as I am in dealing with Henry. I know his devious ways too well.'

'I wish he was dead and Edward were King,' she said passionately. 'How could he start a truce by giving our manors to Roger Mortimer? I never liked that greedy unbridled young man. Edward you could control.'

He gave a deep sigh and winced at the pain in his shoulder. His leg seemed to be on fire. 'I might have done once but I think Edward is now become too much our enemy. He had ideals – perhaps he still has – but nothing could hold him back from his father when it came to the choice. And now they will all work on Louis, the Queen will influence her sister, and I am not there to speak for our cause.'

He was in such distress of mind as well as in body that Eleanor rose. 'I have a potion of my own that will help you sleep, my heart. I won't share our bed tonight in case I should cause you pain, Dionysia shall make me up a truckle bed here at the foot.'

She made him drink her concoction of herbs and after a little more restless talk, his voice faded and his heavy breathing told her that he slept. She went softly into the adjoining bower to reassure the Demoiselle who was sitting up, despite the lateness of the hour, full of anxiety for her father. Then she returned and lay fully dressed on her pallet. Philip, her page, came to curl up by the fire and keep it replenished through the night.

Eleanor slept little, her mind tormented by Simon's injuries, by the vital moment lost, by tearing anxiety for the future. In the morning he was feverish and it was a week before the hectic flush left his face. Eleanor prayed, sent Roger Foliot to the shrine at Walsingham, with offerings for the Blessed Virgin, and through the cold January days watched beside her husband. Snow fell, the mere froze and she looked out on to a white landscape. In the courtyard men's feet trod the snow to slush which froze overnight and proved a trap for the unwary next morning. The cook was laid up with a twisted ankle and directed operations from a stool.

Dionysia complained of chilblains and the Demioselle had a cold in the head.

The younger Simon proved himself indispensable, taking command off his mother's shoulders, leaving her free to nurse his father. He sat in the manorial court, dealt with offenders, listened to complaints and handled all affairs with a commonsense beyond that which his mother had expected of one not yet twenty-three.

Guy stamped restlessly about the place, went hunting in the snow, finding little game and wearing out the horses. Eleanor wished Amaury were at home for she found her youngest son a comfort to talk to, but Amaury had at last abandoned hope of becoming a proficient knight, realizing that his tastes lay in a more scholarly direction. He had become a clerk in minor orders and was now in Rouen occupying a prebend's stall, with his head no doubt happily immersed in books of theology. She missed him and determined that when the country was quiet again he should come home to a position in the English church.

The weeks went by and the snow gave way to a mild spell. On an afternoon when a pale winter sun lit the room Simon was at last sitting up in bed, his leg still unhealed but all danger past, and Eleanor was giving him an account of their estates when they heard the sound of hooves.

'Guy back from his hunting,' she said, but Simon shook his head.

'He's not been gone half an hour. See who has come to visit us, my love.'

But Eleanor had got no further than the door when she heard feet coming up the stair three steps at a time and her eldest son came hurrying along the passage. She gave a little start of pleasure but even as he kissed her she saw the unusual gravity on his face and asked hastily what had happened.

Instead of answering he asked in return, 'How is my father? Is he well enough to see me and hear my news?'

'Jesu!' she said. 'Is it so bad?' And when he nodded she drew him into the room.

There he told them both the worst they feared to hear. Without Simon, the baronial pleas had carried no weight with King Louis. In fact from the first he had been totally biased in favour of his brother king. Louis believed in the sanctity of kingship, the holiness of the anointing oil, the power he saw as God-given. He dismissed the Provisions, held that Henry was in no way bound by what he had been forced to sign, that he might appoint whom he willed, filling his offices with men of any nationality. This the French King gave as his ruling and the Pope supported his verdict: King Henry's subjects had only to obey in all things and there would be peace.

'Peace!' Simon exploded and smote one hand against the other. 'My God, Louis has given us not peace but civil war. This – this ruling will unite all our old supporters, every man who would see justice done in this land.'

'You are right, my lord,' Harry said. 'Englishmen will have none of it. The call to war has already gone out. Gilbert the Red is summoning his men and my cousin Derby has a good force in arms. De Bohun is gone to the west to keep Mortimer in check.'

'Then we must make plans – at once. Send Sir John Penrose and Sir Roger Foliot to me and call in the abbot. I shall need funds and supplies.'

Eleanor came to him. 'Dear heart, you are not yet fit for all this. You cannot sit a horse.'

'Maybe not.' The lines about his mouth were grim. 'But I can direct from my bed. Better still, I'll have a wagon turned into a bed on wheels and that can carry me to London if necessary. I'll not lie here while all I have dreamed of lies in the balance.'

He sent Harry off to join de Bohun, the young Earl of Hereford, and Simon to hold Northampton Castle, called in his stewards and armourers, his fletchers and grooms, and set the castle on a war footing.

It seemed to Eleanor that the place rang all day to the sound of hammers on anvils, the comings and goings of horsemen. The baileys seethed with men answering the call, more mouths to feed than ever. Lawless bands, seeing in the mounting hostilities a chance to enrich themselves, ravaged and plundered, burning cottages and slaying innocent people. Simon despatched his third son to deal with one such band pillaging Leicester land and Guy came back reporting with fierce satisfaction a bloody skirmish and a dozen men swinging from trees as a warning to others.

Harry returned a few weeks later, utterly dejected. The Lord Edward had marched on Gloucester and though they were in greater strength Harry and de Bohun had treated with him. To Harry he was still the loved cousin, and he extracted from him an oath that he and his father would once more adhere to their promises at Oxford. Harry had believed the Prince and withdrawn his forces, but he had not reached home before a breathless messenger chased after him to say that Edward had not kept his word above a day, that he had seized the city of Gloucester and every penny in it for his father's cause.

'By God,' Simon said, 'you must learn, my son, not to let your good nature make you so gullible. Edward loved us once but he is as much our enemy now as his father is.'

Harry, red with shame at this failure of his first mission, said to his mother later, 'How was I to know Edward would cheat us? We have always been friends since we were children.'

'You are not children now and family affection is lost in greater matters,' she said sadly. 'Once I would have thought nothing could have separated me from the love of my brothers, but now I hate the King for what he has done to your father, and as for Richard – I thought he would be the one to make Henry see how foolishly he has acted, but Richard is against us too and that I find hard to bear. Please God Simon will hold Northampton for us.'

But her prayer was not answered. The Lord Edward had got a taste for warfare and he and his father came storming up to Northampton and attacked the castle. Young Simon defended it well and led a sortie against the besiegers, conducting himself bravely as became a son of the Earl of Leicester, and it was sheer misfortune that in the thick of the fight his horse reared, he lost control, and falling backwards was seized by several of his cousin's men. Yelling with triumph they bore him away to the King and Henry sent him to Windsor Castle, a prisoner. Those of the Leicester force who escaped fled back to Kenilworth with the news.

With a set face Simon had himself carried to his wheeled car, his standard fixed to one of the poles holding the canvas covering. 'It is time I showed myself,' he told Eleanor. 'Our men need a rallying point if we are not to lose all. Keep this place while I am gone. I shall leave an adequate number for your defence.'

Eleanor clung to him for one last moment, so fearful for him in his injured state that she had to force back a plea that he should not go. Harry and Guy were to ride with him, and with Simon a prisoner and Amaury in France she felt suddenly bereft, left with only her twelve-year-old daughter. But as Simon was settled against the piled cushions, fully armed, his helm and shield beside him, his stiffened leg supported, her pride in him rose, stronger than fear. She held the Demoiselle's hand firmly and stood back from the procession waiting to move out.

'God go with you, my lord, and all of you,' she said clearly. 'You have the right on your side and He cannot be against us.'

And only when he had gone, when the last man-at-arms had marched out of the bailey and over the drawbridge, leaving the castle horribly empty, did she shut herself in her chamber and give way to weeping.

As the weeks slid by news came. Now he was at Leicester, now at St Albans, and at each step he did the unexpected. When Richard sent forces to cut him off from Oxford he circled the city and crossed the Thames. When they looked for him in London he went south to encourage the barons of the Cinque ports, and when Henry made for Kent, Simon entered London where the people greeted him vociferously. They had wrecked Richard of Cornwall's manor at Islington, ruining his new fishponds, and with wry amusement she imagined how such waste would annoy her careful brother. Henry had sent the Queen to Ponthieu, out of reach of the mob, and her train of Provencal hangers-on with her. Eleanor heard this news without regret for the sister-in-law she had never really liked.

She tried to concentrate on daily business at Kenilworth, waiting for tidings, praying for Simon to defeat their enemies, to send for her to share his triumph. If he triumphed this time bow much it would mean for him, for her, for them all. She dreamed of him in the seat of power, yet all the while was fearful of bad news, afraid of his incapacity to sit a horse, to escape if things went against him.

Spring gave way to early summer. She interested herself in the spring sowing, talked with the shepherd of the tally of young lambs, with Jack in the bakehouse and Nell who brewed their beer. She worried in case a late frost should spoil the prolific blossom on the fruit trees and was thankful for the support of Finch in all she did.

Simon had promoted him from the stables, leaving these in the care of his son, Martin Finch, and had made him a steward in charge of all huntsmen and grooms and stableboys responsible for the purchase of horses and for seeing that all the men were suitably clothed in their lord's livery. Martin had gone with the rest and Finch was proud of his son, proud of his own position. He wore a long belted gown and carried a staff; his lord had entrusted him with the care of his lady and Eleanor leaned on him as on an old friend.

She was more abstemious now over her own wardrobe, but had several new gowns made for her daughter. Simon must see about the girl's betrothal, she thought, and chose blue damask, white sendal trimmed with miniver, yellow velvet with gold embroidery. The Demoiselle was growing very pretty with a clear soft complexion and thick dark lashes to eyes that were so like her father's. The barbette and crespine of Eleanor's youth had given way to the wimple which she appreciated now that there were streaks of grey in her hair, but she placed only a simple veil on her daughter's head, letting the dusky plaits fall free to her waist.

Adam Marsh came to visit her and lectured her on the danger of making the Demoiselle too concerned with worldly things.

'We live in the world, Brother Adam,' she answered, 'and a sorry place it is now. I pray only that it will be more peaceful when she is wed and taking her place in it.'

'Amen.' he said, but his tone was not hopeful. 'I grieve to hear that your husband has found it necessary to plunder innocent landowners, even holy houses.'

'He takes only what he needs,' she retorted. 'He must have money and food for his men. Do you doubt he fights for justice? Or that God will pardon what must be done in that cause?'

Brother Adam gave a heavy sigh. 'There was never a war yet, lady, in which both sides did not believe equally that they had the right.'

For once Eleanor was glad when he went. It was no more than three days after his departure that there was a frantic clatter of hooves over the drawbridge and into the inner bailey and a knight flung himself down from the saddle. Eleanor was in the hall near the open door and her heart turned over as Roger Foliot ran up the steps, pulling off his helm. He was dripping with perspiration, his hair clinging to his forehead, his cheeks flushed. He looked up at her with his face glowing, his eyes alight.

'A great victory!' he cried out. 'Lady, our lord has won a great victory!'

She clasped both hands at her breast. 'God be praised! Tell me – tell me quickly. Where? How?'

'At Lewes. Oh, it was beyond anything how fortune favoured us. We had thought everything going so badly after the Lord Edward took Tonbridge Castle. He seized all my lord of Gloucester's treasure and arms and his wife into the bargain.'

For a moment Eleanor's attention was diverted as a brief memory came back of Edward flirting with Alice in this very place six years ago, and she wondered what the meeting had been like. Gilbert the Red must be very angry that his wife was in Edward's hands. But she must know it all. 'And my lord? Is he well? How did it all happen?'

'The King had a great army and he was marching on London.' Foliot paused as those in the hall gathered round to hear the news, servants pushing by the buttery screen, grooms and kitchen lads crowding the outer steps to listen, a buzz of excitement growing. He went on, 'Some of our leaders thought my lord Simon made a great mistake in trying to intercept the King, for our army was much smaller. My lord of Gloucester was all for racing the King back to London. But our master proved to be right for the men of Kent came out in their hundreds to join us. We hid ourselves in the Weald and the King did not know where we were. He sent out a few scouts and those he did send somehow never got back to him! And when we came up on to the Downs north of the town we only found one sentry and he had fallen asleep under a bush. We saw that the fellow told us what we wanted to know before we sent him to sleep again, for good.'

How like Henry, Eleanor thought, to be so slack, so overconfident. 'Go on. You have not told me about your lord.'

'He is much better, madame. He can sit a horse now, but he let no one know that until the last moment. He kept his standard flying on that chariot of his, but instead of lying in it himself he put four prisoners in it, and when the Lord Edward drove the Londoners back in the battle, his troops slew the prisoners, thinking they had found Lord Simon. But I'm getting ahead of myself. I've not told you how it started.'

He looked so hot and so weary that Eleanor made him sit and Finch, his wrinkled face wearing a satisfied smile, summoned an usher to bring ale. Roger drained the mug before he went on, and eager as she was for news, it was enough for Eleanor to know that Simon was well, that he had won a victory.

The Demoiselle, hearing the commotion, had run down the stair and was listening wide-eyed. Now she cried out, 'Oh pray go on, Sir Roger. Tell us how father won the battle.'

He wiped his mouth with the back of his hand. 'It was dark when we came to the top of the Downs. We thought if the King's men had the hill they call the Black Cap there would be little chance for us. My lord Simon said it was the point he would have made for if he had been in the King's shoes, but it seemed they thought us far away, for they were all asleep in the town, except that one fellow I've told you of. We moved quietly, my lord forbade us to speak, but there were no royalists anywhere outside the walls and soon our men held the cut through the hills as well as the heights and no one the wiser.'

Eleanor found herself glowing too. What a leader Simon was, out-marshalling the enemy, seizing the right place, the right time to strike! 'What happened then?'

'Well, he gave the centre to my lord Gloucester and your sons, lady, held the right wing while Sir Nicholas Segrave and the London bands held the left. My lord was with the Earl of Gloucester and I with him. I swore to myself that I would not leave him, whatever happened.'

'God will bless you for that. And was it still dark?'

'Aye, but the dawn came soon after and then they saw us. The King and the Lord Edward and the Earl of Cornwall brought their army out of the town. Everyone says the Lord Edward will be a great leader one day. I saw him slay a dozen men, but he is still too wild,' Roger added as if he himself was a veteran. 'His men broke the Londoners and went chasing off, pursuing them half way to Fletching where we were the day before. I suppose he has never forgotten how they stoned his mother, for he took a bloody vengeance. He thought he had found my lord in the carriage and – but I've told you that. Anyway he paid for that revenge, by God, for he left their flank exposed.'

'And my lord? He was able to fight?'

'Able?' Roger laughed, his face lit with pride. 'He sat his horse as if his leg had never been injured and he was in the thick of it. No man ever fought as he did.'

'Oh, brave, brave!' Eleanor exclaimed. She could see it all in her mind's eye. The battlefield, the close-locked men in armour, the hideous clash of weapons, the dead and dying, and her lord in the saddle once more, the victor. 'Did my sons do well?'

'They fought to make their father proud of them,' Foliot told her, 'particularly Sir Guy who drove a great gap in the enemy line. Nothing can stop him when he has that look of blood-desire in his eye.'

No, she thought, she had seen that look out hunting, and then something in her cried out in relief that none of those she loved had fallen. Her thoughts turned to those others for whom she had once cared so much.

'And my brothers, the King and the Earl of Cornwall?'

Foliot gave a boyish grin. 'The Earl of Cornwall, lady, saw that things were going badly and he took refuge in a windmill which we soon surrounded. We – we called him the Miller and asked him to grind our corn for us! And when he came out at last he was all over flour and cobwebs and a sorry sight. They're singing a song about it already.'

Eleanor could not keep back a smile but she felt pity for Richard, the cool, the dignified. How he must have hated that surrender. 'Was the King taken too?'

'Aye, we found him in the Priory of St Pancras, but before that the Lord Edward had come back to find our standard over the castle instead of his father's and the day ours. He did manage to reach the Priory but he could do naught to aid his father and by the time darkness came again they yielded and it was all over.'

Eleanor was silent, her hands still clasped, unable to take it all. The Demoiselle questioned Roger again about her brothers and their prowess, crowing with delight as he told how they had held their own, and ending by saying how mortified Simon would be that he had not been there with them. But he would be freed now, father would see to that!

Eleanor shared her daughter's exultation, dwelling on the tale. She wished she had been near enough to ride to Lewes and share in her lord's triumph. She knew little of warfare but she could guess how great a gamble Simon had taken, how startled his enemies must have been at his sudden attack. She could imagine Edward returning from his wild pursuit and his fury at finding the battle lost. But Henry had never been a soldier and Richard had only toyed with warfare, and now Simon had vanquished them, repaid all the broken promises with blood.

'Did you go with my lord to the surrender?' she asked, breaking into his description of Guy's tempestuous attack.

'I did attend him, lady, he and my lord of Gloucester sat half the night with the King and his brother and the Lord Edward. They drew up a paper which the King signed and the others too. And then we all slept. Jesu, but I was weary! My lord left the King under guard at the Priory and we slept at the castle. It was a great victory, my lady, even the Lord Edward owned it.'

A thought struck her and she asked if Henry of Almaine had been there?

'My lord Richard's son? Yes, madame, he was in the mill with his father – the miller's boy!'

Her hands clenched. 'Fickle. My lord always said he was fickle. So much for his word. He deserves to have his spurs struck off for breaking such a promise. What has my lord done with his prisoners, Roger?'

'He has taken them all to London, lady, the King riding beside him and held in respect, I assure you. Your lord will have no insolence, though' – he admitted apologetically – 'we do make jokes. The men will sing their songs of it. Your lord has sent trusted knights to hold all the castles in the realm. There will be peace now, my lady.'

'Peace!' she echoed. 'But for how long?'

'Please God our lord will see all well done. He has ordered men on both sides to go home and wage no more war, and he has sent me to say –'

'Yes? What message has he for me?'

'His greeting and his dear love, madame, and his wish that I should escort you and his daughter at once to London.'

The Demoiselle exclaimed in delight and Eleanor at once gave orders for them all to be ready in the morning, except the garrison which must remain behind. She acknowledged the eager congratulations, the delight of her household, and then went up the stair to her bower, setting Mary and Dionysia to search out the very best gowns for herself and her daughter.

While they busied themselves, chattering excitedly, she stood looking out over the mere, blue under a summer sky. She was almost too happy, too proud to think clearly, for this consummation of all her prayers was overwhelming. She leaned her head against the cool stone of the embrasure, trying to see into the future. It had been worth all the struggle, the anxiety, all his earnest endeavour, and with Henry his prisoner, what would not come to them? She and Simon were on a pinnacle of power, and her love and her ambition for him rose within her. He was the greatest man in the kingdom and she, Eleanor Plantagenet, was his wife.

CHAPTER TEN

Richard, Earl of Cornwall and King of the Romans did not relish captivity, though when one of his jailers was his own sister it made it a little more palatable. And he was hardly treated like a prisoner, more as an honoured guest. He had a fine bedchamber, servants to wait on him, luxuries ordered from London to suit his taste at table, everything he could possibly want – except his freedom.

His escapade in the mill at Lewes provided ample fodder for the impudent writers of scurrilous verse and a song was circulating:

'The Emperor of Germany thought he'd done well,
To make a strong fortress out of a mill. . .
Dick, up to every treacherous trick,
Your crafty career's done in, sir!'

It was humiliating, and even now outside in the bailey he could hear someone whistling the tune. He saw one or two lips twitching at the lower tables but no one dared to sing it openly in front of their Countess. At least, he thought, Eleanor kept his dignity and hers. Only he and she and Edward sat at the centre of this high table and no doubt soon her stern husband, his hand firmly on the nation's reins, would arrange some terms for his freedom. He would be allowed to go back to Germany, to his third wife, Beatrice of Falkenberg, but he reflected gloomily that if he went God alone knew what would happen to his brother. Henry was treated royally, but he was still watched every moment by Simon's men, bereft of his Queen, a lonely worried man pacing the palace of Woodstock.

Richard glanced at his nephew sitting on his other side. Edward's head was full of plans for escape, anyone could see that. A party of knights from Bristol had tried to rescue him from Wallingford where he had first been imprisoned and had nearly carried the day, but the defenders had threatened to shoot their captive over the wall from a mangonel if they did not withdraw. Edward had mounted the battlements himself and assured his friends that his captors meant what they said so the affair had come to nothing, but Richard, watching his nephew's long handsome face, the blue eyes shadowed and deep in thought, was convinced that Edward could not be held for long.

His own son Henry of Almaine was also with him and hard words had nearly come to blows between Henry and Guy de Montfort, Guy reminding his cousin of his promise never to draw sword against the Earl of Leicester. Almaine had retorted that his loyalty to his father came first, and only restraining hands kept Guy from attacking his unarmed cousin. Now Guy scowled and ignored Almaine, seldom speaking even to his uncle Richard.

Richard reached for his cup. It was empty and Eleanor beckoned to an usher to bring wine. Richard liked the light wine from Gascony and nothing but the best was served to him. Tonight he had eaten of crane's flesh, served with parsnips topped with honey and baked so that they were deliciously browned, a pie of lampreys and this at their most expensive season, hashed duck and hard boiled eggs, salted salmon in a piquant white sauce, and now he was biting into a tasty honey and almond and raisin tart.

'An excellent supper, my dear sister,' he said. 'You keep great state here at Kenilworth.'

'How should I not when I have such guests.' She answered courteously but her relations with him were more formal than they had once been, their talk more edged.

'Guests?' He raised an eyebrow. 'Well, I'll not comment on our status yet again, but I confess I grow weary with sitting here doing nothing.'

'And I,' Edward agreed. Only today a pedlar with a pack of silks and ribbons, belts and shoes, on his way from Bristol to the north, had stopped briefly at the castle. Something about his expression as he looked at the prince made Edward inspect his wares. Under cover of the purchase of an embroidered belt, the man had told him in a low voice that despite her lord's banishment Roger Mortimer's lady was devising a plan of her own for his rescue. His mouth widened as he thought of the Lady Maud, fiercely proud, beautiful and utterly unscrupulous – God send a good result of her scheming and then he would find a way to repay the indignity of Lewes and its consequences.

In a sudden spurt of irritation at the whole miserable business he said, 'I hear Harry is busy setting up as a wool merchant. Perhaps he cannot spare the time to sit in Parliament.'

'Your tongue is sharp,' Eleanor retorted with asperity. 'Harry is entitled to take dues on the wool shipped at Dover. Being warden of the castle he must raise money for its defence, but that is no reason why he should not attend Parliament. Simon has his affairs in hand at Porchester so no doubt they will ride up together. Knights from all the shires will be there.'

'We gathered all and sundry were to be invited,' Richard said. 'God's teeth, what are we coming to?'

'A better way of doing things,' Eleanor replied. She turned her head to look closely at her brother. He had grown heavier but he had not lost his hair as Henry had done. He was still enormously wealthy and had sunk a fortune in his brother's struggle to keep his crown. He, like Edward, was irrevocably Simon's enemy now and yet she found herself longing for something of the old love between them.

'Richard,' she said again in a softer tone, 'I know we have talked of this before but can't I make you understand Simon cares only for what is best for England?'

'Do you say so?' Richard's retort was dry. 'Not everyone thinks it for the best that the merchant and the goldsmith and the cooper should have as much right to sit in Parliament as their natural lords.'

'No one wants to upset the standing of their natural lords.' Eleanor lifted her head. 'Simon will never be other than master here, but he will have all his people able to speak for their own needs and rights.'

'High sounding phrases, but men think he has feathered his own nest pretty well since Lewes.'

'And rightly so. He must have means for his work.' She broke off abruptly. 'Pray, brother, take some of this cheese from Brie. It is very good. My lord' – she turned to a young man with thick, wildly curling dark hair and eyes that were almost black. 'Will you not sing us one of your Welsh songs? They are so charming.'

'A marching song perhaps?' Edward said under his breath, his hands curling themselves as if grasping a sword. He disliked the presence at this table of Llewellyn of Wales, but Simon had made a treaty with the young prince to keep the marches safe and Llewellyn was perhaps a more welcome guest than he, the Lord Edward! His own friends and closest supporters were the marcher lords and one day, when he his way, he would drive the turbulent Welsh back into their hills. But for the present he must sit and listen to this unruly fellow who called himself a prince playing the lute and singing a song in a language that was beyond understanding.

As he played Llewellyn's black eyes were on Edward's cousin, the Demoiselle, now blossoming into womanhood and beautiful womanhood at that. She blushed and looked down at her folded hands and wished she knew what the words meant, for she was sure they were a love song.

Eleanor watched them both, smiling a little and listening. She had something to say to her daughter on that score.

The company in the hall had quietened now, for a pleasant melody was coming from the lute under the Welshman's able fingers and he had a singularly sweet baritone voice, singing from the heart as all Welshmen seemed to do. Eleanor let her thoughts drift away, as always, to Simon. She had wanted to go to London with him but he wished her to remain here at Kenilworth to keep watch on their illustrious captives. She was troubled for him. He was fifty-seven now and the great burdens on him were at times almost insupportable; yet he worked with fury as if he saw the opportunity as brief, the years passing. This Parliament was indeed the culmination of his great dream, but it was not easily won. There was constant trouble for he had to contend with the jealousies of the barons who wanted to yield nothing, not one jot of their power. Gloucester was the most discontented of all, his most loud complaint that he had taken Richard of Cornwall prisoner and therefore had the right to him and his ransom yet Simon kept him at Kenilworth. Eleanor wished he would try to handle that dangerous young man with more tact, but when she spoke of it, Simon brushed the suggestion aside. Gloucester must abide the agreement made or suffer the consequences.

But the common folk loved the victor of Lewes. In the London taverns they raised their tankards of ale to 'Sir Simon the Just', and not a few, she suspected, would be glad to see her at Westminster and Simon beside her. Yet she knew he did not want that, had never wanted it, though there were times when she herself had dreamed of it, Plantagenet ambition rising in her. Simon was worthy of a crown and was she not the daughter of a king?

She gave a little sigh and turned her attention to the singer. The last notes ended, the lute strings died on a melancholy chord and the Welsh prince smiled across at the Demoiselle as, politely clapping her hands, she raised her eyes to his.

After supper Eleanor retired to her bower with her daughter and there put a hand to the girl's cheek. 'You are hot, my little coney,' she said and the blush returned. 'Do you care so much for him?'

'Oh!' The Demoiselle clasped her hands together. 'Mother, how did you know?'

'How? Child, I have been in love.'

'But – but my lord Llewellyn – does he, I mean – would father –'

Eleanor laughed, finding the girl's confusion charming. She drew her to sit on a stool at her feet. 'Your father has already discussed the matter with me, when he was last here. He has also spoken to the Prince and your betrothal will be announced when he next comes home.'

The Demoiselle gave a startled gasp and then laid her head against her mother's knee. 'I did not know. I am so happy – I did not think I could be so happy.'

'You will be happier yet, please God.' Eleanor said, stroking the long plaits. 'If one is fortunate in marriage, as I have been, there are joys to come beyond your imagining. Llewellyn is a brave young man and our friend. Your marriage will bind him to us and then between him and your father the marcher lords will be kept to a truce. There is policy in this match as well as your inclinations!'

The Demoiselle was enough a maiden of her generation to understand, but she scarcely paused to consider this point of view; her thoughts were all for those black eyes, the lilting voice, the square strong hands that had held hers in a dance this evening. The next day Eleanor brought the prince to her bower and allowed them a few moments together. Llewellyn was to leave after dinner on his way back to Wales and the eager girl stood within the circle of his arms to be kissed for the first time, her young body responding to that swift eager touching of the lips. When he had gone she craned from the tower window to watch the dragon banner fluttering over his head until she could see it no longer, and for the rest of the day sat in a dream, unable to set a stitch in her embroidery while Eleanor smiled at her indulgently.

Some weeks later on a cold February day, Eleanor sat reading a long letter from her lord full of the doings of Parliament, of Henry's forced concurrence in the achievements there. Edward and Henry of Almaine, summoned to London, were nominally released and Edward gave to his uncle the wealthy earldom of Chester as an earnest of his good behaviour. 'But,' Simon wrote, 'I do not trust his youthful impulses. He will seek an opportunity to destroy me and I keep my own men constantly outnumbering his in his retinue.'

There was however another matter engaging him. Before the long debates were over their three elder sons, always easily wearied with too much talking, organized a tournament with Gilbert the Red, to be held at Nottingham. Overstrained and in no mood for frivolity, Simon forbade it, at least until Parliament had ended its deliberations. Harry and his brothers were much put out of countenance by this, but they glumly obeyed their father, 'like tiresome children,' he added, 'but Gilbert has taken it as a personal insult. It is time he grew a wiser head on his shoulders for he stands second to me among our barons.'

Eleanor was troubled, more deeply than she allowed anyone to see. She wrote back to Simon, entrusting the letter to her faithful messenger, Truebody. 'Keep Gloucester at your side,' she urged him. 'If you will, my dear lord, you can win him back to you.'

But would he do it? Harry came home and told her of the angry words exchanged between his father and Gilbert, both equally unbending. Gilbert called the Earl of Leicester's attitude high-handed and was now retired to Hertford, simmering with indignation. 'I have given myself and my substance to the cause,' he had said at one point, according to Harry, 'and yet you treat me as an untried squire.'

'To which my father replied,' Harry went on, 'that behavior made the man, which Gilbert did not like at all.'

Eleanor could see that flaming red head, the angry freckled face – the Earl of Gloucester would make a bad enemy. She wrote an urgent letter to Simon bidding him be careful, and sent Harry back to his father's side with an injunction to be obedient in all things.

The spring days lengthened and her anxieties increased, turning at last to immense relief when Simon asked her to meet him at Odiham so that all the family might spend Easter together. Amaury rode down from York to accompany her. He was still the same dreamy youth, but since he had been made treasurer of the Minster in that city there was a streak of ambition appearing, a desire to rise in the Church. They set out together through the awakening woods and fields, the first green buds bursting on the hawthorns, anemones growing under the great oaks, violets showing in the banks, and Eleanor felt her spirits responding to this rebirth, the loveliness of the countryside emerging from winter.

Guy was already at Odiham when she rode over the lowered drawbridge and as he came dutifully to assist her from the saddle she asked where his elder brothers were.

'Harry is with Edward in my father's train and they may be here tomorrow. Simon should be on his way too, if he can tear himself from the lady he is chasing so persistently.'

She shook out the folds of her mantle and gave her whip to young Martin Finch. 'What lady? I have heard nothing of this.'

'Isabella de Fortibus, William's widow.'

'The Countess of Aumale ?' She was astonished. 'She is the richest widow in England. I wonder what your father will have to say about that.'

'I can tell you what the lady has said.' Guy's tone was dry. 'She will have none of Simon and she fears to be abducted as he is always turning up at her door with armed men and a spare horse.'

'What a way to conduct a courtship.' Eleanor could not keep back a smile. She went into the hall and called to her steward, enquiring if all the arrangements for their stay were well in hand, and that night she slept in her bed in the great chamber, hoping the morrow would bring Simon to share it with her. He came as dusk was falling, a long train of knights behind him, including his eldest son, the Lord Edward, and Henry of Almaine. In their chamber while he changed his travelling clothes and washed the dust of the road from his hands and face she studied him, thinking how the last months had aged him, but she forebore to question him while Peter was shaving his cheeks and his servants laying out a rich gown of red sandal with white scalloping and the white cross of his cause on the shoulder.

Supper was announced and they went down together, the hall so crammed tonight that many of the lesser folk were forced to eat out in the bailey under the stars. Because it was still Lent the fare was restricted but as varied as Eleanor's cook could make it, and her sons and their royal cousins certainly did justice to it.

The talk was mostly of the doings of Parliament and the latest threats from the Pope, but with such opposing views at the high table Eleanor soon guided the conversation into pleasanter channels. Simon said little and it was not until they were alone at last in her bedchamber that she was able to sit down by the fire and beg him to tell her how matters stood between him and Gloucester, the subject uppermost in her mind.

Simon stood leaning against the stone hearth, one thin hand held to the blaze, the firelight catching the gold of the ring she had given him on their wedding day. He was so gaunt that she wondered if he ever paused in the midst of business to eat enough to keep his health. He suffered much from indigestion and she made a mental note to instruct the cook to prepare a junket for that always lay well on an uneasy stomach.

In answer to her question Simon said, 'There is so much to be done that it is particularly irritating that Gilbert should be behaving like a willful boy at the moment. The country must be settled, and with speed. There has been too much pillaging and lawless raiding and men need security again. Gilbert does not aid me by his attitude. But' – he gave a heavy sigh – 'no doubt he will come to heel when he has got over his sulking. I wonder if he really thought I should hand over Richard to him?'

'He is eaten up with pride,' she said. 'Where is he now? Still at Hertford?'

'No, he has gone to Monmouth, and because I want an eye kept on him I have told Harry and the others they may organize their tourney now that Parliament has ended. Gloucester has been invited and his coming or not seems to be a test of his friendship. If he will not meet us I must deal with him. Such an enemy I cannot have at my back.'

'No indeed, but' – her hands gripped the arms of her chair – 'I could have him beaten for so defying you, after all you have done for him, for them all.'

'It has not come to a betrayal yet,' he said wearily.

The next day he seemed to make an effort to put aside his depression, to be more the father of his family than the man in control of the state. His displeasure with his sons was forgotten as he went hawking with them and singing together, complimenting his daughter on her voice.

Lifting her chin he said, 'You are fast becoming the beauty your mother was at your age, and still is in my eyes. Perhaps a certain Welshman has been teaching you to sing and putting that brightness in your eyes at the same time.'

She looked up at him, a little smile curving her mouth. 'My lord, I am nearly fifteen now and a woman. Mother said you considered it time – my lord Llewellyn –' She broke off, a pink tinge in her cheeks, and lowered her eyes.

Her father smiled. 'Since when did a Demoiselle of nearly fifteen arrange her own marriage plans?'

'But mother said she was wed to the Earl of Pembroke when she was only fourteen, wasn't she?'

His smile widened into one of his rare laughs. 'Child, do you love Prince Llewellyn so much?'

'Oh yes,' she said and turned her face to kiss her father's hand.

'Then you shall be wed as soon as the country is quieter. This marriage pleases me too, for reasons you would not consider important.'

She responded to his teasing. 'Father, I know what must be considered for the daughter of a Princess.'

'Do you indeed?' he retorted. 'Thank God, you have your mother's spirit.'

The Easter feast was celebrated, a choir of boys singing an anthem to the risen Christ in the chapel, the assembled family and their noble guests kneeling together where shafts of sunshine slanted through the splayed windows. The younger Simon had joined them in a bad temper, for his widow had fled from his attentions and gone to friends in Wales, but he forgot his disappointment in the rare pleasure of a shared feast.

For Eleanor there was joy and a poignant sadness in this Easter Mass. She was not blind to the grave anxieties disturbing her lord's sleep so that he often tossed and turned, muttering to himself. She was aware too of Edward's restlessness, of her own sons' ambitions to share in their father's exalted position, wanting the rewards without the labour, and listening to the words of the Easter anthem– 'Surrexit Christus, spes mea . . . tu nobis victor Rex. .

.' she thought of Henry hearing the Easter Mass at the same hour, surrounded by Simon's watchdogs. Did he hate them both now? Could this Easter day bring no hope of peace, of the healing of wounds? But as the Host was raised and she bowed her head her prayer was all for the rigid, absorbed figure at her side. God send him at least a little rest.

A few days later Edward left with Harry and Almaine and a large following of knights to join his father at Gloucester where the court had spent the feast. Before his departure he came to take leave of his aunt.

'God go with you, nephew,' she said and then paused, her eyes on his face. He met her look straightly, no longer a boy but a cool, wary young man who had learned some hard lessons from the man best able to teach them.

On an impulse she rose and laid her hand on his arm. 'Trust your godfather, support him. He wants only what is best. Remember all that you and he used to talk of. One day it will all be your responsibility.'

'I have not forgotten,' he said, 'but my lord of Leicester has chosen a hard path.'

His use of the title instead of the more familiar address did not escape her. 'Edward, if I could only make you see . . .'

'I see more clearly than I used,' he answered and shut his mouth hard. How could he speak of the feelings he now had for her husband? 'My dear aunt, never will I forget your love and kindness to me. Be assured at least of that.'

He bent to kiss her and before she had the chance to say more he bowed and left the bower. A few moments later she saw him ride away to the west and as their cavalcade disappeared into the leafy green where the road wound between woods, a lonely heron winged its way across the river. There seemed to her something ominous about the slow flapping, the solitariness of the bird. It had been nesting nearby and she wondered why it was deserting its young, watching it as it vanished into the blue distance.

That afternoon her two younger sons left to busy themselves with their tournament, and it was less than a week later that they sent a message to say Gloucester had refused to come. He no longer trusted his person among them. At the same time news reached Odiham that Mortimer was back and that William de Valence had landed at Pembroke with quite a considerable following.

'Then I must leave at first light,' Simon said to his wife. 'I must have the King under my hand and scotch the danger in the west before they can raise too great an army against me.'

He could do nothing else, she thought. His enemies were gathering and she was aware of bitterness, of aching disappointment, of frustration that no one wanted what Simon had to give them. They feared him yet, she thought with Plantagenet pride. If she and Simon sat at Westminster the barons could scarcely be worse off than under Henry who got sillier with age.

'I must make my position stronger,' Simon said, as if reading her thoughts. 'After all, legally I hold no position at all, except Steward of England. I think I shall write to my great-aunt Loretta. Incredible woman, she is past ninety and still as lively minded as ever! I had that office from her husband and perhaps she will know some detail of how I may use it to gain my way.'

Elinor said, 'So much has gone wrong since you won the fight at Lewes. I thought then all would go well.'

He gave a wry smile. 'Did you? Then you were more sanguine than I. Let us not deceive ourselves: I have more enemies than friends.'

'If Edward had stayed loyal –'

'Perhaps we might have held the peace,' he finished. 'But Edward has too great an ambition, too high a heritage to want to stand in my shadow, even for a few years.' He looked very weary and at supper seemed to have no appetite. Later, when she had seen the Demoiselle settled into bed and allayed as far as possible the girl's fears for her father, her brothers, her lover, Eleanor went to her own bedchamber. Simon was not there and knowing intuitively where at this late hour she would find him, she slipped a mantle about her shoulders and went across the bailey to the chapel. The sentries on watch stood stiffly as she passed, well-drilled men alert at their posts, knowing their lord's stern penalty if they were slack about their duties. The dark night was heavy with rain clouds, the first drops falling. It was darker still inside the little building for knowing every stone of it Simon had carried no light. But he was there as she expected, kneeling before the enshrined Host, only the tiny sanctuary lamp burning, his hands clasped, his eyes fixed, deep set and hollow. She knelt, signing herself and he turned his head.

'Come away,' she said. 'My heart, you need rest.'

'Rest?' he queried in a low voice. '"Arise and let us be going for this is no place to rest". Is that Job, or perhaps it is Micah? But it is true for me. It is better that I watch for I think my hardest hour is yet to come.'

'Even Our Blessed Lord had to sleep,' she said and felt the tears stinging her eyes. 'You cannot lead our people if your strength is wasted.'

'Perhaps not, yet I think my strength lies here, in God's hands, to give or take away.'

'You have watched long enough. His blessing is on you, my love, I know it, but come away now. Sleep for a few hours at least.'

He was silent for a moment, his head bent. Then he crossed himself and rose stiffly to his feet. 'I have asked Walter to say Mass at dawn, so I will try to sleep until then. Indeed, to rest in your arms would be balm before I leave.'

Together they left the chill dark chapel and went slowly up to their bedchamber, undressed and lay in bed, naked, side by side. His body was painfully thin and she drew his head, as so often before, to rest on her shoulder. The spring rain was falling heavily now and she said softly, 'Do you remember how it rained the day we played backgammon in this very room and you told me that you loved me?'

In her arms the tension seemed to be leaving him. 'I remember every moment of that day; and the day of our bridal. We said bad weather was our good fortune.'

'Perhaps it will be again. Can you hear the rain?'

'Aye,' he said dreamily. 'I have always liked the sound of it. Beloved, there is so much I would say to you, but I am too tired tonight and tomorrow I'll be gone, so it must wait until I come again.'

'What is it, my heart? Not further trouble?'

'No,' he said unexpectedly. 'It is only that I have been so busy, so overwrought of late, all of England in my care and yet – tonight I feel that nothing else is so important as loving you. You have always been, you are, the wife I desired that day so long ago, nearly thirty years.'

She had not heard him talk like this before and in sudden fear her arms tightened about him. 'And you are life to me. Nothing, not even death could separate us.'

'Not even death,' he answered and for a little while they lay in silence, close to each other, every curve and shape known and loved.

Neither could help but be aware that he was riding away to a final confrontation, that he must have victory or lose all he had striven for. And, if he lost, his chance of survival would be small. Mother of God, she prayed desperately, give him victory, keep him safe, bring him back to me.

His hands were pressing her body even closer now and she could feel his bones starkly as he possessed her once more. But his love-making was quiet, with less of passion than of a desire for a union that might sustain him when he was gone, a union born out of the shared years, a need in the face of what the future might bring.

He gave a long deep sigh and presently she thought he slept, but she lay awake in the darkness, torn with fear for him, longing to keep every moment of this night, feeling the loved warmth of him close to her, the weight of his head against her shoulder. She turned her lips into his hair, grey now but thick as always. Ah, whatever came, she would not change one hour of her life with him!

She slept at last, fitfully, and awoke as the first glimmering of light lifted the darkness of their bedchamber. His face was softened in sleep, the anxious lines smoothed, the mouth gentle, and she looked long as if to impress every line into her memory, a dull ache of dread heavy on her. She bent to kiss his lips and he stirred into wakefulness. 'It is getting light,' she said and he answered, 'Then I must go.'

CHAPTER ELEVEN

A silent army was riding westwards led by men nominally at peace, their reconciliation blessed by the Church, but with very different feelings in their hearts. Simon rode with his chin on his breast. Gilbert, Earl of Gloucester had broken openly with him now, jealous and bitterly offended, and Simon saw, too late, the wisdom of Eleanor's words. Gilbert, young as he was, was a better man than his father had ever been, and it might have been worth the effort to cultivate his better qualities, take the trouble to keep him loyal. But there had been so many other matters on his mind and now the breach was beyond mending.

He had Henry and Edward with him, mainly that he might keep them under surveillance, the three of them supposedly reconciled. Gilbert and Mortimer with de Valence were skulking in the Forest of Dean, and one last bid for terms carried out by Simon's close friend, Bishop Cantelupe of Worcester, had failed. The King's cousin, de Warenne, Earl of Surrey, slipped away to join the rebels and their forces grew. It would come to a fight soon, Simon thought, and wondered how far the father and son riding either side of him would be assets in the conflict. No, the agreement between them was not worth the parchment it was written on, for they wished him dead.

It was Maytime and the peasants tending their fields watched the passing army with dulled eyes.

They knew only too well that if those great lords astride their destriers, dressed in chain mail with swords at their sides, were to join battle with their enemies, the carefully sown crops would be trampled and poor men would face starvation next winter. But in one or two villages men cried out God's blessing on the Lord Simon, for if they suffered loss he would punish the marauders and see them recompensed, whereas if the King won he would make promises and do nothing.

Henry also rode in silence, his face as sullen as those of his meanest subjects. He hated the loss of power, of luxury and comfort, for Simon in his preoccupation cared little for such things. He hated the separation from his beloved Queen whom he had not seen since last year, and he hated the helplessness he felt in the company of his brother-in-law, his wishes counting for nothing any more.

'How far is it to Hereford?' he asked petulantly. 'Are we to have no rest today?'

Simon answered, 'There is bread and meat and wine ready, sire, but I will not pause longer than to rest the horses. I will be in Hereford before dark.'

'I am tired,' Henry said. 'Surely is some suitable lodging between here and the city.'

'None that I consider safe.'

The King sat slumped in the saddle. 'Jesu, will you never be at peace, nor let other men be?'

Simon turned to look at him, a shaft of memory carrying him back to the early days of their friendship when he could do no wrong. 'I have always wanted peace,' he said, 'but not at the price of my honour – no, nor of England's welfare.'

It was nearly dark when they reached Hereford and the King lodged in the best chamber of the castle, demanding that supper be served to him when he was in his bed.

Simon sat in conference with his most able lieutenants, the Earls of Norfolk and Arundel, the Justiciar Hugh Despenser, and one or two others. If they could deal quickly with Gilbert and Mortimer there was a fair chance that the King and Edward, robbed of these powerful allies, would settle for a permanent truce. At last Simon sought a pallet in the ante-chamber outside Henry's room and when Harry, coming to bid him goodnight, asked if he and Edward might race their horses outside the walls in the morning to settle a wager, Simon gave his consent, too weary to consider so trifling a matter, stipulating only that Harry should take sufficient armed men with him.

It was a brilliant morning when the cousins rode out, seemingly on the best of terms. Edward made great play of his new charger, sent to him by Roger Leyburn, now with Gloucester. He beat Harry easily and then tried out several other mounts owned by the knights accompanying them. The young men lolled on the ground, watching their lords, relaxing in the warm sun, and when Harry ordered ale to be brought, they all drank together. He flung his arm about Edward and said how glad he was that there was no more enmity between them.

Edward looked deep into his mug of ale and said, 'You're a good fellow, Harry, but you've much to learn about –' he paused and a smile crossed his face as he finished the sentence, ' – about horses.'

'Then let my grey race yours again,' Harry said. 'Give me a chance to win back my wager.'

'Ten marks then,' Edward agreed. 'You are wealthier than I now for your father keeps a tight hold on my purse strings.'

'I wish you would not say things like that. When we have beaten the rebels all that will be altered.'

Edward lay back on the grass, his hands behind his head. He seemed inordinately long stretched out thus on the turf. 'By Our Lady, you always were over-sanguine, Harry. Did you note that minstrel who came after supper last night and sang so sweetly?'

'I saw him. Why?'

'Naught.' Edward was laughing. 'But I adjure you to think of him now and ask yourself if his shape was not somewhat voluptuous for a man.'

Harry gaped. 'What are you saying? Do you tell me he – she – was a woman? And what should that signify but a freakish jest? Or,' he grinned amiably, 'did this minstrel beguile your bed for you?'

'I only wish there were more like her,' Edward said ambiguously.

'You are talking nonsense. Only a woman of no virtue would dress thus and sing before the court.'

'My great-grandmother once put on man's clothes to elude my great-grandfather's vengeance,' Edward told him. 'And they say old Henry's vengeance was something to be feared. She was caught and shut up in Winchester Castle, but my minstrel is long gone. Only remember her.'

'In God's name, why?' Harry laid down his mug and jumped up without waiting for an answer. 'Aren't we here to race?'

'Indeed,' Edward agreed, 'but my groom has a black I've not yet tried – a poor enough mount, I fear, but he needs exercise.'

'Are you so eager to throw your money away then?' Harry mounted his own percheron and Edward's man brought up the black. For a brief second it crossed Harry's mind that the horse was not so poor a specimen as his cousin claimed, but though his own grey was already tired for a while they went neck and neck. And then suddenly Edward set spurs to the black. The horse, quite fresh, leapt forward before Harry realized what was happening, and Edward was away, galloping across the springy turf towards a clump of trees.

Startled, Harry dug in his own spurs, but on his blown horse he could not hope to catch his cousin. Some instinct warned him and he yelled to his companions who scrambled to their feet, dashing for their wandered horses, seizing reins, leaping into their saddles.

But it was too late. A large group of horsemen appeared from the trees and Edward rode into their midst, disappearing at once into the thick green foliage.

It was a hopeless pursuit and Harry drew rein. His knights and armed men came up and cursing them with rare savagery he sat breathless in the saddle, beating his fist and again on his pommel.

Simon was furious. He treated Harry to a diatribe such as his son had never heard from him, and knowing he deserved it be stood still, scarlet-faced and ashamed.

'Do you know what you have done?' Simon thundered. 'By your folly you have put us all in danger. Edward has gone to Gloucester, that's plain enough, and now they will raise a great army with Edward's banner to float over it. By the arm of St James, I did not think any son of mine could be so stupid, so gullible. I am tempted to whip you myself! As for this tale of a woman minstrel, that is how it was planned! Did you not at least suspect when Edward told you of her? No, I suppose you would not. How sure Edward must have been of your credulity to tell you of it! He will laugh over this for the rest of his life.'

'I thought he was boasting of a conquest,' Harry muttered.

'A conquest! Edward has more craft in his little finger than you have in your whole head. I would have guessed there was some meaning in what he said. God in Heaven, he may well have a different sort of conquest to boast of before long. He was a prize in my hand and you have lost him to me. You have served me very ill this day, my son.'

When the angry words ceased, Harry, unable to stem the tears of shame and bitter remorse, stumbled away to his own quarters, and when Guy also told him he was a fool Harry for once lost his temper and struck Guy across the mouth. And Guy, the fiery, flung out of the chamber, letting the blow pass with rare forbearance, but he notched up the incident as one more in a list of items to be avenged one day on his royal cousins.

Simon sent for young Martin Finch and despatched him to Odiham. Eleanor was in the still-room when a servant came to announce the messenger from her lord. She loved this narrow stone chamber near the wine-cellar, with its aroma of spices and herbs, the large jars of nuts and dried fruits. She spent an occasional half hour here distilling concoctions of her own against the fever, purges for stomach troubles, crushed almond milk for the complexion. Such ingredients were expensive and she carefully locked the door with her own key before going up the stair to find young Martin Finch.

He poured out the story of Edward's escape and she listened in growing consternation, aware only too well that the charisma of Edward's personality and the tale of his daring bid for freedom would bring young men flocking to his banner. Martin ended by saying that his lord desired urgently that she should go at once to Dover Castle, take charge of that vital stronghold herself and send her son, Sir Simon, to raise all the forces he could from Kenilworth.

She needed no time to consider. 'I will ride at once. Get a fresh horse and come with me, Martin.'

'Aye, my lady, but it will be dark soon and I don't know this part of the country.'

'Then find Dobbe the shepherd. His cottage is the one by the bridge. He knows every inch of the land about here and he will guide us.'

Without further question Martin ran to do her bidding while she hurried to her bower, changing her fine gown for a plain dress belonging to Dionysia and a plain black cloak and hood. She gave orders for the rest of her household to pack all moveable goods into wagons and join her at Dover as soon as they might. The Demoiselle begged to come with her but her mother shook her head.

'No, my dear. You told your father that you are a woman now and you must act as one. I leave you to see that all is properly done here. We will leave only a small garrison, everyone else must come to Dover; your father would not have sent such a message it if was not imperative that I should get there with all speed and I shall do it best without any encumbrances.' She kissed her daughter and hurried away to the bailey where Martin stood holding the horses, old Dobbe regarding his with suspicion for he was unused to riding.

'You must lead us,' Eleanor told him. 'You have eyes like the night owl.' Martin helped her into the saddle and looking down at him she thought how like his father he was, silent and dependable.

Dusk was falling as they rode out and after the first mile it became quite dark. The summer night was warm, the sky like velvet above them. They rode carefully, Dobbe watching for pot holes and uneven stretches in the track that served for a road. He seldom spoke, sitting like a sack uneasily in the saddle, his eyes on the ground, but he enabled them to keep up a good pace. About midnight they rested the horses and again at three o'clock. Martin helped his lady from the saddle and she sat on a hummock of grass, stiff and a little cold now in the chill of the small hours, a prey to hideous anxieties but concentrating on what her beloved asked of her.

She thought of Edward's escape and could have cried with vexation at Harry's trustful folly. How could he have been so mad as to let Edward slip away? Now indeed Simon faced a formidable enemy and in the low spirits of this night hour, without sleep, chilled to the bone, she knew the depths of fear and doubt. They rode on again and odd memories came to her during that silent ride, headlong now that they were on the main road. She thought of how once she had said to Isabella that Odiham would be easy prey for an enemy and laughed at the idea she might ever be attacked; how she had joked with Edward at Kenilworth, said she could not imagine he would ever want to besiege her. Now he was her enemy and Simon's in reality and the knowledge was hard to bear, but there was fighting spirit in her still and between her prayers for Simon's desperate situation she urged Finch and the shepherd on.

By dawn they had reached the hill above Dover, a mist from the sea heralding another warm day. The grey castle stood out strongly on ·the cliffs. In a short while she was within the walls and storming up the stair to her son's bedchamber. A scared servant tried to go before her, to assure her he would rouse Sir Simon but she thrust him aside and opened the door. Simon was in bed, sprawled beside the body of a girl whose pale hair fanned out across the pillow.

As she pushed the door shut in the face of a stupefied page, Simon roused himself, blinking in surprise. Eleanor flung back the clothes and seized the naked girl by the arm, thrusting a wrap towards her. 'Get up – go!' she commanded. 'Leave at once!'

The girl, pitchforked from sleep to be confronted by this urgent, angry woman, grabbed at her gown, covering herself as best she could and stumbled from the room while Simon sat staring at his mother in astonishment.

'In God's name what is all this about?' he demanded. 'I am no boy, mother, that you should –'

'Get up!' she repeated. 'Why are you sleeping at such moment?' She had forgotten that he did not know what had happened. Hastily explaining she bade him take all the troops but those she needed for defence and hasten to raise the men of Kenilworth for his father's aid.

Simon got out of bed and began to dress, unimpressed by the need for such urgency. 'Father is more than a match for Edward, and the King was never any good at fighting,' he said casually and Eleanor stamped her foot.

'Simon, you do not know how bad it is. The King is still with your father, and it is Edward and Gloucester and Mortimer and de Valence that are against him now. All the marcher lords are joining the rebels. Go – go, or it will mean your father's life.'

He thought her hysterical, overwrought and tried to soothe her, assuring her that he held the Cinque Ports and no help could come from across the channel.

'You will be safe here,' he assured her and she cut across his words.

'Do you think it is my safety I care for?' She caught him by the arms, half shaking him. He must not fail now, this second son whom she had always thought so reliable.

But it was the very slowness of his nature that was to prove his undoing. He went, taking a fair body of men with him but on the way paused to sack a priory, bang a few opponents and, still smarting from the loss of his rich widow, to amuse himself with the wife of one of the knights he slew, wasting a day and a night instead of marching on.

He came to Kenilworth at last and settled his considerable forces in the grounds of the abbey, about the gatehouse, and some in cottages in the village. In one of these he held a conference with his leading knights over supper, ordering the march for the morrow. They drank deep and he decided to sleep there instead of returning to the castle; for Finch had come with adequate supplies of food and drink and was busy bringing out fresh mounts. He rolled in his cloak by the fire and slept, snoring gently.

An hour before first light every man in the place was awakened by the sound of trumpets. Simon catapulted himself from his bed, yelled to Finch to know what was happening and together they burst into the road. Everywhere men were tumbling from the cottages, from the bivouacks on the ground where they had slept. Simon seized a foot soldier, pelting towards the castle gate.

'What is it? God's curse on you, what is it?'

'The Lord Edward,' the man gabbled, 'the Lord Edward! He is on us, I saw his banner!'

'Jesu!' Simon said and felt the colour drain from his face. 'I thought he was at Worcester.'

The confusion was awful. Men were scurrying about, trying to find armour and weapons, to form into some sort of order, knights yelling to their followers, struggling to mount in the darkness, shouting orders that no one heard as the remorseless enemy drove down on them.

Simon ran from one group to another, bawling at them to run for the castle, but before he or they could get to the gates, Edward's men were upon them and the castellan had hastily to raise the drawbridge against friend and foe alike.

The street, the abbey grounds, the meadows had become one mass of struggling men; Edward's voice was heard shouting in triumph and Simon had one glimpse in the light of the waning moon of his cousin's tall figure beneath the banner of England. He saw several of his friends struck down, saw the Earl of Oxford seized and dragged away, saw Finch with some of his old strength try to pull an enemy from the saddle only to be spitted with .a sword, falling beneath the hooves of the rearing charger.

The surprise had been complete, the fight lost before it ever began. Turning, Simon ran by paths he knew as well in the darkness as in the light and with one or two who joined him flung off his shoes and plunged into the waters of the mere. Swimming strongly he reached the walls of the castle and the step to the postern gate. Ahead of his companions he reached down to help them out and a moment, later, dripping and breathless, they were inside.

He leaned against the stone wall, sick with humiliation and shame, most of his army lost, utterly helpless. But even he, at that moment, did not know the enormity of his failure. He staggered up the steps, calling for dry clothes and went to the turret of the keep where he could look down on his cousin's banner, planted firmly in the ground not fifty yards from the pool.

CHAPTER TWELVE

All through the hot day the long lines of men waded the River Severn. They were tired and hungry and in hopes of finding food and shelter on the far side where Hereford would be open to them.

There were few boats but one of these ferried the King and the Earl of Leicester to the far side. Henry sat slumped, weary with being carted about the marches by this pale gaunt man who had no thought for food or rest, but Edward surely was on the way to rescue him? Edward was proving himself a soldier, from all he heard, and he would deal with this rabble of some four thousand tired men, no great army! During the last weeks, treating with Llewellyn of Wales, he had never seen Simon smile, seldom a lift to the grim expression and now, sitting side by side in the boat, they did not speak.

Once on land Simon held a conference with his closest associates, the Earl of Arundel, John de Vescy, loyal as ever, Henry Percy, and Hugh Despenser the Justiciar.

'My son Simon will be marching to join us with all the forces from Kenilworth,' he said. 'We must go east to meet him and then we will have men enough.'

'But the Lord Edward is not at Worcester where we thought he was,' Arundel objected. 'Your scout told us the town was empty. Where has he gone? Can he have marched on London – or to besiege Kenilworth?'

'The scout could not get close enough to see which road he took. Edward has learned some lessons,' Simon said. 'He has not forgotten his one sentry at Lewes. But if we march for Evesham we shall cut off his route to London and we shall be half way to Kenilworth.'

'We're in no fit state for battle,' Percy put in. He was a hard-headed blunt Northumbrian with a shock of red hair, and though his loyalty was unshaken his commonsense told him the sands were running out unless some drastic action was taken.

'Surprise is worth a thousand men,' his north-country companion de Vescy told him briskly, little guessing how right he was as far as Edward was concerned. 'The Lord Edward does not know what we will do any more than we know his movement at this moment. And as my lord of Leicester says, Sir Simon may well be on his way to us by now.'

'Providing he got to Kenilworth,' Arundel added gloomily.

'Of course he got to Kenilworth.' Still ashamed of his own failure to hold Edward, a failure which had brought the present situation on them all, Harry refused to believe his brother would not be more alert. In any case they knew for certain Edward had made Worcester his headquarters and was surely unlikely to know of Simon's march from Dover.

'The men of Kenilworth are at least well trained,' Guy said in his arrogant manner. 'Don't fear, my lord Arundel, they will be with us soon.'

Arundel, plainly wishing he was anywhere but where he was, gave him a sour look. 'We may all well pray that your brother understands our need.'

The men were across the river now, their wet clothes drying in the hot sun, and Simon gave the order to move on. He rode in the van, his eyes fixed between his horse's ears. He had wasted time in the marches, of that he was sure, but he had gone to link up with Llewellyn, to receive some of the much needed gold that Llewellyn had promised as part of their agreement, but the Welshmen had only been able to raise half of the money and he had had to accept what that likeable but unreliable young man chose to give with only promises for the rest.

Simon thought of his daughter, her eyes bright with young love. He would hate to take that light from her eyes but if Llewellyn did not fulfil his side of the settlement it might have to be done. As always his thoughts went then to Eleanor, far away in Dover, for that she had done what he asked he had no doubt. When would he see her again? He was under no illusion as to the gravity of the situation. His enemies –Edward, Gloucester, Mortimer and the rest, with de Valence raising the men of Pembroke – had an army that must amount to more than twice the number under his command. All he could do was to try to repeat the surprise of Lewes and by God, if he took Gilbert the Red that young man would repent of his treachery! By late afternoon the last of the baronial army had filed through the pleasant vale of Evesham, taking apples from the trees to allay their hunger – though the fruit was scarcely ripe, and before darkness came all were safely in the town and scrambling for lodgings.

Simon slept in a merchant's house with Henry in the same room, a brief exhausted sleep, but by dawn he was up and dressing. A man came to his chamber and announced that there was good news.

'We can see an army coming, my lord, and your own banners at the head of it. It must be Sir Simon.'

'God be praised!' Simon was tying the strings of his jack. 'Have the horns sounded. Sire, it is time to be up.'

Henry sat up slowly, his face pink and puffy with sleep, his thin grey hair disordered. 'We have not heard Mass. If you will summon my chaplain –'

Simon hesitated and then went to the door. Now that his son was here, haste was not so imperative and he was never willing to forgo what was due to God, but before he could call for the King's priest, there was a further commotion below. A voice cried out desperately that he must see the Earl and the fear in that sharp cry made Simon order him up the stair, asking, 'What is it? Out with it, man!'

'My lord!' The fellow scrambled up, tripping on the last step in his haste. He was a barber by trade and he had once served at Kenilworth. 'My lord, I went up the abbey tower to look, to rejoice that Sir Simon has come, but – but – they are your banners, my lord, but captured. It is a ruse. The Lord Edward is on us, with all his army.'

'Jesu!' Simon stood still for one moment, paralysed by the unexpected blow. Harry and Guy had tumbled from their beds and come to find out what was happening and Harry cried out, 'Oh God, is Simon dead?'

Pale and grim, their father gave his orders, the men to be assembled at once in full battle array. There could be no surprise now, for Edward had seized that advantage, and if he had marched so swiftly to destroy the Kenilworth reinforcements and then return here, he was becoming a general beyond Simon's reckoning.

Deep in his anxiety for his second son, Simon swung round on the King. 'Dress, sire. There's no time for Mass now but commend your soul to God for you will stand with us in battle, and in plain harness.'

'Mother of God!' Henry cried out. 'Would you have my own men, perhaps my own son, kill me?'

'God shall decide between us this day,' Simon retorted. Two squires had brought his hauberk of mail and were helping him into it. He pulled his mail hood over his head himself and set a flat-topped helm firmly over it. Another squire had brought a soldier's gambeson and mail tunic for the King, and Simon watched as he was hurried into it.

'You have brought all this on us, your subjects,' he said sternly, 'and by the arm of St James, you will face it with us.'

A hasty consultation was held below. Scouts came hurrying to their leader, reporting Mortimer on one bank of the loop of the river, Gloucester's troops on the other, and ahead on the flat ground between the two banks lay the whole strength of Edward's own division. Their only hope was to try to cut their way through that centre and make for the Alcester road and Kenilworth.

A sudden breeze had risen, storm clouds driving up from the east and hiding the blue of the summer sky. Simon called his sons to him. 'We are in a desperate position,' he said in a low voice. 'Pray for God's protection this day, for without a miracle our bodies are at the mercy of our enemies. And if the day goes badly one of you must try to reach your mother.'

Impulsively Harry embraced his father while Guy stood gripping his sword hilt; his swarthy face grim.

From Evesham Abbey came the sound of chanting. Despite the imminence of a battle at their very gate the monks were singing the office of Prime, some pale and fearful, but discipline keeping their hands folded, the procession into the choir as orderly as usual.

Simon heard the sound and his mouth tightened. The King said with sudden passion, his voice shaking, 'If I am slain you will burn in hell, Simon de Montfort, and my son will wreak such a vengeance as you and yours have never seen.'

Simon answered, 'It is in God's hands,' and turned his attention to positioning his men. A few large spots of rain fell and there was a clap of thunder overhead. Some of the men cried out that it was an omen, but for or against which side they did not know.

The army filed out in a tight block, no diverging to deal with Mortimer or Gloucester. Simon's experience told him that the centre was his only hope, where Edward had drawn up, this time taking the advantage of a small rise in the ground. There seemed to be no end to that daunting mass of enemy soldiers.

Simon set Henry slightly to the rear of himself, in the centre of the horsemen. He knew it was unjustifiable yet he did not reverse the order. Henry was the author of twenty years of trouble, of enmity against himself and Eleanor, and this was to be the reckoning. He bowed his head and crossed himself and with one last brief prayer, for Eleanor as well as for himself, he commended them both to the care of the Blessed Virgin and gripped his lance in his gauntleted hand. There would be no half-measures now – it would be victory or death. His years seemed to slide away, the weariness, the disillusion gone. He would make something of this fight, by God, and if it was to be his last at least he would die for a cause he believed in. And that cause would surely, somehow, survive him in the years to come, for he had fought for it for so long.

With his sons one on each side of him he led the first attack against Edward's knights. On horseback, his knees pressed hard against the animal's flanks, reins twisted round the pommel, he plunged forward. Beside and behind him some hundred and sixty cavalry followed him and such was the force of their attack that Edward's line sagged in the middle. Simon struck out and saw a man go down, broke his lance on another's shield, drew his sword and brought it down in a great thrust, using his shield painted with his emblem to deflect a blow. The battle was joined in earnest, and added to the clash of weapons, the battle cries, the screams of wounded horses and men alike, was the noise of the thunder. Sudden shafts of lightning illuminated the scene and while the fight raged below a summer storm shook the sky above.

Simon was in the thick of it now. He sensed the enemy rallying after the first shock and shouted encouragement to his men, though it was doubtful if they could hear him. He saw Hugh Despenser go down and after him both Arundel and Percy. He fought on, swinging his sword with the accuracy for which he was famed, losing none of his skill with the years, and he was spattered with the blood of those he had slain. He became aware of Gloucester's banner nearby, implying the

Earl had broken his flank, and in an access of passion sought to cut his way through to it, to use his weapon on Gilbert so that more than Gilbert's hair should be red, but before he could do so he heard a sharp cry. A lance thrust with deadly aim had pierced Harry's chest, and with both hands at it, he was swaying in the saddle. A slash from a sword had bloodied his face and as he fell horses trampled him under foot.

Simon gave one sharp anguished cry and tried to reach him but it was too late. In an agony of grief he struck at an enemy horseman, his sword deep in the man's belly.

Somewhere behind him a high-pitched voice was calling, 'I am your King! I am Henry of Winchester – don't slay me – don't slay your King!'

Momentarily distracted he paused. Had the enemy fought their way through and cut him off? But that pause was fatal. A terrific clap of thunder overhead seemed like a stark pronouncement of doom and he cried out involuntarily, 'God's grace!' as a battle axe came down on him, cleaving him at the joint of neck and shoulder. He swayed, his mouth full of blood, his throat burning. He tried to raise his shield but his enemies were encircling him now; a sword was driven with unerring aim at his chest, forcing the chain mail inwards. Choking on his own blood, in an agony of pain, he fell from his horse and was aware of someone standing over him, a two-handed sword poised. From out of the roaring in his ears, from the smell and taste of blood, he saw the blow coming, but of its fall, swift and sure, he was no longer conscious.

The rain began to fall, heavy summer rain, washing the blood from dead faces.

The Lord Edward, with his father free, his first great victory under his hand, his men hailing him as a great soldier, found as many had done that victory was not all triumph and joy. That night he stood beside the monks in Evesham Abbey and watched the body of his cousin Harry lowered into a grave below a paving stone in the nave. He had loved Harry, despite everything, and now he remembered only their youth together, Harry's laughter, the hunting, the shooting at the butts, the drinking and feasting, and he wept, the tears running unchecked down his face.

Outside, one of Mortimer's men bore the head of Simon, Earl of Leicester, stuck high on a spear for all to see. One of those who saw it was the younger Simon, breasting the rise with the remaining men of Kenilworth gathered after Edward had raised the siege. There was no mistaking that iron-grey head, the loved features. He rocked in his saddle in a paroxysm of grief, of shame and horror and bitter remorse, and then he and his small army turned and fled from the tragedy he might have prevented.

Eleanor sat alone in a small square room in Dover Castle. Beyond lay the sea, blue and calm today under an October sky, a ship waiting to sail, loaded with all the goods and furniture and money that she had left. Her face was pallid with grief and strain, her eyes shadowed, no tears left now, only numbness and a chill in her that neither sunshine nor fire could warm. She wore a russet gown once more and she smoothed the skirt, remembering Cecily de Sanford and the dreary days after William's death. Then she had been young, and youthful resilience had come to her aid, grief passing with time, but today she felt old, with nothing left to live for.

She had wept until she could weep no more, crushed by the enormity of the holocaust that had swept away Simon and Harry. Young Simon was besieged in Kenilworth, Guy wounded and a prisoner. Only Amaury and the Demoiselle were with her. They tried to offer comfort, but there was no comfort anywhere. Even gentle Adam Marsh was dead and though her chaplain here tried to speak soothing words she cried out in rebellion against God – until she remembered Easter and how she had implored Him that He would give Simon rest. He had answered that prayer indeed, for He had taken Simon to the longest rest of all.

When she could think again, she had appealed to Henry. He was after all still her brother, but in the stern vengeance that followed Evesham, he would not listen. She wondered if he even read her letters. Now she was banished, to leave England today with no more than the possessions she had here in Dover Castle, and she had sent her daughter and her women out of the room, intolerable sorrow threatening to take away her reason. She knew it all now, all the horror of the battle, the shame inflicted on that dear body she had loved. If she could have killed in her own revenge she would have done it. He had not deserved that desecration – was it not enough for them that he was dead? When she asked for his body, they had said that Mortimer's men had so mutilated it, it had been hard to find the remains for burial.

She sat quite still, her hands gripped together, trying to shut the awful images from her mind – the blood, the smashed bones, the brutality of the victorious on the battlefield. Out of his one hundred and sixty knights only twelve survived.

She set both hands before her eyes, gasping with dry sobs yet again, the pictures tormenting her into an agony that seemed insupportable, and in her grief she did not hear a step outside, nor the knock on the door.

In a moment, a hand was set on her arm and a familiar voice said, 'My dear aunt, don't – I beg of you. Let me get you some wine.'

She made an effort and recovered herself sufficiently to look up. Edward was on one knee beside her, as tall as an average man even in that posture. He had a cup of wine in his hand, concern on his face.

She took the cup with a shaking hand and drank. 'I – I did not think you would come to me yourself. Once my castellan had surrendered – '

'I can never forget you are my aunt.' His voice was gentle. 'Nor that you were so often kind to me at Kenilworth. I could not let you go without saying farewell.' He got up and finding a stool sat down facing her. 'I have things to say that may cheer you a little.'

She set the cup down on the table by her side. 'There is nothing left for me in this life.'

'Perhaps not, but I have heard news of my cousin Simon. You know we were besieging him in Kenilworth? Well,' he smiled a little, 'he always was a good swimmer – I remember you and I watching him from your window. Now he has swum the moat again, this time away from the castle and it seems likely he has joined a group of reb– friends of his who are holding out on the Isle of Axholm.'

A little life came into her face. 'Pray God he at least is safe.'

'My uncle Richard told me he owes his life to Simon.' When she looked up, startled, he went on, 'Perhaps you did not know that Simon nearly reached the field in time? But he saw it was all over and rode back to Kenilworth with any that had escaped. They wanted to be avenged and my uncle says that they would have hanged him from the gatehouse if Simon had not stopped them. So even if we take Simon he will receive at least his life – though I cannot promise his freedom.'

She gave an unsteady sigh. 'That was noble of him. I would not have wanted Richard to die. And Guy?'

'He is recovering from his wounds.'

'Thank God. Edward – ' she made a great effort – 'I wish I could find it in me to forgive what you have done but I can't. You destroyed a man who was greater than you can know, and you and my brother and all your lords have exacted a terrible retribution. You have soiled victory with cruelty – I know, I have heard.'

'I am sorry,' he said and for the first time his voice was cold. 'War is a harsh business and my father will have no more rebellion while he lives.'

'Rebellion!' she echoed. 'Simon fought only for what was right. Even you cannot fail to see that your father –'

He interrupted her. 'I'll not listen to a word against him after all he has suffered at my uncle's hands. Earl Simon made a mockery of kingship. This last year, since Lewes, he made my father – nothing!

And God has punished him and all those who fought under his banner. Not one of them will be left with enough substance to defy us again.'

'You are cruel,' she said again. 'I did not know you could be so cruel.'

'Not so,' he returned, 'only realistic. And you know what he did to my father, setting him in the centre of the battle in plain harness. He wanted him killed.'

'Oh no, no,' she cried out, 'I'll not believe that. If he did, it was only that Henry might know what his folly had brought on him.'

'We had best not talk of it,' Edward said heavily. He thought of the dying moments of the battle, the thunderstorm, the sweeping summer rain, and Mortimer's men closing in, hacking Leicester's body to pieces. He had put a stop to that at least, and going back to the door he picked up a small casket he had set down on a stool there. 'I have brought you this. It contains his right hand.'

Shock made her reel for a moment, clasping the arm of her chair, but she reached out, trembling, to take the box. For several moments she held it, and then, slowly steeling herself, she opened it. Yes, that was his hand, the wrist wrapped in a piece of red silk, the hand that had so often caressed her, bearing still the ring she had given him. Still slowly she bent and set her lips to it, finding it marble cold. Then she closed the box. 'This shall be sealed. No one else shall see it.'

She steadied her voice and went on, 'I do not know why it was God's will that he should be struck down, but this I do know. He is with God now, but none of you will forget him.'

Edward was silent for a moment. Then he said, 'I will try to remember the past, when we were friends, before this bloody reckoning. And not all he worked for will be lost, I will see to that. As for you, dear aunt, I am sorry you must leave England, but at least you have your freedom.'

'I have only grief and loneliness,' she said. 'Tell them below I will be ready in half an hour.'

He put her hand to his lips without speaking again and when the door had shut behind him, she went to stand by the window.

Her people were embarking; she could see Martin Finch, looking so much older since that wild night ride and the loss of his father, helping Mary and Dionysia with their baggage, and then the Demoiselle, sobbing again, and Amaury with his arm round her. Poor child, Eleanor thought, she wept as much for her lost lover in far away Wales as for her dead father and brother.

And then Eleanor too wept, one last fierce storm of tears, crying out his name again and again. Memories beat at her consciousness, memories of him at Odiham, on their wedding day, his face when he beheld their first-born, in sleep when he lay beside her. All through the years they had been one in thought, the few sudden and flaring quarrels dying as quickly, always healed by the night's passion. What was it he had said on that last night, neither of them knowing it was the last? Or had he had some instinct that his course was run. 'Nothing is as important as loving you.' It had seemed as if there was more, as if he wanted, before parting, to talk of things for which there had been no time. Now there would never be time.

Dear God, she thought, could such grief be borne? She was a Princess of England, but it was as Simon's wife that she was being banished and at least she could have pride in that. She would have it no other way – if men remembered her it would be as Simon's widow.

She straightened her dress and tidied her wimple, and then holding the casket as if it was a holy relic, opened the door and went with slow dignity down the stair and out to the waiting ship.

HISTORICAL NOTE

Eleanor spent the rest of her life in the convent at Montargis living on a small pension from Henry. Simon and Guy eventually escaped to the continent and in 1271 murdered their cousin Henry of Almaine at Viterbo in Italy while he was at Mass. They could not forgive his betrayal of their father. Simon died in hiding and Guy in prison a few years later, leaving only daughters of his marriage to an Italian lady.

The Demoiselle was married by proxy to her Welsh Prince shortly before her mother's death in 1272, but on her way to join him her ship was captured by her cousin, now King Edward I, and it was not until three years later that he made terms with Llewellyn and allowed the marriage to take place in fact. She and Llewellyn were happy together but sadly she died in childbed four years later. Her daughter was taken to England to the nuns at Sempringham; like the Maid of Brittany she could be considered a danger and was never allowed her freedom. The line of Simon de Montfort died with her.

THE PLANTAGENET LINE
CONTINUES

Available on Amazon.

Printed in Great Britain
by Amazon

54837717R00170